THE
FAMILY
HOLIDAY

BOOKS BY SHALINI BOLAND

The Secret Mother

The Child Next Door

The Millionaire's Wife

The Silent Sister

The Perfect Family

The Best Friend

The Girl from the Sea

The Marriage Betrayal

The Other Daughter

One of Us Is Lying

The Wife

My Little Girl

The Couple Upstairs

THE
FAMILY
HOLIDAY

SHALINI BOLAND

bookouture

Published by Bookouture in 2022

An imprint of Storyfire Ltd.
Carmelite House
50 Victoria Embankment
London EC4Y 0DZ
Uniter Kingdom

www.bookouture.com

ISBN: 978-1-83888-152-8
eBook ISBN: 978-1-83888-151-1

For my beautiful family

PROLOGUE

I stare over the balcony at the blur of movement. It's fast and slow all at once. There's no time to consider what's happening, yet there's time enough to feel a shiver of night air on my skin. Time enough to take in their expression of tumbling shock, then fear, then horror, then nothing.

The body below is finally still. Finally quiet. A red stain pooling.

Silence screams in my ears.
Did I really do this?
Did I have a choice?

ONE

BETH

'Beth! That you?' My husband Niall calls down from his office. 'Come and look at this!'

'Just putting the shopping away!' I dump the shopping bags on the kitchen table, blowing on my hands to warm them up. Thankfully, the heating is on full blast. Our eighteenth-century cottage is always draughty, which is great in the summer, but not so good in freezing February.

I head up the creaky stairs towards Niall's office. Usually his door is firmly shut, but right now it's wide open, giving me a view of the back of his head. He's sitting at his desk looking at a website on his laptop. The dull wintry scene through the window beyond does nothing to illuminate the room so I switch on the overhead light.

I step into the room and stand by his side. The room is cluttered but cosy, like the rest of our cottage. Two walls are lined floor-to-ceiling with oak bookshelves. Another is adorned with framed prints of his book covers. My husband is a historical fantasy fiction author of a popular long-running series – The Witching Chronicles.

'Check this out.'

Niall points to the screen and I find myself gazing at stunning images of swanky houses in gorgeous locations.

I read aloud what's written at the top of the page: 'Relax in your own beautiful home away from home.'

'What do you think?' Niall asks, swivelling around in his chair and fixing me with an excited grin. His brown eyes are alive with anticipation.

'A holiday?' I ask, hardly daring to hope.

'Uh huh.' He turns back to the laptop.

I've been craving a holiday for years, but Niall always prefers to spend his limited free time at home. We live on the outskirts of Sherborne in north-west Dorset, which is a beautiful place – and also happens to be the setting for Niall's book series – but I'm itching for a change of scenery. As an author, Niall often takes trips at home and abroad for work – book signings, conferences, panels and other events – so travel isn't relaxing for him. Trouble is, I'm a stay-at-home mum so I never get to go anywhere.

'What's the website?' I ask. 'Holiday homes?'

'Better than that,' Niall declares. 'It's a house-swap site.'

'A *house swap*?' It sounds straightforward, but I'm not entirely sure what he means.

'Yeah, you know. We stay in someone else's house while they stay in ours.'

Even though I'm desperate for a holiday, I'm not sure I like the sound of that. Maybe he's joking. 'You mean strangers would be staying here? In our home?'

Niall tuts and turns to me with a frown. 'I thought you'd be pleased. You're always going on about wanting a holiday. These house swaps are supposed to be great. I think it was Paul who mentioned the site. But I've seen a few articles about it too.' Paul is Niall's editor and he's always telling Niall about the latest trends. My husband loves to keep up to date with these things.

I blink and try to get my thoughts in order. 'I am pleased. Course I am.' I squeeze my husband's shoulder. 'I'm just trying to wrap my head around the idea. You've only just sprung it on me.'

'Look...' Niall clicks a few tabs and brings up the testimonials page. He points at the screen and reads out some snippets. *'Best experience of our lives... we didn't want to swap back...* Here's another one: *From the moment we arrived, we felt at ease. It was like being in our own home, but in another country and on the beach. We'd definitely do this again.'* He looks up at me. 'See?'

'It does sound good,' I reply. I don't voice my opinion that they're hardly likely to put bad reviews on their website.

'Don't sound too excited,' Niall huffs.

'Sorry.' I give an apologetic laugh. 'It's just that, well, my idea of the perfect holiday is relaxing in a luxury hotel, not staying in someone's house.'

Niall shakes his head. 'I stay in posh hotels all the time for work and, believe me, they all feel the same after a while – corporate. A house swap would be more authentic. You know, we'd get to experience what it's like to live in that particular town, rather than be in a bland hotel.'

I nod, unconvinced. The thought of strangers coming into our home and treating it like theirs makes me uneasy. But I know what Niall's like once he gets an idea in his head; he never lets it go. I tell him about my worries anyway. 'It's just... well, it's not a break if I have to shop and cook and do the housework. Do you know what I mean?'

Niall's shoulders tense and he sucks in a frustrated breath. I worry he's about to get annoyed with me. I do feel bad for my reluctance, but if we're finally going to have a family holiday, I'd like one that we can all enjoy.

'I thought cooking was your passion?' he says, leaning back in his chair.

'It is, but not on holiday.'

There's an awkward silence. One that I'm just about to fill when Niall speaks instead.

'Okay, how about if I promise there'll be no cooking or housework. We'll eat out in fancy restaurants every night. Deal?' He turns to me and lifts a dark eyebrow.

I smile and start to feel a flicker of excitement. We haven't been on a proper family holiday for about ten years. The last one was when Connor was a toddler, and that was a disaster. He got sick on day two, and I spent the whole week in the hotel room looking after him. 'When were you thinking of going?' I ask. 'July, August?'

'How about April?' he replies.

'Ooh, okay. That's only two months away.'

'I know, but I'm sick of this cold weather. I think we should go abroad, somewhere sunny. Don't the kids have Easter holidays around then?'

My heart lifts at the thought of a warm escape. I'd been picturing a house swap in the UK. If I'd known he was talking about a holiday abroad, I'd have been more enthusiastic from the start. 'Have you got anywhere in mind?'

'How about Italy?' he suggests.

'That sounds amazing!' I can picture it now – lemon groves, a Tuscan farmhouse, or maybe an apartment overlooking the sea.

Niall grins. 'It does, doesn't it. Grab a chair from the kids' room and we'll have a look at some of the properties available.'

I do as he suggests, and soon we're scrolling through the website. Frustratingly, most of the homes we like the look of have already been booked. I guess it shouldn't be surprising. After all, we're trying to book for one of the busiest times of the year. All that's left now are the grottier places where we wouldn't want to spend an afternoon, let alone two weeks.

'Are there any other house-swap sites?' I ask. 'Or maybe we should pick a different country. I think Cyprus is supposed to be quite warm in April, Sal's been a few times.'

'Hang on, what's this?' Niall clicks on a listing and we're greeted with the image of a stunning white modern villa with a turquoise pool beneath an azure sky. The pool furniture is contemporary and looks very expensive. Everything appears to be immaculate.

'That's gorgeous.' I sigh. 'But I doubt they're going to want to swap with *us*. I mean, I know our house is lovely, but it's not in the same league as that one. It's pretty much the exact opposite.'

'That's the whole point,' Niall says. 'Why would you swap for something the same? They'd be getting a cosy cottage in Dorset. We'd be getting a sunny villa on the Amalfi Coast.'

'Do you think so?' I'm not convinced the owners would go for it. 'Is it available on our dates?'

'Yep.'

'Who owns it?' I ask. 'Does it say who we'd be swapping with?'

'Hang on.' Niall clicks on the 'About Us' tab.

Together, we read what they've written. According to their info, Amber and Renzo Mason are British ex-pats who've lived in Maiori, Italy for years. They have two children, and they're looking for a two-week holiday in the countryside.

'Shall I register our house on the site and get in contact with them?' Niall asks.

Anticipation leaps in my chest. 'Okay, do it.'

I never in a million years believed the Mason family would agree to swap their villa with our little house – quaint as it is. So when they actually show interest, we get the swap locked down before they can change their minds.

Two hours later, it's all agreed.

Now all we have to do is book our flights, and we'll be good to go.

I absolutely cannot wait.

TWO

BETH

I stand in the bedroom surveying the scene of devastation, trying not to panic. I'm looking forward to our upcoming Italian holiday, of course I am, but I'd forgotten how stressful packing can be. Especially as we can't leave the place in a mess, not with this holiday house swap we've arranged. Our home will have to be left in pristine condition. Well, as pristine as a tired three-hundred-year-old cottage can ever hope to be.

I messaged the Masons plenty of photos of our home, so they should know exactly what they're letting themselves in for. Amber Mason said it looked divine – just what she'd envisioned — but I can't help worrying what they'll think once they're actually here. What if they feel duped? Our cottage isn't exactly spacious. Their place, by contrast, has vast airy rooms and four bedrooms, as opposed to our two. We also have Niall's study, but that will be locked and out of bounds. Our boys, Connor and Liam, share a room at the moment. We have a long-term plan to build an office in the garden, so that we can regain a third bedroom, but Niall's reluctant to have builders in as they'll disturb his work. Anyway, that's a plan for the future; for now we have two bedrooms and that's that.

The Masons also have two children, a boy and a girl, so their kids will have to share the boys' room. We're definitely getting the better deal in this house swap and our two can't wait to have a room each. Not to mention the sunshine, the pool, the hot tub, the balconies and their convertible Mercedes. A bit different from my knackered old Renault Clio, which they'll have use of while they're here. I hope it holds out. I've left the phone number of our local mechanic, just in case. I did hint that maybe Niall should let them use his Audi TT, but even our kids are banned from going in it, except for very special occasions, so there's no way he's going to lend it out to strangers.

Bubbles of anxiety float around my stomach as I knock twice on Niall's office door. I flinch when he replies with an irritated, 'Yes? What is it?'

I ease open the door. My husband sits at his desk in front of the window, his dark head bent over his keyboard, his screen open at an empty Word document, the cursor flashing. His desk lamp casts a pool of light over papers, books and empty coffee mugs. I hate to interrupt him while he's writing, but I don't have much of a choice.

'Can you come have a quick look at the stuff I've laid out for you on the bed? All I need is a yes or no.'

We're flying out tomorrow and, for the past week, he's been brushing off my requests for him to pick out his holiday outfits and now I'm running out of time to get everything sorted. I'd choose his clothes myself, but he'd complain if I packed the wrong ones.

Niall straightens up, links his fingers, and stretches his arms out in front of him with a loud sigh before getting to his feet and turning around. 'I've got sod all done today.' A scowl lines his features for a moment, then he softens his expression. 'Okay, I guess I could do with a break from thinking about the next chapter. What do you want me to look at?'

He follows me along the uneven landing into our room,

ducking his head beneath the doorframe. Our bedroom is pretty but small, with just enough room for a double bed, wardrobe and chest of drawers. It currently resembles an explosion in a textile factory. My heart pounds at the thought of everything I have to do before we leave tomorrow.

'These are the shirts, T-shirts and shorts I was going to pack for you.' I point to the various piles on the bed.

'Not those, Beth.' Niall shakes his head. 'What about a suit?'

'I packed the grey one.'

He wrinkles his brow. 'I prefer the navy. Not that shirt.'

My husband spends the next twenty minutes turning up his nose at most of my choices. It would have been so much easier if he'd done as I'd asked and picked out his clothes in the first place. I'm breaking out in a sweat just thinking about what's left to do.

Finally, Niall has made his choices and I can relax a bit.

'Thought I'd order us a takeaway?' I suggest. 'It'll save on washing up and get the holiday started early. What do you think? Italian to get in the mood? The boys would love pizza...' I hold my breath, willing him to say yes.

'Sure, pizza sounds good. And maybe some garlic bread.'

I let out a sigh of relief. I don't think I have the energy or time to cook tonight. I've been baking and cooking for days, stocking the fridge and cupboards with homemade goodies for the Masons. I didn't have to do that, but I really want their stay to be enjoyable. Maybe, if they love it here, we'll be able to do this again as an annual thing. That would be amazing. I'm determined to make this swap as successful as possible.

'Mum, when's dinner?' Connor pokes his head around the door. I still can't get used to his newly cropped hair. Our eleven-year-old son started senior school last year and apparently his gorgeous brown curls weren't cool, so I reluctantly made an appointment with our neighbour Sal – who's a mobile hair-dresser. Connor now has the same generic hairstyle that all his friends have. Another sign that he's growing up. At least he seems to be happier at school now.

'How about takeaway pizza?' Niall asks him.

'Yesss! Can we, Dad?'

Niall's dark eyes sparkle. 'I just said so, didn't I?'

Connor races away down the stairs yelling the good news to his seven-year-old brother. 'Liam! Dad said we can have pizza!'

As if going away isn't exciting enough, the boys are also buzzing at having three extra days off school. The holidays don't start until next week, but our flight is tomorrow so I wrote to the headmaster and asked if it would be okay. Mr Walton said that officially it's absolutely not okay, but unofficially he wished us a happy holiday.

Niall's eyes scan the bedroom as if seeing it for the first time. 'Bloody hell, Beth, it's a bit of a mess in here. It'll need to be tidier than this before the Masons arrive.'

I swallow down the retort that it wouldn't be a mess if he'd packed his stuff last week when I first asked him. 'It's fine,' I reply with a wave of my hand. 'Why don't you go and order the pizza. I'll make a start here.'

'Oh.' Niall sucks air through his teeth.

My shoulders sag at his expression.

'I would order it, Beth, but I've still got this tricky chapter to write. Would you mind? Anyway, I haven't downloaded the delivery app on my new phone yet.' He gives me a regretful look before walking out of the bedroom. 'Oh, large pepperoni for me, Beth. Thanks!' he calls back from the landing.

I stare at the chaos on the bed. I guess it's fair enough that I sort out the dinner and the packing. After all, Niall has to get his work done. But I suddenly wonder how I managed to turn from confident young chef into stressed wife and mother. The plan was for me to work towards opening a restaurant, while Niall worked on getting a publishing deal. We used to share the household duties between us – an equal partnership. Then, when I was pregnant with Connor, Niall got his book deal. His series was a worldwide success, and he was called away on book tours and interviews. I was thrilled for him. It was an exciting time for both of us. But somewhere along the way, my career goals were forgotten. I gave up work and poured all my energy into our children. I love my family, I really do, but I didn't think I'd miss working so much. And now that the kids are at school full time I could probably go back to it. But Niall is reluctant. He says we don't need the money, and the boys need their mum at home. What would happen in the holidays and on weekends? He's probably right. I've been out of the game so long that I wouldn't know how to get back in.

I shake my head, wondering why I'm even thinking about all this right now. What's done is done. I have a lovely life. A life most people could only dream of and one I'm grateful for. And I don't have time to mope about. We're off to Italy tomorrow. I need to order food and then get the house in order. I pick up my phone from the bed and open the delivery app.

As I type in the details, I can't seem to concentrate on what I'm doing. The words on the screen keep blurring. I know Niall and I decided that I wouldn't return to work, that I would stay home in order to keep things running smoothly. I told him I was fine with that decision. So, if that's the case, then why does this dissatisfied voice keep rearing its head? Why do I have to keep squashing down these insistent thoughts? Maybe I need to have another conversation with my husband. Perhaps this holiday will give me the opportunity to do just that.

THREE

AMBER

I stand on the balcony and breathe in the scent of an Italian spring. It's the first truly warm evening so far this year. The first evening I can be outside without a jacket.

'Have you got enough warm clothes?' Renzo calls out from the bedroom. 'You've only packed three jumpers.'

I sip my wine. 'I can always buy more when we get there.'

'What? I can't hear you, Amber! Can you come in a minute?'

I sigh and turn, head back through the French doors into the air-conditioned bedroom.

'Close the door. You're letting the mozzies in and the cold air out.'

I do as he asks.

'Give us a hand. I'm doing everything here at the moment.' Renzo eyes the bed critically, looking at all the neat piles of clothing.

'You know you love it,' I drawl. 'Whenever I help, you always end up re-arranging everything. I've learned to stay out of the way.'

'That's because you don't pack, Amber, you shove stuff into the case and then moan when it's all creased.'

'True.' I nod and give him a teasing smirk.

He shakes his head, his dark hair falling forward. I can't tell if he's annoyed with me or concentrating.

I take a breath and try to show willing. 'Okay, so direct me.'

'No, don't worry. You're right, I'll do it.'

'See! You love it. Want some?' I hold up my glass and waggle it from side to side.

'Not until I've finished this. Pick out another couple of jumpers from the closet. We're there for two weeks, not two days. The forecast's sleet and rain. I don't know why we had to go to England. Couldn't you have chosen somewhere warmer?' He starts placing rolled up T-shirts at the bottom of the case. According to my husband, they crease less if you roll rather than fold them.

I move a pile of his shirts and sit on the end of the bed, knowing this will irritate him, but I can't help myself. He loves me so much that he won't say anything, but I see him wince at my casual destruction of his well-planned order. I take his hand and place it around the stem of my glass. 'Here, have a sip. I want the kids to spend some time in the UK and practise their English. Get to know their roots. We hardly ever go back.'

My husband does as I ask and takes a sip of my wine. 'That's because England's cold and expensive. It's the reason we live in Italy, remember?'

I pout and let my shoulders drop. 'So you don't want to go? I wish you'd said something earlier.'

Renzo hands back my glass. He's barely touched it. 'Of course I want to go. I'm just not looking forward to the weather.'

I tip back my head and close my eyes for a second. 'It's a cosy cottage. We can have romantic evenings in front of the fire, and go for walks to the local pub. There's a castle in Sherborne apparently. Beth whatsherface sent me a whole email of "fun things to do". The kids will love it. Anyway, I thought you wanted to get away for a while.'

'I do want to get away. Ignore me. It'll be good. Not sure if I like the idea of strangers in our house though. It'll be weird thinking of another family in our space.'

'We'll be in their space too.'

'Yeah, I guess so. Didn't you say he's a famous author?'

'Apparently.'

'I've never heard of him.' Renzo screws up his face and I detect a hint of jealousy.

'Papa...'

We both turn at the sound of our six-year-old daughter's voice. I tilt my head at the sight of her in her nightdress, thumb in her mouth, teddy wedged under her arm.

'You should be asleep in bed, young lady. It's very late.' I give a mock frown.

Flora is our youngest and then we also have Frank, who's eleven. They were both born here in Italy, but they're completely bilingual. We speak mainly English at home to keep up their fluency.

'Is it time to go to England now?' she asks sleepily, her thumb still in her mouth.

'No, Miss Flora.' Renzo sweeps her up in his arms, making her giggle. 'It's time to go back to bed. Off we go.' As he takes her back to her room, I return to the balcony and gaze out over the pool. It's been cleaned and refilled for the season, the lights below the surface ripple and glow. Off to the side, beneath a plant-covered gazebo, the hot tub bubbles invitingly. Our home is beautiful. A sanctuary.

I freeze as the fence at the end of the garden rattles and a movement catches my eye. My heart stutters and sweat beads on my back and chest. I grip my wine glass in one hand and hold onto the balcony rail with the other. I swear in Italian when I see that it's only next door's cat. It's probably here to do its business in our garden again. I exhale, steadying my breathing, annoyed with myself for being so jumpy. Oh well, Niall and Beth Kildare can deal with the cat for the next two weeks. They'd better not start feeding it. The last thing I want is for them to encourage the bloody thing.

I think back to Renzo's words about not wanting strangers in our house. I hadn't been worried about it before but suddenly, the thought of another family here makes me nauseous. They'll be sleeping in our bed, opening our cupboards and drawers, eating off our plates and using our cutlery like it's theirs. I have a vision of their kids playing in our pool as Beth lies on a sun lounger, her husband rubbing sunscreen on her body.

I turn away from the view and go back inside, fumbling to close the balcony doors behind me as my hands are shaking so badly. I drain my wine glass.

This holiday swap was my idea. I'm the one who persuaded Renzo to agree. So why am I now having second thoughts?

FOUR

BETH

As we walk towards the departure lounge, I take my phone from my bag.

'Just sending a quick message to Amber.'

'Mum, I'm hungry.' Liam takes my free hand and starts tugging me over towards the staircase. 'Can we go there?' He points to the food hall upstairs.

I let go of his hand and start typing out a text message.

We're at Gatwick!

'You're messaging Amber?' Niall frowns.

'Just letting them know we're at the airport.' I fix my husband with an excited grin. He looks so handsome in his new jeans and cable knit jumper, even with a frown furrowing his brow and his lips pressed into a thin line.

I can't believe we're finally here. The bags have been checked in, and we've got two hours to spare until our flight leaves for Naples. It's been fun planning the trip over the past few weeks, messaging back and forth with Amber. Swapping information about our home towns and the various quirks of each other's houses. Apparently their air conditioning can be a bit temperamental. I let her know that our hot water can take up to an hour to heat up. Thankfully, she's originally from the UK so she's used to the plumbing. I warned her that despite being April, England still thinks it's the depths of winter, so they'd better pack warm clothes. My phone pings with a message back.

Exciting! We're just doing the last bit of packing. Hope you like it when you get here.

I'm sure we'll love it. Happy travels! x

Thanks. You too! X

I think back to the past chaotic twenty-four hours. I thought we'd never get packed and tidied. But after staying up until almost two this morning, our cottage is now as immaculate as it's ever been or ever will be again in its life. The heating is timed to come on two hours before they arrive, the wood store is full, kindling in the fire grate has been laid. Everything has been tidied, vacuumed, dusted, bleached and polished. I only wish it looked as beautiful every day. I even spent last week weeding the front garden and cleaning the windows. The whole experience has been exhausting.

Not for the first time, I wonder why we couldn't have simply gone to a hotel or rented a villa – it's not like we don't have the money – but I've been trying to get Niall to agree to a holiday for so long, that I didn't want to criticise his suggestion in case I put him off the whole idea.

But now... now that the cleaning and tidying is done, our two-week holiday stretches out ahead of us like a sparkling jewel. I inhale and exhale, revelling in a rare warm glow of contentment.

'Mum!' Liam reaches up and snatches my phone away.

'Liam, give that back.'

'I'm hungry.' His dark eyes narrow and he looks exactly like his father. 'There's a Wagamama up there.' His expression changes to hopeful.

I take a breath and hold out my hand. Liam plops my phone back into my palm, a resentful scowl settling back on his face. Niall and Connor are walking on without us, oblivious to Liam's strop. 'Don't take Mummy's phone without asking.' I realise that if we don't sit down and get some food into the kids, a meltdown will be imminent. It's been a long morning, what with last-minute tidying, making snacks, driving to the airport, getting parked and checked in. The boys sniped at each other in the car the whole way and Niall lost his temper more than once while I tried to be peacemaker.

I resolve that things are going to be different from now on. We're not going to be one of those stressed families who argues in public. We're going to be calm and happy. Composed and carefree. I've been looking forward to this trip for so long that I'm not about to let something as simple as a hangry child ruin the first day.

'Wagamama?' I ask Liam with a frown. 'What's that? Never heard of it.'

'Mu-um!' He grins and gives my arm a gentle knock, knowing that I'm well aware it's his favourite place to eat. Niall's parents took him there for his seventh birthday and he loved it.

'Come on then. Let's catch up with your dad and brother.' Liam and I quicken our pace. I'd been hoping to browse in some shops first, but I'll do it after we've eaten. I realise I'm actually looking forward to sitting in a restaurant, having a nice cold glass of wine and socialising as a family. It's been so long since Niall and I had an actual conversation about anything that isn't domestic, I'm determined that we're going to recapture the romance in our relationship. And I also want to be a fun parent again instead of a nagging mum. My heart expands with all the possibilities that these two weeks could offer.

'Niall!' I call after my husband who's chatting away to Connor. It's great to see him paying attention to the kids. These past few years he always seems to have been working away from home or shut in his office.

Liam reaches them before I do. 'Mum said we can go to Wagamama for lunch,' he pants, his eyes bright, excited to be imparting such momentous news.

Connor looks back at me for confirmation.

'If your dad says it's okay. We are on holiday...' I smile up at Niall.

'Sure. I don't see why not.'

My shoulders relax. Everyone's happy again. 'It's upstairs, let's go grab a table.' I pull ahead, Liam matching my stride.

'Beth...'

I turn.

'The thing is. I still have quite a few emails to catch up on. Would you mind taking the kids while I find a quiet spot to work?'

'You need to eat too,' I reply. 'Why don't you come with us, have some lunch, and then work on the plane?'

His eyes darken. 'Because I'd like to get it out of the way before we leave. The last thing I want is to have to start working on the flight over. It's supposed to be a holiday for me too.'

I swallow the lump in my throat. 'Sorry, of course. Yep, you go and do what you need to do. I'll get the kids some food.'

'It's not as though I want to work, you know. I'd much rather be relaxing with you and the kids.'

'Of course. Do you want me to get you anything – a sandwich, or...'

'No, I'll find a quiet spot in either Jamie's Italian or

Juniper's. Come on, the quicker we go, the sooner my holiday can start.'

As we troop up the stairs, the boys are quiet. They're just as disappointed as I am that their dad won't be joining us. But I remind myself that it's only one meal, and Niall would rather be with us than working. At the top of the staircase, he turns and heads towards a posh-looking restaurant while we head towards Wagamama.

I know it's ridiculous, but there are tears prickling behind my eyes. I tell myself it's only tiredness. I push away the unwelcome thought that maybe Niall doesn't actually want to spend time with us. That he would rather be on his phone, or laptop. I need to stop this self-pity. It was his idea to book this holiday swap in the first place. If he didn't want to spend time with us, why would he have suggested it? I take a deep breath and try to conjure up some enthusiasm for the boys.

'Who's hungry?'

Connor stops and folds his arms across his chest. 'Why can't we go to the same place as Dad?'

I sigh. 'Sorry, Con, but Dad needs quiet to do some last-minute work.'

'He's always working! Why does he always have to work and you don't? Can't you do the work and then Dad can come and eat with *us*?'

My stomach turns over at his words. Even the boys feel sidelined by their dad. I can't let their disappointment spoil the start of our holiday. 'It's only for a couple of hours. We've got two whole weeks in Italy. Dad will be eating with us every night when we get there, okay?'

I fervently hope that's the case. I have a niggling doubt that despite this being a family holiday, Niall will still want to take himself off to work. Hopefully the boys will be distracted enough by the pool and the beach. But if that does end up being the case, what will distract *me*? What will this mean for our relationship? For our family? Will I sit back and take it, or will I be able to find the courage from somewhere to speak up for myself? To inject some hope, some *life,* back into our marriage.

FIVE

BETH

The novelty of eating in a restaurant soon takes the boys' minds off their disappointment at their father's absence. I let them order what they like – including three rounds of fizzy drinks – and splash out on fancy desserts for all of us. Two glasses of cold white wine in quick succession take the edge off my worries. I barely notice the food as I'm too preoccupied with my thoughts. The boys are quiet while they eat. I let them look at their phones, feeling like a bad mother. I tell myself that we'll limit screen time once we're in Italy.

I check my own phone. Still an hour until our flight leaves. I text Niall to see how he's getting on with his work. There's no immediate reply so I think I'll leave him be and take the boys back downstairs. I'd like to pick out some pretty underwear and a sexy holiday outfit. I need to do something to get Niall's attention. He used to adore me. He'd want to spend all his time in my company. Now, I feel like I'm nothing more than an irritation. When I speak to him, I can almost hear him willing me to hurry up and finish what I'm saying so that he can get back to his work. But I can hardly blame him because all we ever talk about these days are chores and kids. This holiday has become a bright spot in a never-ending cloud of domesticity.

I need to get him to notice me. At thirty-seven, I'm still reasonably attractive. My hair is long and dark, my skin is clear. My boobs have held up pretty well after breastfeeding two babies. I'm not a size 10 any more, but then he's not in the same shape he was twelve years ago either. We need to have fun again.

I pay the bill and try not to worry about the expense. It's not as if we need to watch the pennies – at least I don't think we do. Niall has never specified what he earns from his books. He organises the finances and I've always accepted that, even though I'd rather take a more active role. I'm justifying my imminent spending spree as a means to get our marriage back on track. Also, I'm tipsy and it's making me a little reckless. I'm not used to lunchtime drinking.

'Okay, boys, we're just going to pop into a couple of shops. Let's go.'

'*Shopping?*' Connor's lip curls and he sinks further into his seat. 'Can't we sit here and wait for you?'

'No. It won't take long. Come on.'

'Can I get some Lego?' Liam asks, his eyes hopeful.

'Not today.' I get to my feet and wait while my sons reluctantly peel themselves from their chairs.

I ignore their twin grumbles as we walk out of the restaurant and back down the stairs. I'm picturing something silky and lacy to wear under a slinky dress that will flatter my body and accentuate my curves in all the right places. I think I'll treat myself to some red lipstick too. I hardly ever wear lipstick any more, and when I do it's usually a nude colour or a lip gloss.

I think back to the woman I used to be. Energetic, fun, hardworking with a successful career as a respected chef in a London restaurant. I had so many friends back then. My life was full and vibrant. I want to reclaim some of the old me and remind Niall why he married me in the first place.

I smile as I remember how hard Niall worked to convince me to go out with him in the first place. He noticed me in a bar one evening, came over and told me he thought I was beautiful. My friends and I all laughed, thinking it was a cheesy pickup line. I politely turned down his offer of a drink. The following week he came up to me in the same bar and this time we got talking. He told me he was a writer. I looked at him properly this time, and decided he was interesting, even a little bit handsome. I let him buy me a drink.

He wasn't deterred by the fact that, as a chef, I worked long, unsociable hours and had very little free time for dating. He persisted, and I was won over by his quiet charm and his ambition and passion for writing. He told me I inspired him; that since he'd started seeing me, the ideas were coming thick and fast. I was flattered.

Months later, I learned that he'd based the main character in his Witching Chronicles on me – a dark-haired, dark-eyed girl with red lips and a haughty stare – his words, not mine. I mean, who isn't going to be won over by something like that? But while his fictional witch has remained young and glamorous, the real me has not.

I head towards a shiny-looking store that oozes exclusivity with its sparsely populated racks and shelves, and no visible price tags. Everything is bright and flimsy, designed for sun-drenched beaches or cocktail evenings on warm terraces. I'm drawn to a jade silk dress with emerald-jewelled straps and a plunging back. I can picture myself wearing it with a pair of killer heels. The image in my head is of a younger me, but surely I can channel that vision to give myself more confidence.

There are two of the jade dresses on the rack – a small and a medium, both hopelessly tiny. If this is a medium then I must be an XXXL.

'Mum, I need the toilet.'

I look up from the clothes rack. Liam hasn't reached the jiggling-around stage yet, so we should be okay for another few minutes. 'Okay, sweets, hang on a moment.'

'Can we go now? This is boring,' Connor adds.

A svelte shop assistant heads over. 'Everything okay? Can I help?' She smiles what looks like a genuine smile. 'That dress is gorgeous. It would look amazing with your dark hair.'

'I'm worried about the size. The medium's a bit small for me.'

'We've just had a new delivery, let me check for you.' She strides off into the back and I gaze around half-heartedly at the other dresses. None of them are grabbing me like the jade one. I check my phone. Still no reply from Niall even though I can tell he's seen my message.

'Here we are, you're in luck!' The sales assistant hands me the dress and points to the fitting room. 'Sorry the dress is a bit creased; I haven't had a chance to steam it yet.'

I glance at the label. It's a large so I hope it fits. 'That's great, thanks so much.' I glance at my phone again. Time is getting tight now. I wonder if I'll even have time to try on the dress. I hesitate and then decide that I'll regret it if I don't. 'Boys, wait outside the changing room for me, I won't be long.'

I step into the cubicle, strip off and slip the cool satin over my head. I stare at myself in the mirror. It's absolutely perfect. I can't remember the last time I tried something on that suited me so well. I place a hand on my heart and take a breath. If Niall doesn't react to me in this dress, then all hope for our marriage is lost. Maybe I'll wear it tonight. We can all go out together as a family. I picture the evening – Niall in his suit, me in this dress, the boys handsome in their new shirts.

Okay, I'd better get a move on, pay for the dress and check the screen to see if we've been allocated a departure gate yet. I quickly slip back into my jeans and sweatshirt, drape the dress over my arm and leave the fitting room.

'Mum, I really need a wee.' Liam's jiggling now.

'I'm not surprised after all that lemonade. I'll pay for this and then we'll get your dad to take you both to the loo.'

'Can we get him now?' Liam's voice is becoming desperate.

'Hang on.' I pull my phone out and check the screen. Still no reply from Niall. I bang out another text.

The boys need the toilet. Can you come down now? Meet at the bottom of the stairs.

'Mum!' Liam's face contorts and he runs into the changing room that I've just come out of.

'Liam, come out. What are you doing in there?'

Connor looks up at me, white-faced. He leans towards me and whispers, 'I think he's wet himself.'

'*What?*' My heart sinks. We have no spare clothes. I'm going to have to buy him something. He can't sit on a plane for two and a half hours with sodden jogging bottoms. 'Liam?' I follow him into the cubicle.

He's crouched in the corner with tears streaming down his face. 'I told you I needed the toilet,' he croaks.

'I'm so sorry, sweets. You did tell me, and I didn't listen. Don't worry, we'll get you a change of clothes.'

'Will we still be able to go to Italy?' he gulps.

'Of course we will, baby.' I crouch down and put my arms around him. Kiss his tear-stained cheek. I check my phone again. Niall has finally replied.

Be there in five.

'It's gone into my shoes and socks,' Liam sobs.

'Everything okay?' The sales assistant calls into the cubicle. 'How was the dress?'

'Don't tell her what happened!' Liam hisses.

'Of course not. Don't you worry. Tie your hoody around your waist,' I say in a low voice before calling back to the sales assistant. 'Thanks, but it's no good.' I step back out holding Liam's hand and pass her back the dress.

'Oh, that's a shame. I was certain it would look incredible on you.'

I give her a regretful smile trying not to remember how beautiful I felt in it.

She sniffs and wrinkles her nose, and we hurriedly leave the shop before she realises the source of the smell.

Outside the store, I glance over at the staircase, but Niall isn't there yet. I take the boys into a surf shop and pick out some overpriced joggers, socks and trainers. Liam is being picky about what he wants and Connor is whingeing about how it's not fair that Liam's getting a new outfit. I snap and say that if he wets himself he too can have a new outfit. My voice is louder and angrier than it should be and we attract a few unwanted stares, but at least the boys have gone quiet again.

Guilt hits me. Why didn't I take Liam to the bathroom sooner? I was being selfish, more concerned with buying a sexy dress than with my child's comfort. This isn't like me. I always put my kids first. What's wrong with me? I guess it shows how much I need a holiday. I shake my head. 'Okay, let's go to the changing room. We'll strip off your bottom half, clean you up with these hand wipes and tissues and stick all your wet stuff into a bag.'

My phone pings. It's another message from Niall.

Where the hell are you? I'm at the bottom of the staircase and our gate number has come up on the screen. We need to go now.

I inhale and try to stop myself from letting out a frustrated growl. If Niall had stayed with us instead of escaping for a nice peaceful lunch on his own, then none of this would have happened in the first place. Where's the fun start to our family holiday that I'd pictured only a short while ago? How did things descend into such a chaotic disaster so quickly? I only hope we manage to make it to the departure gate in time.

SIX

Love isn't simply a feeling. It's a physical, tangible thing. A **terrible** *thing. The ache in my guts is real. It's with me day and night.*

I thought that time and space would knit the wound together. That I'd be scarred, yet somehow able to carry on. But that's not the case.

I'm still paralysed. The pain increases week on week. Shifting and twisting like a knife, or a burrowing creature.

The knots in my stomach tighten, the acid in my throat burns. Some days, like today, I'm so blinded by hatred and fury that I can't see straight. I can't focus on anything else.

. . .

There's only one way I can think of to ease it. One way to make things better.

I know what I have to do...

SEVEN

AMBER

After last night's wobble, today is better. I'm feeling far more positive about our upcoming trip. Check-in was smooth and the four of us are having a late dinner at a restaurant in the departure lounge at Capodichino Airport.

'You're quiet,' Renzo observes, his dark eyes filled with love and a tinge of concern.

'I'm fine.' I reach across the table and take my husband's hand. His puppy-dog eyes were what drew me to him in the first place. I met Renzo at a friend's winter wedding in Ravello twelve years ago. He was crying during the church service and he caught me staring at him. I raised an eyebrow and he shrugged and smiled through his tears. After the service, he sought me out and explained that the bride was his younger sister who'd been through a lot recently and he was just so happy for her. I liked the fact that he wasn't embarrassed to show his emotion.

I remarked on his perfect English, and said that I'd assumed from his looks that he was Italian. He explained that his father is English and his mother was Italian, but she had died the previous year, making today doubly emotional. I told him that I was a friend of Federico, the groom, and didn't know his sister personally, but I assured Renzo that she was marrying a good guy. I'd worked with Federico on and off for years and all his friends and acquaintances had only lovely things to say about him.

After the meal and wedding speeches, we spent the rest of the evening talking about our lives. I told him I worked in PR. He told me he'd recently come out of a long-term relationship. He said he owned a couple of jewellery stores – one in Amalfi, another in Maiori – and would love to chat about a possible publicity campaign for them. I was living in Rome at the time, but arranged to come back down the coast the following month for a meeting. It's not something I would normally have done. All my regular work was in Rome. But there was something about Renzo that drew me in.

Frank was born later that year, and we were married eight months after that.

'Amber?' Renzo prompts.

I realise he's been talking to me. 'Sorry, miles away.' I look out through the restaurant window at the travellers going by. Some ambling along comfortably and others hurrying past with anxious expressions. My breath hitches at the sight of a man staring at me from a souvenir store opposite. But then he waves and the woman at the next table to us waves back. I need to calm down and stop being so jittery.

'Earth to Amber. I was asking how's your spaghetti?'

'Sorry.' I drag my gaze and my attention back to my husband. 'Mm, good. Full up, but I will have another glass of Falanghina.' I clamp my jaw shut as I realise my voice sounds high and shaky. I tell myself to get a grip.

Renzo signals to the waiter who immediately comes over with the bottle. That's the other thing about my husband, he commands situations. People take him seriously.

'Papa, can we have ice cream?' Flora always asks her father

for things before she asks me, because she knows he's more likely to say yes.

Renzo pinches her cheek. 'Of course we can, my little sugarplum. Franco? Ice cream?' Renzo always reverts to the Italian version of our son's name. It's also what all his friends call him.

Franco gives a single nod. He's sulking over the fact that we said no phones at the dinner table when he was in the middle of playing a game online.

'Was that a yes please?' Renzo asks with a smile. 'Because I need to hear the actual words.'

Franco mumbles an almost inaudible yes. Renzo catches my eye and we silently commiserate over our son's gradual descent into teenage grumpiness.

Renzo and the kids have an in-depth discussion with the waiter about ice-cream flavours while I knock back another half glass of wine. It's delicious. My phone buzzes. I pull it out of my bag with a pounding heart. After yesterday's doubts, I'm now convinced we did the right thing in booking this trip. I need to get away. To relax.

'That's not fair!' Franco points at my phone. 'You said no phones while we're eating.'

Renzo nudges him softly. 'We meant no socialising and games with other people, Franco. Your mum's phone is either for work or sorting out holiday stuff – both of which are so you can have a nice life. Come on, cheer up, we're going on our holidays.' Renzo pulls a stupid face and Franco cracks an unwilling smile.

'It's just a work message,' I confirm. 'But I might send Beth a quick text to let her know we'll be getting on the plane soon.'

Renzo nods.

Our flight is later than the Kildares'. It'll probably be the early hours of the morning when we finally arrive in Sherborne, but I'm hoping the children will sleep most of the way. I tap out a message:

Hope you guys had a great flight. We'll be boarding soon!

I cringe at my overly cheery tone. I come across like some kind of holiday-camp entertainer. But I've been imitating Beth's manner to make her feel more at ease. If she met me in real life, she would soon see that the real me isn't like that at all. I have to be personable and professional in my career as a publicist, but I'm certainly not what you'd describe as bubbly. I've always preferred to be quietly confident and hold back. I think it yields better results. Makes people *want* to do things for you. Makes them yearn to please you. If you give sparingly, the recipient will feel as if they have a spark of stardust in a dark night.

I wait for Beth's return text. Normally she replies within seconds of me sending one. Not this time. They must already be in the air.

I wonder if Beth is as annoying in person as she comes across on email and text.

I think she probably is.

EIGHT

BETH

'There they are! Look!' Connor points to our cases, which have miraculously come onto the conveyor belt at the same time.

'I saw them first!' Liam insists.

'No you never.'

'Boys, that's enough.' Niall reprimands them without taking his eyes off his phone.

I shift around to the side of our luggage trolley, preparing to grab one of our suitcases. 'Niall, can you get one of the cases?'

'What?' He frowns and looks up distractedly. 'Uh, yeah, sure.'

'I can get it,' Connor says, taking a step closer to the belt.

'Can I get one, Mum?' Liam asks, shouldering his way in front of me.

I take his hand. 'Liam, can you move back, darling. The cases might be a bit heavy for you.'

'Not too heavy for *me*,' Connor asserts, leaning forward, hand out ready.

'I can do it too,' Liam insists, his voice getting higher.

Niall is staying out of it. My shoulders tense. If I let Connor take a case and not Liam, there'll be a full scale argument.

They're overtired and overstimulated and I haven't got the energy to deal with it right now. 'Boys, I need you both to step back—'

'But—'

'But nothing. Dad and I are going to get the cases, I need you two to guard the trolley for me. Make sure no one takes it.'

Connor scowls. He knows I'm fobbing him off. But Liam puts a hand on his hip and moves over to take charge of the trolley, thank goodness.

Connor leans in front of me and takes the first case, swinging it triumphantly onto the trolley and bashing my ankle in the process.

'Good lad!' Niall says.

Connor glows under his father's praise.

'That's not fair!' Liam's face reddens.

I grab the second case and dump it onto the trolley before walking round and taking hold of the handle. 'Right, let's go.' I'm hoping that if I ignore the drama, it might go away. The after-effects of the wine, plus two gin and tonics on the plane, have given me the beginnings of a headache. I need some water. 'Hey, guys, can you believe we're in Italy?' I try to get their moods to lift. I want us all to chatter away, to get excited about our holiday.

No one responds. Connor and Niall are walking alongside me, but Liam's face is red and sweaty, his arms folded angrily across his chest.

'Do you want to sit on the trolley?' I ask him, coming to a halt.

I can see the idea appeals, but he's torn – wondering if he should stay mad. Thankfully the appeal of a trolley ride wins out. He grins and plops himself next to the two cases. Relieved, I resume pushing. The added weight makes one of the wheels spin out and I have to keep pulling it back. I think about asking Niall to help, but his phone is pinging like crazy with messages and his eyes are on his screen. I haven't turned my phone back on since we landed.

Finally, we step outside the terminal. The air is thick and warm, tinged with the scent of fuel and tarmac. A canopy juts out from the building, shading us from the afternoon sun. I dump the trolley with a stack of others and pass one of the cases to Niall, who reluctantly slips his phone back into his pocket and pulls out the handle so he can wheel it.

As we leave the shade of the building, I pull at the neck of my sweatshirt. I knew it would be warmer here than England, but I'm not prepared for the white brightness, the heavy heat. I wish I hadn't worn jeans. I should take off my sweatshirt, but I'm carrying too many things. Taxis and minibuses trundle by in non-stop succession so we head for one of the zebra crossings.

'It's hot!' Liam declares with a puff of his cheeks. He stops where he is and wipes his brow.

Suddenly, we're all laughing at Liam's red little face and serious expression. I catch Niall's eye and he gives me a smile that makes my stomach flip. I'm so relieved the tension's finally gone.

'Naples isn't normally this warm in April,' Niall says. 'Did you look at the forecast?'

I nod. 'Supposed to be a storm tonight. But then it said sunny weather for the next few days, so that's good.'

'A storm? That's why it's so sticky. Where's this car? I hope it's got air con.'

'I should think so, but in any case, it's a convertible so we might not need it. Amber said they'd park it in the short-term car park in front of the terminal. Actually, she said she'd send us a photo of the parking spot, like we did for them. Let me check if she's sent it.' I take my phone from my bag and wait for it to start up. I swipe the screen and open our chat history. 'Nothing. Maybe the messages haven't come through yet.' I put a hand to my temple. My head is pounding now. 'We need to get out of this sun.'

'You do realise we've got two weeks of sun, Beth? Italy isn't renowned for its chilly weather.' Niall shakes his head and smiles to himself.

'I know, I'm not used to it, that's all. I'll message her.' I fire off a text reminding Amber to let us know where they've parked, but I don't get an immediate reply, so I call her instead. It goes straight to voicemail and I leave a message. I try to sound nonchalant and upbeat, as if this isn't fazing me at all, but my voice comes across as anxious and pathetic.

'Okay, standing here dithering isn't going to do anything. Let's have a look, see if we can spot it.' Niall continues striding across the concourse towards the crossing. He turns. 'You said it was a Mercedes, right?'

'Yes, a navy-blue cabriolet. So it should be easy to spot.' As we follow my husband across the road, I scan the parked cars and intermittently glance at my phone, waiting for a message to pop up.

'It's not a big car park,' Niall says. 'Let's start at one end and work our way down. Okay, boys, we're looking for a dark-blue Mercedes with a soft top. Shout if you see it.'

We spend the next ten minutes trawling the car park, but the Masons' car is obviously not here.

'I hope it hasn't been stolen.' The thought fills me with dread. 'I mean, it's quite a flashy vehicle.'

'Are you sure she said the short-term car park?' Niall asks, ignoring my speculation and wiping a line of sweat from his upper lip. 'Maybe they stuck it in the multi-storey so it's out of the sun. You might have misread her message.'

I feel my stress levels drop slightly. 'Hang on, let me check.' I scroll back through my conversation with Amber, wondering if I did misread it. Niall will be really pissed off if I've made us walk up and down the car park for nothing. 'No, look, here...' I hold out the screen, but he's not interested, so I start to tell him that I didn't get it wrong. 'She clearly said they'd park it in the short-term car—'

Niall waves me away with his hand. 'Fine, I believe you.'

'I'm thirsty,' Liam says with a pitiful expression on his face.

I hand him the last few sips from my water bottle. I realise I should have bought some more water while we were at the airport. 'Share it with your brother. Two sips each.'

'Is that all the water we've got?' Niall asks. 'I could do with some of that.'

I take a breath and try to stop the rising anxiety in my gut. I tell myself that there's nothing to worry about. We're all just tired and hot, and we need to find Amber and Renzo's car. We'll all laugh about this one day. 'Why don't I go and get some more water,' I offer. 'While you guys go and look for the car?'

'I'll be quicker without the kids,' Niall replies. He starts walking away. 'Text me when you're back with the water and I'll let you know when I find the car. This is ridiculous, you know. You should have worked out a better way of doing this.'

'It wasn't my idea, it was Amber's.'

'You don't have to go along with someone's idea if it's no good,' Niall replies. 'We should have got a cab from the airport. I really don't feel like driving anyway.'

I hope Niall doesn't expect me to drive – I'm over the limit after my lunchtime wine and those two G & Ts on the plane. He told me he was looking forward to getting behind the wheel and cruising down to Maiori, otherwise I wouldn't have had any alcohol. 'Come on, boys, let's go and get some water. I might get myself a coffee too.'

As we head back to the terminal building, I try not to think about what a shaky start this holiday is getting off to. I try not to worry about what we're going to do if we can't find the car. And I especially try not to think about how Niall will blame me if this trip turns into a disaster.

NINE

BETH

After a stressful hour at Naples Airport searching for the Masons' car in all the car parks, we eventually give up and decide to take a cab. I guess we can always go back once we find out where they parked it. Although Niall says they can bugger off if they think we're going to waste our holiday going back and forth to the airport to locate their car.

As we leave Naples, heading south, Niall, from the passenger seat, points out Mount Vesuvius, an impressive sight on its own, but even more so with a backdrop of gathering storm clouds. Liam fell asleep on my shoulder five minutes into the journey, but Connor is awestruck by the real live volcano in the distance. We promise him we'll go there on a day trip.

Soon we encounter the winding roads of the Amalfi Coast curving along sheer cliffs and corkscrewing down into pretty coastal villages and back up again. Daylight is fading and lights start winking on one by one.

It should have been a wonderful journey, but after the missing-car debacle I keep having unsettling thoughts that this whole holiday swap might be a scam, and we've actually given our car and house keys to a con artist. I can't enjoy any of the drive due to a heavy dread that's settled in my stomach. I spend the whole time feeling sick with worry that we'll arrive at the villa to discover it's owned by someone else, or that it isn't there at all. I know this holiday-swap idea was Niall's, but I did all of the organising, so I can't help feel personally responsible for the success of the trip.

Soon, we're descending the cliffs again into the town of Maiori, our holiday destination. The cab driver cruises along the seafront where the promenade is lit up with garlands of lights. Despite the rows of loungers and sun umbrellas on the beach, the brightly lit shops, the bars, restaurants, hotels and apartments, the whole place has an out-of-season, low-key feel.

'Is this where we're staying?' Connor asks, his nose pressed to the cab window.

'It is,' Niall replies. 'What do you think?'

'Are there boats? Can we go in one?'

'Maybe,' Niall replies. 'If you're good.'

'I'd love to go to Capri,' I add. 'There are supposed to be some amazing restaurants over there. Maybe we could pop over for the day.'

'We're almost there,' the driver says, turning off the main drag and heading away from the beach. We pass shops and squares, hotels and apartment blocks. The roads grow narrower and steeper, and I catch glimpses of the dark sea below. Amber assured me their place was close to the beach, but it feels like we're already quite a distance away. I'll be so relieved once we're in the villa and I can set my anxieties aside. I've already sent a text to Amber and Renzo's neighbour, Paola, who's going to let us in and give us the keys.

Our driver takes a few more turns. The road we're now in is narrow and tree-lined, the houses spaced widely apart, semi-hidden behind hedges and tall gates. The cab slows.

'This is the one, yes?' the cab driver asks. 'Villa Della Luna?'

My gaze lands on the slate name plaque attached to a stone

pier. 'Yes, this looks like it.' My heart skips as I peer through the open double gates. The house is almost as impressive as the local scenery. A large white-and-glass modern villa with an immaculate pale-grey driveway lined with potted fir trees and palms, and lit up with inset lighting. It's all so beautiful I could weep with gratitude. We drive in through the gates and pull up outside the large black front door.

More security lighting flashes on as we approach the property.

'Nice,' Niall comments.

'It's so cool,' Connor cries. 'Is this where we're staying?'

'It is,' I reply, allowing myself to feel a flicker of excitement. I gently shake Liam's shoulder. 'Hey, Mr Sleepy. We're here.'

'Mmm?' His cheeks are flushed and his hair is warm and damp with sweat where he's been leaning against me.

'Liam, time to wake up.'

He opens his eyes, stretches and yawns loudly. Niall and Connor are already out of the cab and the driver is lifting our cases from the boot. I step onto the driveway followed by a rumpled and disoriented Liam. The air is warm and heavy.

'Mummy, I'm thirsty.'

'Here.' I hand Liam a bottle of lukewarm water from my bag.

'Good evening.' A woman's voice catches my attention.

I turn to see an elegant blonde woman walking down the drive towards us. Niall heads over to meet her. I realise the cab driver is waiting for payment, so I rummage in my bag for my wallet and then fumble with a wad of unfamiliar euros, eventually working out the correct fare. The driver leaves, and I join Niall, with the kids trailing behind me.

'This is Paola,' Niall says. 'She lives next door. Paola, this is my wife, Beth.'

'Hi,' I say, wondering how travel weary I look on a scale of one to ten.

'So lovely to meet you.' Her accent is charming. She holds out a tiny, manicured hand for me to shake.

My hand feels clammy in her cool, dry palm.

She looks at me and tilts her head. 'For a minute, I think you are Amber; you look very similar.'

'I guess we're both dark-haired.' I pull at my hair self-consciously. 'So you live next door?'

'Yes, next door. That's our house on the left.' She points to an older-style grey mansion, partially screened by a stone wall and stately cypress trees.

'It looks beautiful,' I say.

'Thank you.' She bobs her head. 'It's not modern like this. More traditional. It was my husband's grandparents' house and now we have our family there.' She turns to look at the boys. 'And how old are you two beautiful children?' Her eyes twinkle.

Connor and Liam both look at me, too shy to respond.

'Connor,' Niall prompts. 'Paola's asking you a question.'

'Eleven,' he mumbles.

Liam grips my hand tight and doesn't reply.

'Connor's eleven and Liam's seven,' I say.

'Wonderful! This is a good age. I have five children, and the youngest, he is fourteen.'

'Wow,' I reply. 'You don't look old enough.'

She laughs. 'Thank you. Now, you must be tired, I will show you the keys and the alarm, yes?'

We follow her up to the front door where she explains which key to use, and how to open it, and then on into the air-conditioned hall as she demonstrates the alarm system. I'm barely concentrating on her instructions so I hope Niall's managing to take it all in. Instead, my focus is on the interior itself.

The house is like a piece of modern art. The floor is white veined marble and the walls are also white. The hallway is double height lit by soft, square inset downlights. But the main light source comes from the white-and-glass staircase, which appears to be glowing. I realise that each open stair tread is illuminated from within – the staircase is a giant light fitting. The overall effect of the space is crisp and cool without managing to feel cold.

'Nice?' Paola catches my dropped jaw and gives me a smile.

'It's stunning.' I swallow as I think of our modest home. Amber's photos didn't do this place justice at all. In fact, I can't believe it's the same place she posted on the house-swap website. She really downplayed it. I'm instantly worried about making a mess. What if the kids break or stain something?

'Okay, I leave you now, yes?' Paola looks from me to Niall. 'You have my number, so you call if you have a problem.'

'Thank you so much,' I reply, still a little dazed. 'It was very kind of you to let us in.'

'Of course, of course. It's no problem. I go now, cook dinner for my children. Ciao.'

'Ciao,' Niall and I reply in unison. I feel like a fraud saying it. I've been trying to learn some Italian phrases over the past few weeks, but I'm nowhere near as good as Niall who's almost fluent. His novels are pretty popular in Italy so he's been on a few book tours here over the years and had to do various media interviews.

The door closes behind Paola and we're left standing in the vast, echoing hallway.

'Pretty nice, huh?' I say.

'It's awesome!' Now that Paola's gone, Connor's voice has returned. 'Where's the pool?'

We leave our cases where they are and cross from the hall to the other ground-floor living spaces. There are leafy plants in white pots, black-and-white framed photographs and a couple of well-placed thick grey rugs. One wall is a floor-to-ceiling bookcase, another recessed wall holds split logs, presumably for the modern white wood-burning stove that sits in the corner of the living room. There are slender black columns throughout, to support the ceiling in the open plan areas.

And there, through a rear wall of glass, is a pale-turquoise pool, gleaming in the darkness, the underwater lighting creating a mirrored surface.

'Can we go in the pool?' Liam races towards the door, his hands pressing against the glass, making sweaty handprints. I try not to think about them. This is supposed to be a holiday. We'll do a proper clean at the end of our stay.

'Mum, can we?' Connor asks.

'Later,' I promise.

'Ah, let them have a quick swim,' Niall says. 'I might join them.'

'It's getting late. We need to have some food,' I reply, wishing I could be more spontaneous. But if the kids don't eat soon, they'll get crotchety, and I'll be the one dealing with the fallout.

'We'll go out for dinner straight after our swim,' Niall says. 'I'm sure there'll be a restaurant nearby.'

'Okay.' I nod. 'Let's have a swim.'

'Yesss!' the boys cry, and start asking questions about swimming trunks and inflatables, and can they jump in, and how cold will it be.

My heart lifts at their enthusiasm. It reminds me that I need to go with the flow. This is what I wanted – our family on holiday doing fun, relaxing things. Well, you can't get more fun and relaxing than having an evening swim in a pool in a fancy modern mansion.

Niall and I haul the cases up the illuminated staircase, allocate a room each for the boys, and locate the master bedroom at the far end. Like the rest of the villa, the room is high-ceilinged and airy. The walls are white, but the upstairs flooring is a dark polished wood. Instead of a window, black-framed sliding doors lead out onto a white-and-glass balcony with two metal-framed sun loungers, matching table and chairs and black stone pots of architectural shrubs and trees. Perfect for a cup of morning coffee, or an evening cocktail.

Our bed is a super king with built-in side tables. The only other piece of furniture is an opulent grey velvet chaise that sits opposite the bed, beneath an oversized photo canvas of the stunning Mason family staring out from a blurred beach backdrop.

'Where are we supposed to hang our clothes?' I ask, looking around the room at the lack of wardrobes and dressers.

Niall opens a door and peers through. 'In here.'

I follow him into a massive his-and-hers dressing room lined with fitted wardrobes and drawers. Every so often, there's an inset in the wall displaying either a handbag, shoes or perfume bottle. It's like a designer store.

Past the walk-in wardrobe is a white marble bathroom with twin wash basins and a wide, deep bathtub. But the most striking feature of all is the wall of glass at the back of the double shower onto which has been superimposed with larger-than-life black-and-white photographs of a naked Amber. One from the rear with her looking over her shoulder. The next one is a side view. And the third photo is of her facing forward with her hands on her hips.

Niall's eyes widen. We're both transfixed for a moment. I try to catch his eye to have a laugh about it, but he clears his throat. He's already heading back to the bedroom. Is my husband shocked? Aroused? Indifferent? I have no idea. I, on the other hand, experience a momentary thud of unease in the pit of my stomach.

TEN

BETH

The restaurant terrace lies beneath a vine-covered pergola strung with fairy lights. Glass and rattan chairs and tables sit on traditional terracotta tiles, interspersed with tubs of lemon trees. Two ancient olive trees with twisted trunks lean into the space as though eavesdropping on all the lively conversations. There isn't one single empty table that I can see, and the four of us hover awkwardly on the edge of the terrace. It looks like we'll have to find somewhere else to eat.

The streets outside were quiet, so it's unexpected to see such a crowded space behind the unassuming entrance door to the restaurant.

'We should probably have booked,' Niall says.

I realise he means that *I* should probably have booked. I swallow. 'Well, it's the first place we've tried. Maybe we should walk a bit further. I'm sure we'll find somewhere else?' I sigh. 'That view though.' Beyond the terrace, the lights of Maiori twinkle below us, and the dark sea ripples beneath an almost-full moon. This restaurant was one of a couple that Amber Mason recommended. If the food's anything like the atmosphere and the view, then I'll have to thank her.

'Buona sera.' A friendly waitress has come over. She looks about my age, with a curvy figure and gorgeous caramel ringlets tied back off her face. We must give off tourist vibes as she switches straight to English. 'Welcome to Terrazza Luciana. Table for four, yes? For dinner?' My shoulders relax. It's almost nine p.m. and I don't think I could have faced walking around trying to find somewhere else. Our evening swim was lovely, but I'd fall into bed right now if I weren't so hungry. The boys are shattered too.

'Yes please,' Niall replies. 'A table out here would be great.'

'I'm sorry, the terrace is full, as you see. We have a couple of tables left inside.'

'Inside's fine,' I smile.

'Please...' She gestures us in.

I take a step, but Niall stays put and places a hand on my arm, a frown darkening his features. 'I'd rather be outside. Can you fit another table on the terrace?' He glances around. 'There, look, by that planter. Surely that area's large enough for a small table.'

'So sorry, we need that space to get past, otherwise it's too narrow for the waiters. Inside is still nice, we can seat you by the window so you have the view.'

Niall is silent for a moment and I hope he's not going to kick up a fuss. 'Fine. Let's go inside then.' His face is like thunder.

The waitress pauses. 'You wait here one minute, okay?' She leaves us on the terrace, hurrying away to talk to an older waiter who shakes his head and then nods. He calls another waiter over and the three of them talk loudly and rapidly in Italian.

I shift from foot to foot and fiddle with my bracelet, hoping we can get seated soon. I can feel Niall's patience stretching. Thankfully, the waitress soon returns and beckons us inside. She seats us at a table by the window. True to her word, the view is still lovely, but the air conditioning feels chilly after the warm evening air.

Niall orders a bottle of wine and the boys each ask for a Sprite.

The waitress gives me a warm smile. 'You have a drink inside while my colleagues arrange for you a table on the terrace, okay?'

'Are you sure?' I ask, feeling like we're rude tourists who've bullied her into getting our way.

She gives me a playful smile. 'Of course. We make it perfect for you.'

My husband gives a small inclination of his head. 'Thank you.'

'Good. I get your drinks.'

Once she's out of earshot, Niall leans back in his chair. 'I knew they could fit us in. They were just being lazy. Didn't want the hassle of moving a table. Sometimes it pays to kick up a fuss.'

I bite my lip wanting to defend the waitress. The place is packed and they're rushed off their feet, I'd hardly call her lazy. But it's not worth an argument so I let it go. 'Isn't this place gorgeous though. Boys, what do you think?'

'It's good,' Connor says, nodding. 'Can we go back in the pool when we get home?'

'Tomorrow,' I reply.

Liam's eyes are heavy. He slips off his seat and tries to climb up on my lap.

'Don't fall asleep yet, sweetie. We're going to have some food first, okay? And a nice bubbly glass of Sprite. That will wake you up.' I help him back onto his chair. I'd love to have him cuddle up on my lap, as it's rare he does it these days, but if I do, he'll be out like a light and I want him to eat his dinner first.

It's been a long day. I can't believe we woke in our bed at home in Dorset and scraped ice off the car windscreen at six o'clock this morning. Now, here we are on the Amalfi Coast in short sleeves with two weeks of relaxation stretching out before us.

The waitress returns with our drinks and we're only inside for another five minutes before she returns to show us to our table outside. The atmosphere is buzzy and happy. I don't hear any English voices around us at all. It seems to be all Italian families and couples. I guess that's because we're away from the main drag down by the seafront, so maybe this is where all the locals come.

'It's warm.' Niall pulls at the front of his shirt.

'Muggy,' I agree. The skin on my arms feels static and I can smell ozone in the air.

'That storm's coming,' Niall pronounces.

'I hope it's not going to rain now we've got a table outside.'

We both stare up at the sky and I try to think of something else to talk about besides the weather. I need to reconnect with my husband. Make him remember why he fell for me in the first place. I think longingly of that jade-green dress in the airport shop. It would have been perfect for tonight. Instead, I'm wearing an old floral maxi dress, the strap of which is safety-pinned to my bra, as it ripped when I was taking it off last summer, and I forgot to sew it back on.

Mugginess and fashion malfunctions aside, the evening is magical. The boys perk up with the arrival of drinks and dinner, and the waiting staff are beyond attentive. Niall admits that the place is a real find. The food is outstanding. Niall has fish, the boys have pasta and I opt for the waitress's recommendation of lemon risotto, which is one of the best dishes I've ever tasted.

'I don't suppose I could have the recipe?' I ask, when she comes to take the plates. 'I understand if it's not possible, but it was absolutely exquisite.'

'I don't know if he'll give away the family secrets,' she replies with a laugh, stacking the dishes. 'But I'll ask. My brother's the chef.'

'A family business. That's nice.' Niall nods.

'Yes,' she replies. 'It was my parents' restaurant. They named it after me – Terrazza Luciana. Now my parents have retired and my brother and I have taken over.'

'That's wonderful.' I suddenly envy her. 'I used to be a chef. It was always my dream to open a restaurant.'

'*Really?*' Luciana looks intrigued. 'What type of restaurant? Italian, I hope.'

I flush. No one at home ever asks me about my dreams. I don't know what possessed me to start opening up to a stranger about my past. Maybe it's the wine. 'I trained in French cuisine, but of course I also love Italian food.'

'Pah, French cuisine!' Luciana wrinkles her pretty nose and pretends to spit on the ground before giving a loud chuckle.

'Beth's a good cook,' Niall adds. 'Maybe not as good as your brother, but...' He shrugs and pokes me in the ribs to let me know he's teasing.

Luciana puts a hand on her hip. 'Maybe we should get you in the kitchen. Are you visiting or you live here?'

'Sadly only visiting,' I reply. 'We're staying for a couple of weeks. It's our very first night tonight.'

'And you found us straight away! Okay, so we'll talk some more. I'm interested in this dream you have. But now, can I get you anything else to drink? Maybe a dessert?'

Niall orders us each a decaf coffee, and the boys order ice cream. I'm still buzzing from Luciana's brief interest. I know she was probably only being polite, but it's been years since anyone asked about my abandoned career. I'm surprised to feel a faint spark of that old ambition still glowing in my belly. It's funny, but I feel an affinity with the woman, like we would become good friends if I lived here. She seems warm and funny. Plus, she looks like she's living the kind of busy, purposeful life I would enjoy.

After Luciana leaves our table, I stare out over the night

vista, feeling a sense of nervous optimism. Today has been so up and down, both tiring and stressful, but now we're here in this beautiful place, I'm hoping that our holiday will be as perfect as I imagined.

I shush the boys who've started bickering about which flavour ice cream is the best. They've been so well behaved so far this evening; I hope they're not getting overtired.

The terrace is emptying out now. Everyone who leaves hugs Luciana. She seems to know everybody here. And yet, for all her chatting, the service is still quick, the tables wiped down, orders taken quickly. Her staff are on it.

'Why did you tell her your dream was to open a restaurant?' Niall asks, dabbing his mouth with his napkin.

'Just making conversation.' I shrug, trying to make light of things. Niall can be funny about certain issues and I don't want him to latch onto my comment, thinking I'm unhappy. I mean, my dream *was* to open a restaurant and Niall knows that. Life just didn't work out that way.

He's quiet for a moment. And then, 'So, you wish you'd done that? Opened a restaurant... instead of looking after our family?' A hurt expression crosses his features. 'Or are you trying to guilt-trip me?'

'Of course not, silly.' I rub his arm reassuringly. 'I made a choice that I'm happy with. It's just, we're in a restaurant, talking to a restaurant owner, so I was making conversation about my career as a chef. That's all. Something in common, you know?'

'Chocolate flavour's the best,' Liam says.

'Chocolate ice cream looks like poo.' Connor screws up his face in mock disgust.

'No it doesn't!' Liam cries.

'Shh.' I lean over to the boys and fix them with a glare. 'Connor, stop teasing your brother. Liam, you can't shout like that. We're in a restaurant.'

'But he said—'

'Uh-uh.' I waggle my finger. 'Both of you, behave or there'll be no ice cream.'

'Dad.' Connor tugs his father's sleeve. 'Which is the best ice cream, chocolate – which looks like poo – or strawberry?'

Niall ignores Connor's question and gets to his feet.

'You okay?' I have a nervous feeling in the pit of my stomach.

'Just going for a quick walk. I've eaten too much; I need some space. It's been a hectic day.'

'A walk?' I ask.

'Here we are!' Luciana returns with two frosted glasses of limoncello for me and Niall, along with a couple of the most enormous ice-cream sundaes I've ever seen. They're covered with chocolate sauce, marshmallows and sprinkles, and have sparklers fizzing away on top.

'No way!' Liam and Connor cry in unison, their argument forgotten.

'Wow, they look incredible.' I give Luciana a puzzled smile. 'We didn't order anything this fancy.'

'It's on the house,' she replies. 'If your boys are like mine, then I know they'll enjoy.'

'Very kind.' Niall gives a cold nod. 'I'll be back in a few minutes.' He squeezes past me.

'Everything okay?' Luciana asks, after Niall has left the terrace.

Heat floods my cheeks at my husband's abrupt departure, but I choose to misunderstand her question. 'Yes, wonderful, thank you. You really shouldn't have spoiled them like this. It's so nice of you.'

'It's nothing.'

'You said you have boys too?' I ask, changing the subject and taking a sip of my lemon liqueur, enjoying the sweet alcoholic tang.

'Yes, two. Similar ages to yours, I think.' She gives them a fond glance.

'Connor's eleven and Liam's seven.' I offer information about my life for the second time tonight.

'Okay, so mine are twelve and nine. It's school holidays right now so they help me in the restaurant.'

'Wow, that's great. You hear that, boys? Luciana's boys help her in the restaurant.'

My children are too consumed with their desserts to pay me any attention, other than a distracted mumble.

'Yes, but they complain about it.' Luciana grins. 'Loudly. They would prefer to be with their friends, causing mischief, jumping off the harbour wall into the sea and other things they think I don't know about.'

'Sounds dangerous,' I reply. I realise this might sound critical. I'm coming across as an overprotective mother, but I can't imagine allowing my two to do anything like that.

Luciana shrugs. 'We all did this when we were younger, but it's more worrying with your children than with yourself. It's hard because I have to work so I can't watch them all the time.'

I realise how lucky I am not to have that problem. Although I'd love to have a career like Luciana's. 'But it must be great living by the beach. Luckily, the house we're staying at has a pool, so these two will be occupied while we're here.' I tip my head in the direction of Connor and Liam.

'Oh, that sounds wonderful. My two would love to have a pool. I think it's going to be hot this year.'

'Not in the UK,' I say with a smile.

'Ah, no. You have rain, yes?'

'Ice and sleet at the moment. Which is why it's such a treat to come somewhere warm.'

'I don't like the sound of that.' Luciana screws up her face and we both laugh.

'This limoncello is delicious, by the way.' I take another sip, savouring the taste.

'My mother's recipe,' she says with a nod.

'You make it yourselves?'

'Of course. Ours is the best. Secret ingredient,' she adds with a knowing smile.

'You know,' I say in a spurt of generosity. 'If your boys ever want to come over for a swim, they're very welcome. You too. Connor and Liam would love the company.'

'You're serious?' Luciana's eyes widen.

'Of course. We're very close by – Villa Della Luna, a couple of streets away.'

'I know it! Amber and Renzo Mason's place. They come here very often. We cater for them sometimes at their house. They're not there now?'

'No. We did a house swap. They're staying at our place in England.'

'A swap? Such a good idea! Their pool is beautiful.' Luciana does a chef's kiss.

'It really is.'

We arrange for her and the children to come round at ten tomorrow morning. I ask if she has a husband or partner she wants to bring, but her face clouds over and she tells me she's divorced. After the arrangement is made, I suddenly worry what Niall might think about it. It's only for an hour or two and it will occupy the boys, so I'm sure he'll be fine.

But what if he's not?

ELEVEN

AMBER

It's late when we pull up outside the Kildares' cottage. The porch light glows invitingly. Even though we'd seen a few photos, I realise that I'd had quite low expectations for the place, but the reality from the outside is that it truly is a beautiful property. A double-fronted, stone-built thatched cottage with leaded windows and twin chimneys. With frost glittering on the roof and front lawn, it looks like something you'd see on a Christmas card.

The drive from Gatwick was okay despite being squashed into Beth's tiny Renault with all our luggage. It took us twenty minutes to wedge everything into the boot. Even so, we still had to put one of the cases on the back seat between the children.

Beth and I mailed a set of car keys to one another in advance. We decided not to post the house keys for security reasons. Luckily, we each have friends who said they didn't mind dropping them over once we arrived.

Renzo and I took turns driving, stopping halfway at a service station for a toilet break and a McDonald's coffee. He did the first leg and I did the second. The kids fell asleep after our rest stop, and Renzo dropped off about half an hour ago, his snores vibrating through the whole vehicle.

Now we're finally here, I feel my body start to relax. I unclench the steering wheel and roll my shoulders. I hope the cottage is as welcoming on the inside as it looks on the outside. Right now, I just want to fall into a comfy bed and close my eyes.

'Looks nice.' Renzo gives a noisy yawn.

'Hello, sleepyhead,' I reply.

'Sorry, I know I was supposed to chat and keep you company.' He puts a hand on my thigh and squeezes.

'It's fine.'

'Did they leave the key somewhere?' he asks, stretching his arms out in front of him.

'I've got a number to call. Apparently the neighbour has two keys for us. Sally, I think her name is. They didn't want to leave the keys under a mat.' I reach across into the passenger footwell to get my phone from my bag. As I do, my attention is drawn by a light coming on opposite the cottage. A figure appears from behind a boundary hedge – a woman in a cream towelling dressing gown and trainers. She's heading our way. 'Hey, Renz. This might be the neighbour. She must have seen us pull up.' I open the car door and step out onto the narrow pavement, gasping as the freezing air hits my face. I'd forgotten how utterly freezing the UK can be in April. After the drowsy warmth of the car, I'm suddenly wide awake again.

'Amber?' the woman asks, coming to stand in front of me. She's short and blonde, around fortyish. Her face has a scrubbed clean look. She gives me an appraising glance, her eyes taking in my clothes, face and hair.

'Yes, hi, I'm Amber.' I hug myself against the cold, and smile.

'I'm Sal, Beth's neighbour. You sound English, I assumed

you'd be Italian. Such beautiful dark hair.' Sal has a soft Dorset accent.

'Thanks. No, we live in Italy but I'm originally from Surrey. Sorry to keep you up so late.'

'It's fine. Beth knows I'm a night owl. I told her I didn't mind at all. Excuse the dressing gown.'

'Hello, I'm Renzo.' My husband comes around to the pavement and holds out his hand.

'Nice to meet you.' Sal shakes his hand and then peers into the car. 'They're out for the count, bless their hearts. Shall we get you all inside and settled?'

I follow Sal down the narrow garden path that leads to the wooden front door, while Renzo gets the kids from the car.

She hands me a set of keys attached to a leather heart-shaped keyring. 'Now pull the door towards you at the same time you turn the gold key clockwise.'

I do as she says. After a couple of attempts, the key turns with a satisfying click, and I push open the door.

'Well done. You have to lock it in the same way, but anti-clockwise, obviously.' Sally laughs at this. 'There are two front-door keys, and a back-door key on there.'

I step into a tiny flagstone porch that's lit by a brass ceiling lantern. On the wall to my left are a row of coat hooks. An empty shoe rack sits on the floor. Next to it are four pairs of green wellington boots. I push open the inner door, which leads into the house. Directly ahead of me is a steep, narrow staircase. Sally reaches out a hand to turn on the wall lights, and I stare about me, taking it all in.

I turn slightly left into what seems to be a hallway that's also a dining room. The floors are dark planks pitted with age, the ceiling is white, embedded with a row of warm wooden beams. There's a huge, impressive inglenook fireplace built from a mix of grey stone and red brick with an inset wood burner.

A cream dresser squats in one of the alcoves and a window

seat curves around a deep bay window, completed by two armchairs and a circular polished wood coffee table. In the centre of the room, next to the fireplace, sits a long trestle table with mismatched dining chairs. It's a warm and welcoming room, but I'm immediately irritated by its artful shabbiness. It reminds me of women who spend hours trying to perfect the no-makeup look. They want you to think that they look like that naturally. This room is the same. Someone has obviously spent a lot of time trying to make it look effortlessly comfortable. But in my opinion it's trying too hard. Or maybe I'm just tired.

'Gorgeous, isn't it?' Sal gushes.

'Mm, it's lovely,' I reply, thinking of my light and airy white villa back home.

'Let me get your bags,' Sal says. 'Are they in the boot?'

'Please don't worry,' I reply. 'You've done more than enough by staying up to let us in. I don't want to take up any more of your time.'

'It's no bother at all. I'll bring the bags in and then get out of your hair.' She bustles back outside. I still can't believe she's stayed up so late to help an unknown family settle into their holiday home. She must be a really good friend of Beth's. Either that or she's a really nosy neighbour and wanted to see what we're like. My neighbour was happy to meet the Kildares, but that was at a reasonable hour.

'Are the kids' bedrooms upstairs?' Renzo comes back inside with Flora in his arms, still asleep, her cheek pressed against his shoulder, her mouth hanging open. Franco is by his side, his sweatshirt crumpled, eyes half-lidded.

'I assume the bedrooms are upstairs,' I reply. 'But there are only two in total. Franco and Flora have to share.'

'Oh.' Renzo gives me a puzzled look. He knows that normally I prefer they have their own rooms when we go away. 'Okay, shall I take them up? Or do you want to?'

'You do it. I'll...' I roll my eyes and jerk my head in the direction of the front door, meaning I'll get rid of Sally so we can all go to bed.

Renzo nods and takes the children up the steep staircase. The boards creak alarmingly as goes.

'Here we are.' Beth's neighbour huffs inside with two of our cases and sets them down at the bottom of the stairs. I have no idea how she managed it. I could barely lift one of them. 'I'll get the other two bags for you.' She disappears before I can tell her it's not necessary.

While she's gone, I poke my head through the door at the end of the dining hall. Looks like this is the kitchen diner. I turn on the light and glance at the old-fashioned painted wood cabinets and the oak breakfast bar at one end, and the narrow kitchen table and benches at the other. The only concession to the twenty-first century are a state-of-the-art coffee machine on the counter, and a set of black bifold doors leading out into the pitch-black garden. I'll explore more tomorrow, but for now, I really just want to shower the journey away, brush my teeth and sleep.

'Amber?' Sally's voice is already grating on me and I've only known the woman five minutes. 'Ah, here you are. The last of the bags are in the dining room.'

'That was so kind of you,' I say, trying to sound grateful. 'You really didn't have to.'

'It's fine. You must be tired after your journey. Bit colder here than Italy.'

'Just a bit.' I fake a yawn, hoping she'll get the hint.

No such luck.

'At least Beth left the heating on for you.' Sal nods approvingly. 'Would you like me to make you both a cup of tea before I go? Save you looking for everything?'

I think I can probably manage to locate some mugs and a teabag. 'No, you've honestly done enough. We'll probably go straight to bed. Thanks so much again for waiting up.' I smile and politely usher her out of the kitchen, through the dining room and towards the front door. 'You're so lovely to have brought all the cases in. You really shouldn't have. Thank you.' I soften my eyes and give her my most grateful smile.

Sal lays a hand on my arm and smiles back. 'If there's anything you need, you just shout. I'm at number six opposite, but Beth has left my number on the fridge.'

'Fantastic. Okay then, bye.'

'Cheerio, Amber. Say night to Renzo and the children from me.'

'I will.' I close the front door with a thankful sigh. I hope she isn't going to be popping over all the time. She seems the type.

I should go upstairs and help my husband with the kids, but I'll quickly check my messages first. I haven't looked at my phone since leaving Italy. I sit in one of the armchairs by the bay window, take a breath and swipe the screen. There are five missed calls, three voicemails and a string of text messages from Beth.

I go straight to the voicemails. The first one is Beth asking me to confirm where we parked our car, because it's not where I said it would be. The second message is more panicked. She's worried that it may have been stolen, but she's not sure what to do. Should she contact the police and report the theft? She says she'd rather wait to hear from me first in case we had to park it elsewhere. She doesn't want to waste police time. The third message is her telling us that they've decided to take a cab to the house for now. Her voice is high and anxiety-ridden. I can hear her husband in the background snapping at the kids to be quiet.

I send a text message back.

Beth I'm so, so sorry. We completely forgot about the car! Renzo ordered a cab to the airport and I just went along with it. It was so hectic getting the kids organised that our car arrangement flew out of my head. The car's safe in the garage

at home, so please do feel free to use it. You have the keys, right?
I hope it didn't cause you too much stress!

It's hectic enough travelling with kids, let alone having something like that happen. They must have been so worried, arriving in Italy and thinking our car might have been stolen.

I lean back in my chair, smile and congratulate myself on 'accidentally' forgetting to take the car to the airport. There's nothing like a bit of travel stress to set your holiday off on the wrong foot...

TWELVE

BETH

My heart thumps uncomfortably in my chest. I was right to be worried about Niall's reaction.

'I don't understand what you were even thinking,' he says coldly. A crack of thunder echoes his sharp words as the rain sheets down on the four of us. The boys are running ahead, revelling in the excitement of thunder, lightning and warm rain.

'Don't run too far!' I call out to their oblivious figures. 'I'm sorry, Niall, I wasn't really thinking at all. It seemed like a nice thing to offer.'

We're on our way home from Terrazza Luciana and the second we stepped outside the restaurant the storm decided to hit. I'm only wearing a thin cotton dress, and the boys are in shorts and shirts. We're already drenched to the skin.

'*A nice thing to offer?*' Niall gives an incredulous laugh. 'It's not even our house, or our pool. Would you want Amber and whatshisname to start inviting random strangers into *our* home?'

'It's not like that...'

'It's exactly like that!'

'I'm sorry. It's just... Luciana and I have so much in

common. I wanted to get to know her. Anyway, she said she already knows the Masons. She's been to their house before.'

'I thought this was supposed to be a family holiday. You keep going on about how you want the four of us to spend time together, and now, when we're finally doing that, you invite other people round. You know, I work really hard, Beth. Now that I've taken a little time off, I'd rather not have to spend it with some waitress and her offspring.' He gives a growl and stalks off to catch up with Connor and Liam.

My shoulders sag and I start to shiver. Am I to blame for this argument? Or is Niall overreacting? Maybe it's because we're both tired and cranky. Surely everything will look better after an early night. I decide to hang back and keep my distance for the moment. Give him time to cool down.

I did have quite a lot of wine earlier, plus the two G & Ts on the plane. I don't normally drink much at home, but I wanted to unwind and relax today. Perhaps it's impaired my judgement. Alcohol does tend to have the effect of making me overfriendly. Maybe that's what's happened this evening. In contrast, alcohol tends to make Niall a bit grumpy. I shouldn't worry. When we get home, I'll make us both a hot drink and try to get him to forgive me.

We turn into our street. Wet branches are strewn across the road. The trees are swaying alarmingly and I'm worried one might even blow down. The wind certainly feels strong enough.

Through the drumming swirling rain, Niall is a dark shape up ahead with our two leaping boys. I feel a disappointed pang that he hasn't even turned back to see if I'm okay. What if I'd been hit by a falling branch, or abducted by a stranger? A part of me wants to hang back. To hide. To make him worry about me. To see how long it would take him to come looking. But I would never do something like that. Besides, he's in such a bad mood that he'd likely go to bed without checking whether I'm alive or dead.

I need to shake myself out of this funk. It won't do me any good. Just get inside, get the kids dried off and into bed and go to sleep. Hope that tomorrow is a better day.

When I reach the house, the door is wide open, the wind and rain surging into the house. I'm gasping and shivering as I drip onto the already puddled marble floor. The wet trail leads up the stairs. I hope the illuminated staircase isn't going to electrocute me. I should probably have stripped and dried off downstairs, but I'm not exactly thinking straight right now.

'Boys!' I call out.

I stop on the landing and listen out. Shouts and laughter filter from one of the bedrooms. I follow the noise and open the door. Connor and Liam are jumping around the bedroom like crazy animals, bouncing on the bed and on the armchairs, dripping water onto the sheets and upholstery from their rain-soaked bodies.

'What's going on in here?' I muster my strictest voice.

'You're not allowed to touch the ground,' Liam replies. 'And you can't stop moving either. It's a game. Connor made it up. You can play too, Mum!'

'Right, stop that now, get down from there. Into the bathroom, both of you. Where's your dad?'

'He went to bed,' Connor replies, leaping onto a low velvet ottoman.

It's only day one and the bedroom's an absolute mess. We're going to wreck this pristine house if we're not careful. We should have chosen a more homely home, something rustic and shabby. Something that doesn't stain so easily.

I eventually corral the boys into a warm shower, get them dry with the plentiful white fluffy towels, and take them into another, dryer bedroom with twin beds. They can share a room tonight. It will feel more familiar anyway. I'll sort out the wet bedroom tomorrow. I'm honestly too exhausted to tackle it right now.

Liam's eyes close before I even turn out the lights.

'Mum.' Connor's voice comes at me through the dark room.

'Yes, sweetie?'

'Is Dad cross with us?'

My heart cracks a little. 'No, of course not. He's tired. It's been a very long day.'

'Okay. Night, Mum.'

'Night, Connor. Night, Liam. Love you.'

'Love you too.' I pull the door so it's slightly ajar. I'll leave the hall light on in case they wake up and get disoriented during the night.

I pause on the landing, reluctant to go into our bedroom. I can't face another argument with Niall. Maybe I should go downstairs for a while, wait till he's fallen asleep.

'Beth? That you?' The door to our room opens. Niall's standing in the doorway in a robe, drying his hair with a towel. 'I wondered where you were. Did you lock up downstairs?'

'I think so. I locked the front door, so that's it, right?'

'Yeah.' He looks me up and down. 'You're still soaking.'

'I know. I had to sort out the kids. They've made a right mess in Connor's room.'

Niall leans against the door frame. 'You actually look pretty hot in that dress, all dripping wet like that.'

I grin, my heart lifting. 'I look an absolute state.'

'You can be a state,' he replies. 'As long as it's a state of undress.'

I walk towards him, our argument forgotten. He kisses me and peels off my wet dress. I'm shivering so he leads me into the bathroom where we take a warm shower together. I try to block out the sight of Amber's naked photo wall, but as Niall makes love to me, I'm treated to an eyeful of our absent host's oversized breasts. I'm not sure whether the image is making Niall a little more enthusiastic than usual, but I try to block out that thought. I'm just relieved that my husband has forgiven me and we can go to bed happy on the first night of our holiday.

We dry off in companiable silence before heading back into the bedroom, sleepy and satisfied.

My phone pings. I lift it off my bedside table. 'It's from Amber.'

Niall doesn't reply. He's pulling on a pair of cotton pyjama shorts.

I skim the text and shake my head in disbelief. 'You'll never guess what.'

'So tell me,' Niall replies.

'They forgot to drive their car to Naples Airport! They took a cab instead.' I sit on the bed and lean against the headboard. 'That's why we couldn't find their car.'

'You mean, I was running around Naples Airport trying to find a car that wasn't even there?' Niall's face grows redder as he speaks.

'Apparently it's here in the garage. At least it hasn't been stolen,' I add. 'And we won't have to go back to the airport to collect it.'

'Unbelievable!' Niall says, pacing the length of the bedroom. 'Who forgets something like that?'

'It does seems flaky,' I reply.

'All that hassle for nothing,' Niall mutters.

'Never mind,' I soothe, feeling relieved that it wasn't my mistake after all. 'Let's forget it.'

'Ridiculous,' he snaps. 'And I'm not sleeping opposite that,' Niall says, pointing to the huge black-and-white canvas of the Mason family. 'Grab the other side, will you? Let's take it down and stick it under the bed.'

'You can't do that. What if we damage it?'

Niall rolls his eyes. 'It's only a photo. Come on. I'm not going to bed with a strange family staring down at me. It's creepy.'

'Not as creepy as having sex in the shower with Amber watching.'

Niall blurts out a laugh. 'I know, right. That was pretty weird.'

'So weird,' I agree, happy I could elicit a laugh out of him. I thought he was going to explode when I told him about the car. 'But I still don't think we should mess around with their stuff. The boys have already dripped water all over their room. We need to treat this place better. I mean, it's like a show home. And here come the Kildares to trash the place.'

'Taking a photo off a wall is hardly trashing the place. To be frank, I'm not going to be walking on eggshells for a fortnight. We're here to relax, not tiptoe around. I can't relax with their smug faces grinning at me all night.'

I'm taken aback by Niall's outburst. It's not like him to be so hung up on stuff like this. 'How about we drape a sheet over it?'

'Fine. But hurry up and do it, then. I'm tired. I need to sleep.'

I spend the next five minutes checking cupboards and drawers in the walk-in closet and bathroom for a sheet, but there's no bed linen to be found. I come across a large silk shawl that should do the job. I attempt to drape it over the photo, but the stupid thing keeps sliding off. I end up tucking the corners of the shawl behind the canvas and it eventually stays put.

'There!' I declare to my husband. But Niall is already stretched out on the bed, snoring.

I pad over to my side of the bed and lie back against the headboard. I wish Niall and I could stay on an even footing. Things between us always seem so precarious. I'm annoyed with myself for inviting Luciana and her family over. For rocking the boat. But surely something as minor as that shouldn't cause such a rift between us. I feel as though I can't do anything right these days. I also need to stop spiralling into this negative thinking. On the bright side, Niall and I made love in the shower this evening! We haven't done anything like that for months. And the boys are happy. Plus, the weather is forecast to be sunny tomorrow. The main thing is that we're all here together, as a family.

I realise that I can still make out the faces of the Mason family behind the thin silk of the shawl. It's creepier than it looked before I covered them up. I wish we'd taken the damn thing down like Niall suggested. My head is spinning. I must still be a little tipsy. I turn off the light and lie in the dark, listening to the pounding rain and the wind shaking the trees. I'm trying not to think about how queasy I feel. I need to clear my head of worries. To sleep. But the day's events keep scrolling through my brain like a movie on a loop.

I try not to think about the little pot of prescription sleeping pills I brought with me. I shouldn't really take any after drinking alcohol. But I can tell that I'm not going to fall asleep without one tonight. I'm too wired. I slip out of bed and pad into the bathroom where I locate my wash bag. I rummage through the contents, but the pills don't seem to be in there. My heart gives a little skip of anxiety until I remember that I put them in my bedside drawer when I unpacked.

I tiptoe back to the bedroom and ease open the drawer, my tension evaporating once my fingers curl around the little pot. Using the light from the dressing room, I shake out one of the pills and drop it onto my tongue, chasing it with a swig of water. I can already feel sleep coming to claim me as I slide back into bed next to my snoring husband.

The white silk shawl covering the Masons' portrait looms through the darkness like a ghost. I squeeze my eyes shut and turn onto my side. Just sleep. Tomorrow is another day.

THIRTEEN

I have to force myself to be restrained. I've been getting too close. Putting my emotions before everything else. Being reckless could jeopardise everything.

Having a plan helps. I no longer feel as though I'm falling off a cliff into emptiness. Instead, I now have a purpose that shapes my days.

A goal that I'm working towards.

An endgame.

FOURTEEN

BETH

I fumble my way through the Masons' bright white kitchen, opening and closing cupboards, uninspired and a little disappointed by what I find. Or rather, what I *don't* find.

Connor and Liam were up early, begging to go for a swim. I'm groggy and a little hungover this morning, but it's our first proper day of the holidays so I forced myself out of bed, splashed my face with cold water and came downstairs with the kids, letting Niall have a lie-in. Last night's storm has left everything fresh and cool, but the sun is already warming up the back garden. I think it's going to be a hot one.

I'm nervous about facing Niall today. I know we made up last night, but he could easily lose his temper again when faced with the imminent arrival of Luciana and her children. I'm surprised at my confidence in inviting her. But she seems like such a sweet person.

My stomach flips as Niall comes into the room. He looks handsome in beige linen shorts and a navy polo shirt. His neutral expression gives nothing away.

'Morning. Do you want coffee?' I try not to sound too bright or too apologetic.

'Yeah, coffee sounds good. Make it a strong one, can you?' He doesn't sound upset. That's good. I'm keeping everything crossed that he's let it go.

I close the fridge door. I'll have to do a quick shop before they arrive. There's cereal, milk and orange juice, and that's about it. No bread, or fruit or nibbles. At least there's a decent coffee machine – vital for my sorry state this morning. I spent ages reading the instructions earlier, so I think I've got it sussed now. 'One decent cup of Italian coffee coming up,' I say, cringing at my forced jolly tone.

Niall pulls out one of ten white chairs and sits at the dark wood dining table.

I tip the coffee into the machine and press the grinder. For a few moments the kitchen is filled with the satisfying whirr of the machine, and the pungent aroma of fresh beans. I stare out through the sliding doors at the boys splashing in the pool. This all feels like something out of a John Lewis advert.

'Is that waitress still coming over?' Niall asks, jolting me from my daydream.

My stomach drops.

'I hope you've seen sense and cancelled.'

'Uh, no.' I turn away and busy myself with his coffee. 'She's still coming.'

'That's a shame. It's bad enough with our two making a racket, never mind *four* screaming kids.' He sucks in a breath. 'So what time are they arriving?'

I swallow. 'We said ten.' I glance at my watch. 'It's almost nine fifteen now.'

'Is there any toast? Or fruit? Some scrambled eggs would be good. I'm starving.'

'There's some cereal.'

'Is that it?' Niall screws up his face. 'Didn't we leave them shitloads of stuff in the fridge and cupboards back home? Wasn't that part of the house-swap deal?'

'Not really,' I reply. 'I just thought it was polite to leave them some meals to get them started.' I don't tell him that I put my heart and soul into creating several mini feasts for them. That I probably went a bit overboard. I guess I probably should have checked that they were at least leaving us the basics.

'You should have arranged the same for us. I mean, a loaf of bread and a few eggs isn't too much to ask for, is it?'

Privately I agree, but I need to calm Niall down, not rile him up. I bring him his coffee and set it on the table. I should really use a coaster, but I can't see any lying around. 'It's no problem. I'll nip out and get us something. Do you remember seeing any shops nearby? I need to get some snacks for this morning anyway. I don't want to be a bad host.'

'Oh yeah, heaven forbid you be a bad host,' he mutters under his breath.

'It won't be for long,' I try to reassure, ignoring his jibe. 'And, actually, having her kids here will stop ours from sniping at each other. I think hers are a little bit older too, which will help.' I hear the placatory, pleading tone in my voice. Part of me wishes I could tell him to get over it. It's two flipping hours out of his life, for goodness' sake. But I want us to have a nice, peaceful time. If I can smooth this over, then hopefully we can get back on an even keel. 'I thought it would be fun to get to know some of the locals. You always like meeting new people and socialising.'

'Yes, but not their kids. I want this to be a relaxing break for us, not a hangout for local waifs and strays.'

'So *did* you?' I prompt.

'Did I what?'

'Notice any shops nearby.'

'No, but I'm sure there'll be something.' Niall knocks back his coffee. 'Look, don't worry about breakfast. If this place is turning into a creche this morning, then I'll grab a bite in

Maiori. I'll be back later.' He sets his cup back on the table and gets to his feet.

'No, don't do that. I'll cancel, okay?'

He pauses for a second, his dark eyes narrowed. 'Have you even got her number?'

'No, but I'll find it. I'll call the restaurant. Or I can pop over there, tell her in person.'

Niall shakes his head. 'Don't worry. It's easier if I go out.'

'You don't have to do that.'

'I'll take my laptop. May as well get some work done while I'm there. Text me when they've gone, okay?'

I give up trying to talk him round. Once he's made up his mind about something, there's no changing it. 'Okay, well, can you stay with the kids for ten minutes while I nip out to find a local shop?'

He sits back down. 'Fine. But hurry up. I want to be gone when they get here or I'll have to be sociable. She'll think I'm rude if I leave as soon as she arrives.'

'No problem. I'll go now.'

Once I return from the shop, Niall leaves immediately. I managed to find a small grocery store in the next road. It didn't have the best selection, but at least I managed to get bread, snacks and more milk and juice. I have to admit I'm relieved Niall won't be here when our visitors arrive. At least this way I can relax while they're here without worrying that they're annoying him. Although, I'll probably have to carry on grovelling later. He won't let me off the hook that easily.

A doorbell chimes. I didn't have a chance to look in the mirror and make myself presentable, but aside from being a bit hot and sweaty, I think I'll do. I'm wearing my favourite blue sundress, and my hair is swept up into a half-ponytail.

As I walk along the wide marble hallway to answer the door, I feel like a bit of a fraud. As if I'm playing lady of the manor in my multimillion-pound contemporary show home. The illusion shatters as I have to fiddle with the door to get it to open.

'Sorry!' I call out. 'Having trouble with the door.' Finally, I get the knack and the door swings open.

Luciana is standing there smiling, her corkscrew curls loose and tumbling over her shoulders. Two gorgeous curly-haired young boys stand by her side carrying towels, inflatables and water pistols under their arms.

'Ooh, look at all this! You'll be popular,' I say before realising they might not understand English. But they grin and brandish the guns.

The elder of the two says, 'Thank you for inviting us. Otherwise, we would be in Uncle Matteo's kitchen preparing the vegetables.'

'Well, that was a lucky escape,' I reply. 'Come in.'

The boys head straight out to the pool, where my two are sitting on the side, splashing their feet up and down in the water.

'This is very nice of you,' Luciana says, stepping inside. 'Marco and Gianni are very excited for today, to meet your English boys and swim in the pool.'

'It's my pleasure. Would you like a coffee?'

'Please.' She follows me into the kitchen.

'Looks like they're already introducing themselves.' I nod towards the pool where all four of them are leaning over to fill up their water pistols.

'I hope the guns are okay with you. I told them not to run around or be too noisy.'

'It's fine,' I reply, heading over to the coffee machine feeling doubly glad Niall's gone out. Four boys running around shooting water everywhere would have tipped him over the edge. I shudder at the thought of his reaction to the possible mayhem.

Luciana takes a cardboard box from her beach bag. 'I brought some of my brother's fresh sfogliatella pastries.'

I take the box and peer inside. It's filled with warm shell-shaped pastries. 'Thank you. They look delicious. Is that lemon I smell? What did you say they were called?'

'*Sfogliatella* – they're a traditional pastry. These ones are filled with lemon cream, but you can make them with anything – hazelnut, pistachio, whatever you like.'

'Wow! We can have these with our coffee. I didn't eat breakfast yet so this is a real treat.'

Luciana seats herself on a stool at the long kitchen island while I make our drinks. She glances around the room. 'Your husband isn't here?'

I turn away to fiddle with the machine. 'Niall has some work to do, he sends his apologies and said to say hello.'

She nods. 'He's not happy we come round, no?'

'*What?* No, he's fine. He's gone out to find a café. He's a writer and has to work when inspiration strikes.' I fake an expression of sincerity, but I can tell Luciana doesn't believe me.

She gives a little shrug and selects one of the pastries from the box, taking a bite. 'Mm, these are good. I haven't had them for a long time. What does your husband write?'

The coffee machine whirrs. I'm a little irritated by her assumption about Niall, despite her being correct. I place some of the pastries on a plate and wait for the machine to quiet down before answering her question. I tell her about my husband's fantasy series and feel a little disappointed that she hasn't heard of him. His books are quite popular in Italy, so I thought she might have recognised his name. In fact, she seems quite dismissive and unimpressed, which is strange. Last night I'd found her warm and friendly. Maybe I was mistaken.

I'd planned for us to sit by the pool while the children swam, but I don't think it would be very relaxing out there right now, so instead we take our coffees over to the low grey sofa at the other corner of the room. One side looks through a set of sliding doors to a patio dining set, and the other side looks out onto the pool. I set the plate of pastries on the low white coffee table and sit on the sofa, my bare feet sinking into the soft grey sheepskin rug.

'I apologise if I was a little rude about your husband a moment ago,' she says, her shoulders slumping a little.

'You weren't rude,' I reply, even though she was a bit sniffy.

'Not rude... just... never mind.'

I'm confused. I feel she wants to say something so I prompt her. 'What's wrong?'

'Nothing. Like I told you last night, I'm recently divorced, so I'm off men at the moment, that's all.'

'I'm sorry to hear that. It must have been a difficult time.'

'Take one.' She points to the pastries.

I do as she directs and select one of the warm flaky sfogliatella. I take a bite, and my taste buds come alive. It's sweet and tart and absolutely delicious.

Luciana laughs at my facial expression. 'It's good, huh? Have another.'

I laugh with her and finish my mouthful before replying. 'They're incredible. Tell your brother he's a genius.'

'I won't do that. His head is already too big.' She grins and then grows serious again. 'My ex-husband is not a very nice man. He was... controlling. Not nice to me or the children. Matteo, my brother, helped me to leave him. It was a bit of a scandal because he's a respected person in the area. But I made the right decision.'

'That sounds terrible. I'm sorry you went through that.'

'Thank you. He was not good to me. Not at all.'

I nod feeling a little awkward that she's opened up to me

about something so personal, so soon. But I guess it's nice that she feels comfortable enough to talk to me.

'Your husband, Niall. He was unhappy last night?'

'Oh, no.' I wave away her concern. 'We were all cranky after our long journey, that's all. I was irritable too.'

'You were?' She sips her coffee. 'No. I thought you were very friendly.'

'I must have covered up my crankiness better than Niall did.' I give a light laugh. I can't very well tell her that the reason Niall was annoyed was because I invited her over.

Luciana's expression darkens. 'My ex-husband used to be angry with me all the time. Nothing I did was right. Always he would pick at me. It's not a nice feeling.'

I shift in my seat. I hope she's not insinuating that my husband is anything like her ex. I know Niall can be a bit... set in his ways sometimes, but he's not a bully. He works hard and he gets tired, like everyone does.

Luciana glances up at me and gives me a look that seems pitying. I feel my hackles rise. I need to change the subject or I'm going to snap at her. I take a breath. Maybe I'm overreacting. She hasn't accused Niall of anything, she's simply telling me about her situation. So why am I linking it with mine? Why do I feel as if she's having a dig at my marriage? I've only just met the woman. She knows nothing about me. I'm beginning to think that Niall was right. I shouldn't have invited her over. After all, she's virtually a stranger and this is our family holiday. Whatever was I thinking?

FIFTEEN

AMBER

'What time is it?' I roll over and stretch luxuriously, my eyes still closed against the morning light that's trying to pry me awake.

'Eight thirty.' Renzo's voice comes at me from a distance. He's already up and out of bed.

'Still early,' I mutter.

'It's okay, stay where you are. I'll bring your coffee up. You organised the holiday for us all, so have a morning off.'

'You sure, Renz?' I murmur, snuggling down further beneath the duvet.

'Of course. The kids and I are going to bundle up and have a walk into Sherborne. Give you some peace and quiet.'

I lift my head and open my eyes a crack to look at my husband. He's pulling on a pair of jeans. His bare torso is dark and toned, soft dark hairs shadowing his abs. I wonder what wonderful thing I did in a previous life to be this lucky. If it weren't for the kids, I'd pull Renzo back into bed with me. Make him even happier to be my husband. He catches me looking at him, comes over and kisses my lips. I pull him towards me to stop the dark worries from crowding my brain. Renzo loves me. Worships me. We're here in England now, it will all be fine.

'Papa, the phone charger doesn't plug in!' Franco's panicked voice calls from downstairs.

'Did you pack any adaptors?' I ask.

'Three of the little suckers.' Renzo winks and straightens up. 'Just a minute, Franco!'

'Handsome *and* organised. I knew there was a reason I married you.'

'Papa!' Franco calls again.

Renzo shakes his head at our son's impatience and shoots me a grin. 'Okay, princess, you stay right there. Coffee and croissants are coming right up.'

'Croissants?'

'Yeah, these people didn't scrimp on anything. The cupboards are stuffed, and the fridge is full of all this amazing homemade stuff – lasagne, cherry pie, salads, soup, fresh meats, cheeses. Everything. It's like a deli down there. We don't even need to go out if we don't want to.'

I nod my approval. 'Nice.'

'But we didn't do the same for them.' My considerate husband looks worried for a moment.

I shrug. 'We left them the basics... and some wine. Lots of wine.' I grin.

'Okay, I guess the wine will help. But, Amber, you should see it down there.'

'Okay, I get it,' I snap, rolling my eyes. 'There's a lot of nice stuff. This family's amazing and we're not.'

Renzo's eyebrows lift.

'Sorry, I'm being grumpy. You know what I'm like in the morning.'

'I do. One strong espresso coming up.' Renzo tweaks my chin.

'Yes please.' I lie back down, letting my head sink into the feather pillows. 'Maybe they felt bad because our sunny villa is nicer than their shabby little cottage,' I murmur.

But Renzo has already left the room, his footfalls thudding down the stairs. I doze for a while, letting my mind relax back into a half sleep until, true to his word, he returns with coffee and a croissant, as well as fresh fruit and orange juice.

The kids are up and breakfasted without my help and Renzo assures me the three of them will stay out until midday, so I should just relax. I know it seems as if my husband is too good to be true, but after we first met, when things started to become serious between us, I told him that I'm not the sort of woman who runs around after a man. I'll do my fair share, but that's it. I have my career. I told him I didn't have time for any misogynistic, patriarchal bullshit. He laughed at that and told me he had three sisters and neither did they. That comment sealed the deal for me.

The front door closes with a thud that shakes the house. I eat a few berries and sip my orange juice. From outside, I hear Flora's high-pitched chatter and Renzo's deep-bass replies. Soon their voices fade and I feel oddly unsettled and alone. Here I am back in England for the first time in years, in this strange house in a town I've never visited. And I'm sleeping in Beth and Niall Kildare's double bed while they are in our town, in our house. In *our* bed.

I break off pieces of warm croissant and pop them into my mouth as I gaze around the tiny room that nestles beneath the eaves. The lower parts of the walls are dove grey and the sloping parts of the walls and ceiling are white, interspersed with the same warm wooden beams I noticed in the dining room. But these beams are more pronounced. They jut from the low ceiling as though they're trying to escape. There's a picture window to my left and a Velux window directly opposite the bed through which all I can see are layers of iron-dark clouds that seem to press against the glass.

Suddenly, I'm finding it hard to breathe. Maybe I should have gone to town with my family. I blink rapidly and then inhale for the count of four and exhale for the count of eight. I'm fine. Just a little disoriented, that's all.

My espresso is still nice and hot. I drink it down in a few small gulps, and get out of bed. I'm fully awake now and too restless to lie in. I want to explore this house and see what kind of a place we're going to be calling home for the next two weeks.

The bathroom is traditional with white brick tiles, a clawfoot bath and an old-fashioned toilet with a pull chain. There's no actual shower in the house, other than the shower attachment on the bath. I crouched under it last night – a ridiculously uncivilised way to get clean. Thankfully, the Kildares left the immersion heater on for us, so the water was piping hot, but apparently we have to remember to turn it off once the tank has heated up. I remember having this kind of hot-water system at home back when I was a kid, but I thought that kind of barbarism had gone the way of clothes mangles and food safes. This morning, I think longingly of our three contemporary power showers at home.

Once I'm washed and dressed in black jeans, thick Nordic socks and an oversized forest-green cashmere sweater, I pad around the rest of the house, exploring. I noticed a sizeable balcony off the main bedroom with a couple of Adirondack chairs and some tubs crammed with tulips and daffodils, but it's way too cold out there to make use of it at the moment. It's probably quite nice for the two weeks a year when the temperature rises above freezing.

The second bedroom is larger than the master bedroom, with room enough for two beds – one either side of a thick chimney breast. The walls are mustard yellow, which sounds revolting, but actually somehow works, and a large vibrant red ikat rug covers the floorboards, making the room cosy. It's not how I would have decorated in here, but I guess it isn't too horrible.

The only other door upstairs is closed. I try turning the brass knob, already knowing it will be locked. Beth told me that Niall's study is his sanctuary, the only room in the house that will remain private. I agreed, of course I did. After all, what else was I supposed to say? *No?* But I have to admit that now I'm here standing before this locked door, I'm more than a little curious. I wonder if Niall also keeps it private from the rest of his family, or only from us holidaymakers. I turn the knob again, back and forth, back and forth with a creak and a rattle, but it's locked tight.

A knock at the front door startles me from my snooping. I stay where I am. Renzo told me he was taking one of the keys, so it can't be him. I tiptoe back into our bedroom and peer down out the window. A blonde head. I'm pretty sure it's Sally from over the road. She's bundled up in a smart woollen coat and Burberry knock-off scarf. I step away from the window. She knocks again. 'Piss off,' I mouth. After a moment or two, she does just that and I hear her busybody footsteps retreating along the path.

Once I'm sure she's gone, I head downstairs, gripping the bannister as I go. I'll have to watch Flora on these stairs, they're so steep. At the bottom, I find myself back in the dining hall. I turn left and walk through another door into the living room with yet more beams. The room stretches from the front of the house to the back, with a bay window at each end. There's another impressive inglenook fireplace, and three mismatched Persian rugs cover the dark floorboards. The two sofas are worn, and there's a low table and a clutter of kids toys beneath the far bay window. I'm sure it's cosy once the wood burner's lit, but it feels more like a playroom than an adult space to relax.

After another quick scoot around the ground floor, I realise I've seen the entirety of the cottage. I head back to the kitchen where I can now see the garden through the bifold doors. It must be beautiful out there in summer. Faded wooden tables and chairs have been artfully placed on a large limestone patio. Tubs of plants soften the space and the raised borders contain plenty of shrubs and bushes that screen the neighbours. Beyond the patio a set of wide steps lead onto an endless frosty lawn bounded by all manner of trees and further seating areas. Towards the back, I spy a faded wooden play fort with rope swings. It's nice. Too bad it looks freezing today.

I turn away from the view and focus my attention to the kitchen, remembering Renzo's comment about all the food. I open the fridge door. It's stuffed with earthenware and Tupperware containers. Begrudgingly, I see that it's all homemade things – all my favourites too. The freezer is similarly stocked, along with some plainer food like chicken nuggets and oven chips – presumably their kids' preferences. My two eat the same meals as Renzo and me. I've always insisted on it. There are various notes stuck to the front of the fridge. One says to help ourselves to all the food in the fridge, freezer and cupboards. Another has a list of useful numbers. I clench my fists and try to calm my breathing. I bet Beth was the teacher's pet at school.

Thinking back to the locked room upstairs, I wonder if there's a spare key anywhere. I spend the next hour and a half going through all the cupboards and drawers in the house. Each one is full of mainly useless clutter. If this were my place, I would have emptied them all out before our house swap. I'd hate for other people to see all this crap. Although, I wouldn't have let it get into this state in the first place. As I move methodically through the rooms, I come across several keys, but none that fit the office.

Once I've exhausted all the possible places, I make myself another espresso, twist my lip and muse that a locked door won't stop me getting in there. I have two weeks to figure out a way.

SIXTEEN

BETH

'Coming! Ready or not!' I cry, taking my hands away from my eyes with an anticipatory smile.

It's early evening and we've had a wonderful day at the beach, swimming and sunbathing. Niall even took the boys out on a pedalo, which had its own little slide. Although it was a bit of a shock to discover that most of the beach is privately owned and we had to pay to use it. Afterwards, we came home to relax for a couple of hours and now I'm playing hide-and-seek with the boys while Niall has a shower and gets changed for dinner. I got ready a while ago, and I'm pleased with my outfit tonight – a strapless black jumpsuit and gold sandals, with my hair arranged in a chignon. Niall gave me an approving look when we passed one another in the dressing room, his eyebrows raised, his smirk telling me that I look good.

The boys were getting restless and hungry, so I suggested we play hide-and-seek while we're waiting for their dad to get ready. I'm currently in the boys' bedroom, counting to twenty. Despite having four bedrooms to choose from here, Connor and Liam are used to sharing and decided they were happier in the same room. It's funny because before we arrived, they'd been so excited about having a room each, but once faced with it, they quickly changed their minds – Connor more so than Liam, which warmed my heart. For all their bickering, my sons love one another.

I leave their room and make exaggerated searching motions, pulling back curtains and peering beneath beds. Opening wardrobe doors with a loud 'Aha!' but not finding them. I estimate that Niall will take another twenty minutes or so. He doesn't like to be rushed, so I'll need to string out the game to stop the boys from getting bored.

Compared to yesterday's awkwardness between me and Niall due to Luciana's visit, today has been a dream. Our house swap is finally turning into the idyllic holiday I imagined. The boys have been in heaven, swimming all day, playing with one another without too much arguing, and Niall has been relaxed and attentive. I think it's simply taken us all a day or two to adjust. Getting here was such a mission that emotions were bound to be a bit bumpy at the start.

Despite Niall's reservations, I'm still glad I invited Luciana over. The boys all got on really well. After my initial annoyance of Luciana's insinuation that Niall might be anything like her ex-husband, she thankfully didn't mention anything else about it. Instead, we chatted about our kids, and I quizzed her about running the restaurant. She also seemed really interested in my past career as a chef, and said that Matteo is more than happy for me to visit his kitchen during our stay. The thought of this has really got my attention. I'm even starting to think about the possibility of kickstarting my career in some way once we're back home, but I've yet to mention that to Niall. I'm waiting for the right moment – if that ever comes. It seems each year that passes takes another bite out of my confidence.

In the meantime, Luciana and I have arranged to meet up again next week. My two would have wanted to see Luciana's boys every day of the holiday, but I don't think that would have gone down too well with Niall. I'm hoping that by next week, Niall will be grateful for a couple of hours peace and quiet.

A giggle from one of the spare rooms catches my attention. I smile as I open the door, spying a rumpled shape beneath the covers of a double bed.

'Ooh, this bed looks nice and comfy,' I say with a fake yawn. 'I think I might take a little nap on here.' Another giggle makes me grin. I sit on the edge of the bed and lean back so I'm half lying on my youngest son. I feel a little wriggle beneath my shoulder blades. 'Hm, not as comfy as I thought.' I sit up and pat the bed. 'What are these lumps and bumps?' Quickly, I yank the covers back and cry, 'Found you!'

Liam doubles up on the bed and squeals with laughter. 'You thought I was a lumpy bed!'

'I did! Great hiding place, Liam.'

'Did you find Con yet?' he asks.

'Not yet.'

His face falls. 'Does that mean Connor won?'

'No. It means you get to look for him too. Maybe you'll beat me to it and find him before I do...'

Liam's eyes widen.

'Remember,' I add. 'No going into our bedroom because Daddy's getting ready.'

Liam nods and then races onto the landing.

'And no running in the house!' I call after him. 'Walk carefully down the stairs!' I hear the clatter of his footsteps as I start remaking the double bed, smoothing out the sheets and repositioning the silk cushions. Returning it to its pristine state. I can't imagine living like this, keeping everything so perfect, especially not with children. It's one of those houses where everything has to be kept clean and tidy, or it ruins the aesthetic. Our house, on the other hand, can take a bit of mess – it simply adds to the character of the place.

Idly, I wander round the room. I pull open one of the fitted wardrobe doors. It's empty aside from a couple of items hanging from a chrome rail. One is a beautiful long fitted wool coat that's exactly my taste. I slide it off the hanger and slip it on. The silk lining is cool against my bare arms. The coat is light and warm, beautiful. The inside of the wardrobe door is mirrored so I step back and admire myself. The coat is a little snug. If it were one size larger, it would be incredible on me. Then again, it would look incredible on anyone. I've never worn anything this beautiful. I put my hands in the pockets and turn from side to side, posing. Reluctantly, I return it to its hanger.

I should go help Liam find his brother. Connor will be upset if he thinks I've abandoned the game. But the other item, a deep peacock-blue jacket, is calling to me. It would look great with my outfit. There are a matching pair of trousers on the hanger, but there's no way I could carry off that whole look. The jacket on its own is enough of a statement.

I put it on. This suits me even better than the coat. It's slightly fitted at the waist and adds an extra level of sophistication to my outfit. For a moment, I think about wearing it this evening. Would Amber mind? Maybe. What if someone she knows recognises it and says something to her?

After a couple of nights eating at other restaurants, we're going back to Terrazza Luciana tonight. The other places were nice, but not a patch on Luciana's place. The food, view and atmosphere were perfect.

I wish I were one of those people who could bend the rules every now and again, but I know that if I wore it without asking, I'd spend the evening feeling guilty. I wouldn't mind if she borrowed something of mine. But that's not the point. I don't know Amber. She's trusting us in her house. No, I shouldn't. Plus, knowing me, I'd end up spilling something on it, and staining it, and it feels like it would cost a bazillion euros to replace.

I put my hands in the pockets and admire myself one last

time. As I do, my fingers curl around a piece of thin card. I pull it out of the pocket. It's a photo. A man. Is that...? I frown and study the image, not quite comprehending what I'm seeing.

Surely it can't be.

It is.

It's a photo of Niall.

SEVENTEEN

BETH

The photograph is an old one, taken before Niall's hair started greying. He's wearing a pale-green shirt with the sleeves rolled up to just below the elbows. His skin is tan, and his chin is lightly stubbled. He's in a bookshop smiling at the camera as though he's in love with it. His dark eyes gleam, his teeth are white.

What the hell is this photograph doing in Amber Mason's coat pocket? I turn it over. The back is blank. Nothing written on it.

'Mummy, I can't find him!' Liam's voice floats up the stairs, jolting me from my shock. I'm supposed to be playing hide-and-seek with the boys. 'I'll be down in a minute, Liam! Keep looking!' I shrug off the jacket and replace it on the hanger with trembling fingers. Do Niall and Amber somehow know one another? Is that why we're here? Is there some weird reason behind it? My pulse skitters as I have the unwelcome thought that perhaps something is going on between them. But if that's the case, why on earth would he bring me to the woman's house while she's staying in ours? That makes no sense whatsoever.

The photo feels hot in my hand. I press my other hand to

my chest and take a breath, trying to stem the awful thoughts that are flitting through my mind. One second I think it's a weird coincidence that means nothing, the next I'm telling myself that there's no such thing as a coincidence, and I need to get to the bottom of whatever this is.

'Mum!' Liam thunders up the stairs and throws open the bedroom door. 'I can't find him anywhere. I went into every room, and he's not in any of them. I think he's gone out, but that's cheating. You can't win if you cheat, can you, Mummy?'

'Don't worry.' I tousle his hair absent-mindedly. 'We'll find him.'

'What's that?' Liam ducks his head away from my hand and grabs it, opening my fingers. Before I can stop him, he's taken the photograph from me.

'It's just a photo of Daddy,' I reply, annoyed with myself for letting him see it. But he simply looks and then dismisses it, returning it to my grasp.

'Come on.' He tugs my hand. 'We have to find Connor.'

'What's the time?' I ask myself, checking my watch to realise that only five minutes have passed since we started playing the game. It feels like an hour. I should go and ask Niall about the photo straight away, but the thought of it makes my insides turn to water. My question will sound like an accusation. Even if I phrase it in a light-hearted way, my husband will know I'm anxious and upset. How will he react? Angrily? Defensively? Or will he have a simple explanation?

For now, I tuck the photo in my pocket and follow Liam out of the room. After a good ten minutes of looking, I conclude that Connor is neither upstairs nor downstairs. My heart gives a worried flip, but I tell myself not to be silly. He's an inventive eleven-year-old; he'll have found somewhere good to hide. While searching the house, all I can think about is the photograph of my husband. I also wonder what were the odds of trying on that jacket and finding the picture in the first place. Does this mean there are other photos of Niall in the house?

'Where is he, Mummy? I don't want to look any more. I'm bored.' Liam sits at the top of the stairs, arms crossed, chin jutting out.

'Let's call and tell him we give up.'

'So he'll win?' Liam frowns.

'It's not a proper game,' I reply. 'Everyone knows the first go is just a practise one.'

'Oh.' Liam considers this and gets to his feet. 'Okay.'

I should win medals for my placatory skills.

'Connor!' he yells. 'We give up! You can come out now!'

Ten seconds later, the door to the master bedroom is flung open and Connor stands there red-faced and triumphant.

'That's not fair!' Liam cries. 'Mum said we weren't allowed in her room 'cause Dad's getting ready.'

'Dad said it was okay. So I won.'

'No you didn't. Mum said—'

'Right, that's enough!' I snap.

Both boys stop squabbling for a second and look at me. I don't normally shout, but I'm on edge right now and I haven't got the patience to put up with another altercation.

'Both of you, go and wait downstairs, please.'

'I'm hungry,' Liam whines.

'You can each take a nectarine from the fridge. Make sure you wash it, and don't drip juice on your shirts.' I doubt they'll wash them properly, and I'm ninety-nine per cent sure that Liam's shirt will be covered in juice, but that's the least of my worries.

They both walk sulkily down the stairs, muttering their discontent as they go. Once they're halfway down, I head into the bedroom.

Niall's sitting on the bed pulling on a pair of socks. He's dressed in a pair of grey trousers and a navy short-sleeve shirt.

The scent of his cologne fills the room – a lemony, spicy scent that's as familiar as Niall's face. My hand goes to my pocket and cradles the photo.

'What's all that about?' he asks, nodding towards the hallway.

'Nothing. The usual arguing over a game.'

'They don't stop, do they?' Niall shakes his head.

'It's just normal sibling stuff. Me and my brother used to argue all the time when we were growing up.'

Niall rolls his eyes. 'That's why I'm glad I'm an only child.'

I love my younger brother, Owen, but he's also the apple of my parents' eyes. Growing up, he could never do any wrong and would blame me when he messed up or did something bad. I would argue my side of the story, but then I'd be accused of telling tales. They always believed him, so in the end I kept quiet. Learned not to let it bother me. Niall thinks my brother is a spoiled brat. They don't get on. Consequently, I rarely see him any more. Or my parents, for that matter.

'You ready to go?' Niall asks. He stands and smooths his trousers.

'Look what I found in the other room.' I remove the photograph from my pocket and hold it out for him to see. My voice sounds strange and faraway.

'What is it?' Niall squints and takes the photo from me. My heart beats loud in my ears as I wait for his reaction.

'I tried on one of Amber's jackets and found it in the pocket. What would it be doing in there?' I run a finger over my bottom lip and try to stay calm, watching my husband's face for a reaction.

'It's an old photo of me.' He frowns. 'You found it in a jacket pocket?'

'Yeah.'

'It's one of my promo photos. She must be a fan.' He looks up and grins.

My doubt eases a little at his words. 'She didn't say anything to me when we booked the house swap.'

'Maybe she didn't put two and two together. Or maybe she doesn't read my stuff any more. This photo was taken over a decade ago. We used it on my Italian book tour.'

'Oh.' I try to inject some lightness into my voice. 'That must be it then. Didn't you sign those photos? This one isn't signed.'

Niall shrugs. 'I signed some, but not all of them.' He checks his watch and pockets the photo. 'It's getting late, we should go. Isn't the table booked for seven?'

'I guess I should put the photo back where I found it?'

'What? Uh, yes, sure. I guess.' He takes it from his pocket and hands it back to me. 'Maybe I should sign it,' he quips with a cheeky smile, but there's something guarded behind his eyes.

I don't know why I should feel so uneasy. Niall's explanation makes sense. I have no reason to disbelieve him. But he's been irritable and on edge ever since we left home. I'd been putting it down to him having trouble relaxing, and wanting to get back to his laptop. But what if it's more than that? I don't know. Am I reading too much into this, or could something else be going on here?

EIGHTEEN

AMBER

I'm getting dressed when the doorbell goes. Renzo is already downstairs with the children. I pad to the top of the stairs in just my jeans and bra to see Renzo striding towards the front door.

'Renzo,' I hiss from the landing.

He turns and peers up at me with a raised eyebrow.

'Don't answer it.' I shake my head at him.

'Flora's waving to them out the window,' he replies with a shrug and a smile. 'Whoever it is already knows we're in.' To my dismay, he turns around to open the door. I stomp back to the bedroom with an exasperated grunt.

'Renzo! Good morning. I hope you've settled in okay.'

I knew it! It's busybody Sal from over the road. Doesn't she realise we're here on a family holiday and we don't want her 'popping round' every two minutes. I yank my T-shirt over my head and follow it with a cream roll-neck sweater. I'm all hot and bothered now. I wanted to have a nice quiet brunch with my family. Whatever that woman's here for, I hope she's quick about it.

'Come in!' I hear Renzo offer cheerfully.

Why is my husband so bloody nice? I sit on the bed for a

moment. It's his *one* fault. I mean, he can be nice to me and the children, but that's as far as his niceness needs to go. Of course, I'm not being serious. His warm personality was what drew me in. He wasn't deterred by my forthright prickly nature. I inhale through my nose, and stand. I should go down and see what busybody Sal wants.

Be nice, Amber. Be nice.

I sashay down the creaky stairs and turn into the dining room where Flora launches herself at me.

'Mama! Sal's here with a big cake. She's talking to Papa in the kitchen.' My daughter takes my hand and drags me in there.

'Amber! Hello.' Sal has draped her coat over her arm and is loosening her scarf. She's wearing a pale-pink shirt tucked into a horrible shade of blue jeans and her blonde hair is freshly washed and bouncy. She's also wearing far too much perfume for this time of the morning.

'Sal has brought us round some homemade Dorset apple cake,' Renzo says. 'Isn't that so very kind of her? I've said she must stay and have a slice with a cup of tea.' I'm sure Renzo's winding me up on purpose.

'Sal, you're an angel,' I gush convincingly.

'I didn't want to impose,' Sal says, lying through her imposing teeth. 'I was making a cake anyway and I thought you might enjoy one too, so I doubled the recipe and made another. Then your gorgeous husband twisted my arm and made me stay for tea. How could I say no?' She laughs and we all join in.

What is it with these Dorset women and their hospitality? I thought we Brits were supposed to be standoffish and antisocial? There's Beth with her stuffed fridge and cupboards, and now her neighbour's trying to get in on the act.

'Franco, put your phone away, we have a visitor,' Renzo chides.

'In a minute, Papa, I—'

'*Now*, Franco.'

Our son scowls, but does as he's told.

'How are you enjoying your stay so far?' Sal asks. She walks over to the cutlery drawer and takes out a cake knife while Renzo makes tea. I think it's a bit cheeky of her to treat the place like her own. It may be her friends' house, but for now, it's ours. She should be less familiar.

'We're having a great time,' Renzo answers.

'I'll have coffee,' I call over to Renzo as I slide onto one of the benches at the kitchen table. Flora shuffles in next to me.

'Papa took us to town yesterday,' Flora says to our visitor, 'and we went into a toy shop where he bought me this parrot.' She holds out her new favourite toy, a brightly coloured stuffed bird that says things when you squeeze its claw.

'My name's Percy,' it squawks.

'Well, that's just lovely,' Sal says, slicing into her cake.

'Just a small piece for me,' I say, although I have to admit, it smells absolutely delicious.

'It's best with cream,' Sal says, producing a pot of Elmlea from her bag.

'You've thought of everything,' I say. 'Go on then, cream too. Why not.' I lean back against the wall. 'So how long have you known the Kildares?' While Sal's here, I figure I may as well get her to tell me about them.

'Hm, let me see...' She brings over two slices of cake and places one each in front of me and Flora, along with the pot of cream. 'I moved in over the road coming up to seven years ago now. Little Liam was a baby and wasn't sleeping well, so I used to pop round and help Beth out so she could catch up on her own sleep.'

'That's nice of you,' Renzo says, bringing her tea over. He returns to the kitchen area to make my coffee.

Sal returns to finish cutting the cake. 'Well, it was nice for me too. I'd just got divorced and moved here from Poole for a fresh start. Beth was very kind to me.'

I notice she doesn't mention Niall. 'What about her husband?' I ask.

'A nice big slice for you, Franco.' Sal cuts him a piece that's double the size of Flora's. I hope she doesn't notice or there'll be trouble. 'I don't see much of Niall,' Sal replies. 'He's a writer and keeps himself to himself.'

I don't blame him.

'Although I do cut all the family's hair. I'm a mobile hair-dresser.'

'Nice,' I reply.

'Keeps me out of trouble.' She gives a small laugh.

Renzo brings my coffee over and we all sit round the table.

'This is delicious, Sal,' Renzo says after his first mouthful. 'And it's still warm.'

I take a bite and have to admit that Renzo is right. 'It's really good,' I agree.

The kids polish off theirs in double-quick time and ask to leave the table. Sal takes her time eating her slice.

'So is Beth okay?' I ask. 'She seemed quite anxious about everything when I spoke to her at the beginning of the week to finalise everything.'

Sal's blue eyes widen. 'I think so. She didn't say anything about being anxious.'

'Good. Must have been pre-travel jitters.' I take a sip of my coffee. 'Neither of us have done a house swap before.'

'Yes, I must admit that I thought she was brave to do it,' Sal says before flushing. 'No offence to you, but you're both opening up your house to strangers. I think it was Niall's idea, not Beth's. What gave you two the idea to do it?' She turns to my husband.

Renzo starts talking but I cut him off. 'Oh, we love to try different things. Makes life interesting, doesn't it?'

Sal nods and I notice her looking from Renzo to me with a sharper expression. 'Well, they've certainly got the better end of the deal weather-wise. It's another chilly one out there. Although it's supposed to brighten up later. Got any plans for today?'

'We're off to Sherborne Castle,' Renzo says, his eyes lighting up.

'Honestly, he's like a kid over this stuff,' I say.

'*What?* I like history.' Renzo shrugs. 'I think I'm going to have another slice of cake. Sal, more tea or cake?'

'I'm fine, thanks.' She pats her stomach. 'Which castle are you visiting, old or new?'

'I didn't know there were two.' Renzo frowns.

'The new one is still an old castle, but it's intact and impressive inside. The old one is a ruin, but very atmospheric to wander around.'

'What do you suggest?' Renzo asks.

'You can do both in one day, but if I were you, I'd go to the new castle today as you can stay warm inside. Then maybe you can visit the ruined castle when the weather's better. Next week looks promising. You're lucky, it's only just opened up to the public this week. It's been closed all winter.'

I try to steer the conversation away from castles to dig out some more gossip on the Kildares, but Sal is surprisingly loyal. Even when I tell her that Niall's office is locked and I joke that he might be hiding a deep, dark secret, she doesn't take the bait and speculate. Instead she primly states that he's an internationally famous author, so of course his manuscripts must be kept secure. After that, she gets to her feet.

'Well, I'll let you all get on with your day.'

'Thanks again for the cake,' Renzo says. 'Very sweet of you.'

She dimples and blushes. Honestly, she's behaving like a lovesick teenager over my husband. It's pathetic. I should call her out on it. I won't, of course. But it would be fun to see her squirm.

'We'll return your plate once we've washed it,' he says.

'Oh, thanks.' She shakes her head and waves her hand. 'No rush.'

'So lovely of you, Sal,' I add. 'And thanks for the castle advice. Very helpful.'

She gives me a curt nod.

Oh dear, I think I've somehow offended her. Maybe she didn't like the fact that I asked Renzo to make my coffee. She strikes me as one of those women who treat men like they're gods. No doubt she thinks she'd make him a better wife than me. *No offence, sweetie, but you're not his type.* I give her a sickly smile and see her to the front door.

'Thanks again,' I say.

'You're welcome.' She opens her mouth to say something more but then decides against it and leaves the house.

I hope that's the last we'll be seeing of busybody Sal. I could really do without her popping round all the time, trying to be hospitable and flirting with Renzo. Hasn't the woman got anything better to do? After all, I've got my own plans to be getting on with...

NINETEEN

Sometimes you have to force the issue. People insist that they don't want to do the things that need to be done. But when it comes down to it, they'll thank you for being the only person who has the guts to act.

*I don't like the fact that I had to issue an ultimatum. But I also don't see it as a threat. It's more like a laying-out of how things need to be, in order for everyone to be happy. Okay, maybe not **everyone**. But for the people who matter, an ultimatum is key. It's the only option if you want to move forward. If you're to stand any chance of getting what you want.*

And I know what I want.

TWENTY

BETH

The boys' eyes are out on stalks as we queue up in front of one of the sweet stalls, with its endless tubs of brightly wrapped toffees, bonbons, chocolates and other confectionary. A warm sugary smell tantalises our taste buds.

'I can't decide, Mum. Can we get one of each?' Connor asks.

We're at Maiori's weekly market on Corso Reginna, the main shopping street that leads off the coast road. It's bustling with traders and shoppers, and I can see why. The goods on sale here are fresh and plentiful. There's cheese, salami, pastries, bread, fruit and vegetables. Not to mention clothing, ceramics and, of course, limoncello, the speciality liqueur local to the area. There's a seriousness to the noisy chatter around us, as shoppers select the choicest cuts and freshest produce, and vendors greet returning customers.

Niall isn't a morning person, and the market only comes to Maiori on Friday mornings so I had to coax him from his lie-in to come with us. I suppose I could have brought the boys on my own, but I thought Niall might enjoy it once he got here. I had optimistic visions of us strolling arm in arm from stall to stall exclaiming over all the wonderful things, and picking out delicacies from handsome Italian traders, in a kind of romcom-montage type situation.

Sadly my family isn't being obligingly agreeable. Instead, the children are fractious and my husband looks unimpressed. The image I carried in my head couldn't be further from the reality. Rather than a quaint farmer's market vibe, the marketplace is more utilitarian with white trucks, whirring generators, and covered stalls with plastic awnings. It's heaving with people – mainly middle-aged women and maybe the odd tourist.

I'm still glad I came. I'm looking forward to buying fresh local ingredients for lunch, as well as a few souvenirs to take home. It was Luciana who told me about the market. She said that she comes here really early in the morning each week, and that we should check it out.

We had another lovely meal at Terrazza Luciana last night, but this time Luciana and I didn't have much opportunity to chat. I hope it's not because she's wary of Niall, or because I might have offended her in any way. She seemed friendly enough, she just didn't talk for long. Although, they were busier than the last time we visited, so maybe that was the reason. She did, however, reserve us the best table on the terrace. Even Niall was appreciative of that.

I thought that coming to the market today would take my mind off finding that photograph last night. I know Niall gave a perfectly reasonable explanation of why it might have been in Amber's pocket, but I have this nagging doubt that won't go away. It's tapping me on the head and swirling around my stomach. I want to bring up the subject with him again. To ask him if he might know Amber. If perhaps she was an ex-girlfriend, or maybe he worked with her in the past. But if I ask those questions, I may as well accuse him of lying. And I can't do that. So I'm going to have to put the whole thing out of my mind.

Niall tuts as a local woman cuts in front of him to talk to the vendor. With a sinking heart, I realise he's already losing patience with the busyness of the market. I thought he'd enjoy it. My plan was for us to buy the boys some sweets to keep them occupied while we browse the other stalls. I wish Niall was as enthusiastic about this as me, but I shouldn't be surprised. He's never really been a foodie. Of course he loves my cooking, but he's not remotely interested in how his food is made. He just wants to eat it. As far as I'm concerned, this place is my idea of heaven. Or it would be if I didn't have to entertain a grumpy husband and two restless kids.

'Mum?' Connor pulls at my shirt. 'Can we?'

'Can you what?'

'Get one of each?'

'Umm.' I scan the rows and rows of sweets on offer. 'No, that's way too many. Your teeth will fall out. You can pick six sweets each.'

'*Six*?' Liam and Connor groan.

'Okay, eight, and that's it.'

'O-kaay,' they reluctantly agree.

The boys make their selections, and the vendor throws in two extra for free. 'Don't tell Mama.' He winks at them, and they look up at me with triumphant shining eyes.

I thank the vendor and pay before turning to Niall. 'Why don't you take the boys and chill in a café while I pick up some groceries?' I'd rather we were all together, but letting him off the hook might win me some points.

'It'll hardly be chilling with these two on a sugar high.' Niall rolls his eyes.

'They'll be fine. The high won't hit instantly, and I'll come and find you way before it does.' I can tell Niall wants to leave the boys with me, but he hasn't spent any time on his own with them since we got here. It would be nice for them to have some father-sons bonding time. 'Or you could take them to the beach?'

He frowns. 'No, it's fine. We'll just stay with you. You dragged us here in the first place, remember? I would have been quite happy to have a leisurely breakfast at home with the boys.'

I take a breath and bite my tongue. I could reply that I thought this would be something nice for us to do, that I'm sorry it's such a chore. He's obviously not into it, so there's no point provoking a full-blown argument.

'Let's have one of those sweets,' Niall says, digging into Liam's paper bag.

Our youngest son's eyes widen at the injustice of one of his precious sweets being taken. But he knows not to say anything to his father about it. Niall isn't as gentle with them as me. Which I guess isn't necessarily a bad thing.

'I'll have one of Connor's,' I say, knowing that this will appease Liam somewhat.

'I'm going to go over there,' Niall says, pointing at a leather-goods stand on the opposite side of the market. 'I need a new belt.'

'Okay, great, we'll come with you.'

'No, that's okay. You do your food shopping, if you like. Text me when you're done and we'll meet back up.' He walks off, leaving me with the children. So much for him wanting us all to stay together.

I square my shoulders. 'Okay, come on, you two. Let's choose what we're going to have for lunch.'

The three of us spend the next half hour selecting all kinds of delicious ingredients. To my delight, the boys are really enjoying themselves, especially Connor, who has a surprisingly good eye for fresh produce. We laugh at our poor attempts to make ourselves understood, resorting to pointing, and holding up our fingers for quantities. Connor is also great at using the translation app on my phone and attempting to speak Italian. Liam is probably more interested in eating his sweets, but that's fine.

'I think we might have overdone it a bit,' I say, looking at our bulging shopping bags.

'No, Mum, we'll eat it all, don't you worry,' Connor replies with a serious expression.

'Yeah.' Liam nods his agreement and I can't help laughing.

'Look, there's your dad.' I catch a glimpse of Niall, but then I see that he's talking to someone – a short wiry-looking man in a light-grey suit. They're standing outside a bar and the guy has his hand on Niall's arm. They're animated and laughing, like they know one another.

'Who's that?' Connor asks.

'I don't know,' I reply. 'Let's go and see. Stay close, I don't want either of you getting lost.'

We wend our way through the crowded market and slip between two fruit stalls to emerge on the opposite side of the Corso Reginna. As we approach, Niall catches my eye, shakes the man's hand, and the man walks off without looking in my direction.

'Hi,' I say, feeling slightly out of breath. 'Who was that?'

'Dad, we bought lots of things for lunch,' Liam interrupts. 'And Connor spoke Italian. He's going to teach me some words.'

'That's great, Liam. Sounds like you had fun.' Niall ruffles his hair.

'I did all the translating for Mum,' Connor confirms proudly. 'I used an app. It was really cool.'

'Well done, Con.' Niall gives him a look of approval and Connor glows under the praise.

'They were both so helpful,' I add. 'Thanks, boys. So who was that man?' I ask Niall again.

'Who was what?' Niall looks bemused for a second, and then nods. 'Oh yeah, some guy trying to flog me a timeshare. He cornered me right when I was about to text you. I couldn't get away.'

'Oh.' I think back to their animated conversation. 'It looked like he knew you.'

Niall scratches his chin. 'You know what these people are like, they pretend to be friendly to get you interested.'

But that doesn't explain why Niall was laughing and chatting as enthusiastically as the man was. It isn't like me to doubt my husband's word, but the discovery of that photo has got me questioning everything. I take a deep breath. I need to forget it and relax. 'Did you find a belt you liked?'

'A *what*?' he frowns. 'Oh, no, they weren't really my thing.'

'So what did you get up to in the end?'

'What is this? Twenty questions?' Niall laughs. 'I've just been wandering around waiting for you to finish. Shall we get a coffee somewhere? Here, I'll carry that.' He takes a bag of groceries from me, slings an arm around my shoulder, and we all head off to find a café. Despite the warmth of the morning, I can't shake the sudden chill that's descended, along with the feeling that Niall was trying to sidestep my question.

TWENTY-ONE

AMBER

'I'd like to live here,' Flora states loudly to the amusement of the other castle visitors.

'Lady Flora of Sherborne,' Renzo says with a sweeping bow to our daughter.

She giggles and curtseys as we walk through a burgundy living room with floor-to-ceiling windows, deep red leather furniture, gilt-framed oil paintings and a coat of arms above the ornate stone fireplace.

The sixteenth-century castle is certainly more impressive than I imagined it would be. I'd wrongly assumed it would be an old and dusty relic, uncomfortable and draughty. But it's actually quite stunning and in great condition with its wood panelling, richly painted walls and elegantly comfortable furnishings. I think a family actually lives here. Lucky them. Although, I wonder what they think about having members of the public traipse through their home every day. I smile to myself as I also wonder if it's any less intrusive than a house swap.

Beautiful as this place is, I still don't think I'd trade it for my contemporary Italian lifestyle.

'I wouldn't want to live here,' Franco says, echoing my thoughts. 'I prefer our house in Italy. They haven't got a pool.'

'They've got a lake,' Renzo says, pulling Franco in for a hug. Our son squirms to get free, but I know he likes his dad's bear hugs.

'Yeah, but you can't swim in it,' Franco declares.

'Sure you can,' Renzo replies, releasing his son and ruffling his hair.

'I wouldn't want to swim in that lake.' Franco screws up his face. 'It's green, and it's too cold.'

'A bit of winter lake swimming would toughen you up,' Renzo teases, giving him a playful punch on the arm. 'Flora would join me for a swim in the lake, wouldn't you?'

'We could be mermaids, Papa!' Her eyes light up.

'I'd rather be a knight on a horse,' Franco retorts. 'Or a dragon.'

'You could warm up the lake for me and Lady Flora the mermaid with your fire,' Renzo suggests.

'Shall we find a restaurant?' I ask, bored of the castle now. I want to go somewhere more civilised. More modern. What I really want is to go back home to Maiori and resume our lives. But that's impossible right now. My heart gives a skip of anxiety. This isn't like me. I don't do 'anxiety'. I don't do 'worry'. I run through all the options in my head once more, and come up with the same answer. This was the only possible course of action I could take.

We leave the castle and drive into Sherborne town centre, parking in one of the car parks, and head for a smart-looking bistro that Renzo earmarked when he came into town with the kids yesterday. In typical Renzo fashion, he got chatting with the owner, so today we're afforded a warm welcome by him and his wife – Jeremy and Cindy Hamilton, a good-looking couple in their thirties – who've reserved us a large table in the window, bypassing the queue of people who are having to wait, because none of them is as charming as my husband.

'If you ever come to the Amalfi Coast, you must look us up,' Renzo says to the couple. If I were in a better mood, they would probably be the sort of people I'd like to get to know, either personally or professionally. Their vibe is interesting. But my head isn't in the right space. I ask where I can freshen up, and Cindy directs me to the ladies. Thankfully, I took Flora to the loos when we were in the castle, so I can now have a few moments to myself.

The loo is luxurious – warm marble, brass fixtures and dark-green walls. I take out my phone and open my top-of-the-range camera app.

One thing the Kildares aren't aware of is that there's a hidden camera in every single room of my house. Cameras that only I know about. Even Renzo doesn't know they exist.

I had a nice close-up of Niall fucking his wife in our shower on Wednesday night. It wasn't something I particularly wanted to watch, but it was quite amusing to see her cheek pressed up against my oversized boobs. Renzo commissioned that photo wall for me as a hilarious surprise – he gets my humour so well. Since that first evening, there's been nothing of any interest to see on the cameras. Beth is boring. Niall scratches his balls a lot. Their kids are quite cute, I suppose.

I bring up the multi-feed and see Beth in the kitchen preparing lunch like the good little woman she is. Her husband and brood are sitting on the patio, waiting to be served. The doors are wide open and they're chatting as she cooks. It looks like she's preparing quite a feast. I select the kitchen camera and zoom in on her face. It's clear she's enjoying herself. She keeps casting loving glances over at her family. There's no sound, so I can't hear what she's saying, but it's obviously something funny, because they all start laughing.

I feel a sharp burst of fury. Bile rises in my throat and I'm so close to smashing my phone against the wall. Instead, I close the app, wash my hands and return to the hubbub of the restaurant, making my way back to my beautiful family.

A family I would do anything to protect.

TWENTY-TWO

BETH

The cobbled streets and sleepy atmosphere of the town is like stepping back in time. We've come to visit Ravello for the day and I already feel as if I never want to leave. We took the bus, rather than the Masons' car, as we heard it might be difficult to park. It was a hair-raising journey, overtaking slower vehicles on hairpin bends and blind corners, veering alarmingly close to sheer drops down the cliffside with no safety railings.

The view from the bus window was breathtaking and terrifying at the same time. Everywhere I looked there was something interesting or artistic to see – spring flowers, lemon groves, a wrought-iron fence, a studded wooden door belonging to a home built into the hillside. The Italians certainly know how to allow beauty to flourish, even if they don't seem too hot on health and safety.

Once we reached our destination, the bus stopped in a tunnel and we all disembarked. Vehicles aren't allowed into the town itself. Drivers have to park in a designated car park and walk in.

We have lunch in a quaint restaurant where the table and chairs perch on a grassy bank overlooking the cliffs. The place is peaceful, full of birdsong, and high enough that there's a gentle breeze to take the edge off the heat.

'It feels like we're on the set of *The Sound of Music* crossed with *Jason and the Argonauts*,' Niall says, sipping his Peroni.

'What's Jason and the Astronauts?' Liam asks.

'Argonauts,' Niall replies. 'We'll all watch it together when we get back to England. I watched it with my dad when I was about your age.'

I gaze at the cliffs, their peaks wreathed in mist, ancient turreted buildings clinging to their sides. A momentary sense of peace washes through me and I wonder what it would be like to live here. To be born here and grow up claiming this town as yours. To walk its winding streets, bathe in the sunshine and soak up the tranquil atmosphere every day. Would daily stresses be reduced? Would life feel simpler?

Aside from the discovery of the photograph and that odd situation at the market yesterday, where Niall was talking to that guy, the past couple of days have been magical. Yesterday, I made an incredible lunch with my purchases from the market. We sat at the outside dining area by the pool to eat. Niall was funny and charming, the boys were calm and happy, and the food was absolutely delicious. I felt as if we were one of those Italian families you see in the movies, where everything is perfect.

Maybe the answer isn't to wish for a different life, maybe it's simply to step out of my routine every once in a while. To allow myself to breathe and see the world from another angle. While we're trapped in familiarity, it's hard to see clearly. It's difficult to appreciate what we have. Sitting here in this paradise with my family, I realise that I have everything I need. Life isn't perfect, but there are these rare moments of perfection that, if we're lucky, we can recognise while they're happening and appreciate them. Savour them. I hope Niall feels the same way.

I realise that these aren't thoughts Niall and I ever share. If I said such a thing to him he'd roll his eyes and accuse me of being overly sentimental. But that's just his way. I don't understand why because his parents dote on him – expressing affection whenever they get the chance. They adore their grandchildren, they're generous financially, and love visiting us. Or rather, they love visiting Niall and the boys. With me, they're a little more reserved. I'm sure they think I've taken him away from them, when the reality is that I would love to be embraced by them that way. To be included rather than treated as an interloper. I guess I was hoping that they might give me the love that my parents have always withheld and saved solely for my brother.

In contrast, Niall pushes his parents' affections away. Their declarations of love and pride irritate him. I think he feels stifled by them. Perhaps that's why he's so emotionally closed off to people. Maybe it's also the reason he's such a good writer – he saves all that stuff for his books, for his characters, rather than the real people in his life. The thought saddens me. I wonder if we'll ever get that closeness that he seemed to promise back when we first met. Back when he said I inspired him.

We spend the rest of the afternoon strolling the narrow sun-striped streets, perusing tasteful galleries and quirky boutiques, and eating the most delicious gelato I've ever tasted. Finally, I persuade Niall that we should pay the modest entrance fee to visit Villa Cimbrone. It's now a private five-star hotel, but the building and gardens date back to the eleventh century. I imagine it must be an amazing place to stay. The views over the Amalfi Coast from the Terrazzo dell'Infinito are stunning, with the green of the cliffs studded with tiny villages, the deep blue sea dotted with boats and a clear azure sky stretching on to infinity, like the name suggests.

Too soon, it's time for us to head back to Maiori, and I experience a pang of sadness. A longing for a place that's already claimed a piece of my heart. We head back to the cool of the tunnel where the buses await, swept along with all the other day trippers, banished from the magical kingdom before the sun sets.

The packed, swaying bus is making me feel slightly queasy and I'm beginning to wish I'd only indulged in one scoop of ice cream rather than two. Someone is eating a banana and the smell of the overripe fruit isn't helping my stomach. Liam has fallen asleep on my shoulder, and Connor sits next to his dad, eyes down, playing a game on his phone. My head is throbbing. Probably too much sun. I reach for the water bottle in my bag and take a few sips of the lukewarm liquid. I wish I'd thought to bring some paracetamol.

Finally we reach Amalfi and I step off the bus with wobbly legs, gulping down the fresh air. The thought of getting in another vehicle isn't appealing, but Amalfi is where we have to change buses to get back to Maiori. The concourse is crowded with hot, irritable travellers. There are mutterings about delayed buses and long waits. I hope this doesn't affect the remainder of our journey.

A bus with 'Maiori' on the front waits in one of the covered bays, but its doors are closed and there's no driver in sight. I spot an official-looking woman close by. 'Excuse me,' I say, trying to catch her attention. 'Do you know what time the bus to Maiori leaves?'

'Maiori?' she replies. 'No good. Two hours.' She holds up two fingers. 'In two hours, maybe two and a half hours you go to Maiori.'

'What?' Niall splutters. 'Why? What's the delay?' He says something in Italian, and the woman replies.

'What did she say?' I ask.

'Dad spoke Italian!' Connor interrupts, impressed.

'The driver's not well so we have to wait for the next one to come on shift,' he mutters. 'I told you we should have taken the car.'

I don't remind him that it would have been impossible to park, which would have caused more stress. Instead, I place a soothing hand on his arm. 'Okay, so why don't we go to a café while we wait?'

'Sod that,' Niall replies with a scowl, scanning the area. 'I'll get us a cab.'

'I want to go home,' Liam cries. He's only just woken up and he's sleepy and crotchety.

'Don't worry, baby, we'll be home soon,' I reply, hoping that's the case.

'Wait here.' Niall strides off on a mission.

The bus bays are crowded and there are no free benches nearby, so we perch on the harbour wall and wait for Niall to return. The sun is still so hot but there are no shady spots nearby. I'd like to find somewhere cooler to sit, but Niall will be annoyed if he can't find us. Hopefully he won't be long. I take in the surrounding area. Aside from the crowds, it's a gorgeous place with traditional white-fronted, red-roofed villas built into the cliffside, shaded by cypress trees. Further down, busy shops and pavement cafés draw my eye. We should try to come back here and explore the town properly.

'Forty minutes!' Niall returns with a thunderous expression.

I stand up and shade my eyes.

'No taxis available for at least forty minutes,' he repeats. 'I was lucky to book one. The queue behind me was insane.'

'Shall we find somewhere shady to sit in the meantime?'

'Yeah, okay. Let's get a drink.'

The taxi doesn't arrive for another hour, but at least we're all rested and rehydrated by then. I tell myself it's all part of the adventure of going on holiday. But it's tricky when you have to soothe tired children and calm a tetchy spouse.

Not for the first time this trip, I wonder what happened to the charming, laid-back man I met fifteen years ago. The one who would surprise me with little gifts and thoughtful gestures. I remember after a particularly long and gruelling shift at the restaurant, I'd cancelled our dinner date as I was too tired to see straight. I came back to my flat to find a hot bubble bath, a freshly made bed, a homemade casserole in the oven, my favourite wine and chocolates on the table, and a note from Niall that said he loved me. That was the turning point. The moment I knew he was the one.

When did he become so distant? So irritated by me. At home, he's always working in his office, so we only really talk at mealtimes, or on the odd occasion we meet with friends or family. Otherwise, it's all just mundane domestic stuff. It's one of the reasons I've been desperate for us to go on holiday together. To spend some proper time reconnecting. I only hope it's not too late to save our relationship.

The traffic is heavy as we leave Amalfi, but it gradually thins out and the ride back is smooth and quiet compared to our earlier bus journey. The sun is sinking behind us. It's later than I thought. In the passenger seat, I chat to the taxi driver who's enjoying practising his English while the rest of my family sleep on the back seat. Hopefully they'll wake up refreshed when we reach the villa. I don't think things are truly as bad as I was imagining earlier. After all, our day in Ravello was wonderful, and we had fun at the beach the other day.

Soon, the familiar sight of Maiori beach comes into view, the lights already winking on around us, like glittering jewels. Our cab turns onto the Corso Reginna, the site of yesterday's market, and we turn off again and make our way up the hill towards our villa. I'm looking forward to taking a long cool shower, and maybe having a quick nap before dinner, as long as the boys can amuse themselves without getting into trouble.

As we turn into our road, I'm a little disconcerted to see a police car parked on the road outside our villa. At least I think that's what it is – it's a navy vehicle with a red stripe and the word 'Carabinieri' written on the side, and a blue flashing light on its roof. I hope its presence is nothing to do with us. I don't have the energy to face any hassle. As we draw closer, adrenalin floods my body and I suddenly feel very awake. The Masons' gates are wide open and there are two vehicles parked on the driveway, one of which is a second police car, its blue lights also flashing.

'Niall.' I turn in my seat and prod my husband's knee. 'Niall, wake up. Something's going on.'

TWENTY-THREE

I'm caught in the snarling current now.

There's nothing I can do but let it carry me where it will.

Out to sea or back to shore.

TWENTY-FOUR

AMBER

I take a large glug of Prosecco and try not to keep glancing around the pub. It's a busy Saturday night. Every table is taken, with families perched on bar stools waiting for diners to leave. The pub is a mix of contemporary and cosy, with heritage colours, stripped wood floors, a mix of bistro chairs and velvet bucket seats, and a crackling fire.

Despite the convivial atmosphere, and the fact that I'm fourteen hundred miles from home, I still don't feel relaxed. I don't know what's wrong with me. I've always been able to handle difficult situations. I've never shied away from doing what needs to be done. But tonight this predicament feels like it's getting the better of me. Now that my earlier anger has dissipated, my nerves are shot. Like I've run out of whatever it was that was keeping me going. I think it's because things are getting real now. It's all about to happen and there's nothing I can do to stop it.

'You okay, Amb?' Renzo puts a hand on my thigh.

I jerk away as if I've been scalded. The last thing I need is Renzo being all kind and solicitous. 'I'm fine. Stop fussing.' As soon as I lash out, I regret it. 'Sorry, I'm being a bitch.'

The children look up from their plates.

'Mama said a bad word.' Flora covers her mouth and giggles.

'She said "witch",' Renzo corrects our daughter, giving me a look that tells me I'm forgiven and that he finds my faux pas terrible but hilarious.

'No she didn't,' Franco says, but immediately clamps his lips together when I fix him with a stern look.

'Right, who wants to order some dessert?' Renzo asks, changing the subject. He catches the twenty-something-year-old waitress's eye. Although I think he's had her eye from the moment we walked in an hour ago. The girl smiles and sashays over with her pad and pen.

Another issue I've been ignoring is that Renzo isn't his usual self either. He's always loving and generous towards me and the kids, but since we've come away, he's been even more attentive than usual, letting me get away with being demanding and – if I'm honest – quite brattish. He would never normally put up with such behaviour. I like that about him. Perhaps it's because he can sense I'm on edge and he doesn't want to provoke the tiger. I need to calm down. The last thing I need is for Renzo to start suspecting that something's wrong. The problem is, the more I try to relax and act naturally, the harder it is. Everything feels off. Uncomfortable. As though I have ants crawling beneath my skin.

The waitress offers me a dessert menu but I wave it away and offer her my glass. 'No thanks, but I'd love another Prosecco please.'

'You have to go to the bar for drinks,' she says, ignoring my glass.

I swear silently.

Renzo reaches to take my glass. 'I'll go,' he says.

'It's okay, I think I can manage,' I reply, trying to sound light and breezy, but coming off as deeply sarcastic.

The waitress raises an eyebrow at my husband and I want to

smash my glass in her pretty little face – the second time I've wanted to smash something today. Instead, I force a smile, get to my feet and ask if anyone else wants another drink.

My family give me their drinks orders and then turn their attention back to the dessert menu. Meanwhile, I head towards the bar. Actually, I'm thankful for the breathing space it gives me. I need some time to pull myself together. I take several deep breaths and try not to think about what I stand to lose if this goes wrong. Instead, I give myself a pep talk. This wasn't my doing. I'm not going to second-guess myself. It's all worked out. The holiday-swap plan is perfect.

I sit on a bar stool, toss my dark hair back over my shoulder and pull out my phone. The barman is straight over to take my drinks order. He's young with gym muscles and a cocky smile.

'What can I get you?' he asks.

'Excuse me,' a blonde-haired woman to my right says. 'I've been waiting ages to get served.'

The barman looks from me to her, and back again. He shrugs. 'Sorry, I didn't see who was here first.'

'It was me,' the woman snaps. 'I was here first. But I think you know that.'

He flushes with embarrassment and annoyance.

'Go ahead,' I say to her. 'I'm not in a hurry.'

She glares at me, rather than saying thank you. I always seem to provoke that reaction in other women. Probably why I don't have any female friends. They're jealous.

I slide around on the stool to face away from her and get back to my phone. My heart rate increases as I open my camera app and check the feeds. The house looks empty. The Kildares must be out. But then... I catch my breath. What was that? I click on the main-bedroom feed. A man dressed in dark clothing; his face covered with a dark bandana so only his eyes are showing.

It's him.

Could this be it?

I can't seem to get my breathing under control.

'Hello. Sorry about that.' A male voice cuts into my consciousness. It's the barman.

I can't deal with him right now. I ignore him, get to my feet and head away from the bar, away from my family, out towards the entrance corridor, my gaze focused on the phone screen. On the dark shape ghosting through my bedroom.

Outside the pub, the air is freezing, taking my breath. The town isn't that busy for a Saturday evening, but I guess the weather is pushing people indoors as dusk falls. Light pools on the pavement from streetlamps, and steamed-up bar and restaurant windows show glimpses of drinkers and diners. Just a regular Saturday night. *Not for me.*

I think I'm hyperventilating. No, it must be the cold making me shiver and gasp. All the same, I try to steady my breathing. Concentrating on inhaling slowly and exhaling even slower.

I watch the dark figure on the screen and tell myself not to be so stupid. This is good. This was the plan. This was *always* the plan.

TWENTY-FIVE

BETH

In the back seat of the cab, Niall wakes with a start and throws me a look of confusion. 'What? What is it?'

'There are police here, at the villa,' I hiss, not wanting to wake the boys and worry them. Although I realise that's inevitable as we'll all have to get out of the taxi in a second. It's full dark now, but the villa's powerful security lights are casting a bright pool over everyone, and it looks like all the interior lights are on too. The whole place is lit up like Christmas.

'*Police?*' Niall sits up and looks out the window. 'Why are the police here?'

'Do you want to stay with the boys while I find out?'

'It's a security company,' the taxi driver comments, pointing to one of the parked vehicles with the image of a house on its side. 'Maybe you had a break-in.'

'I don't believe it,' Niall says. 'Beth, did you lock up properly?'

'I, uh... yes, yes, of course.' I open the cab door and thank the driver, leaving Niall to sort out the fare and the boys, which I know he won't be happy about, but he's the one in the back, and he's the one with the cash.

One of the police officers, a young man who looks to be in his twenties wearing a blue shirt, navy trousers and a peaked cap, comes over and starts speaking Italian at me.

'Sorry, do you speak English?' I interrupt. 'Is it a break-in? Did they take anything?' My mind is whirring, my stomach in knots.

'No English.' He shakes his head and gestures to his colleague, a dark-haired woman around my age who comes over.

Niall is already out of the car and striding over. 'I've paid the cab. Can you sort out the kids?'

'Okay,' I reply. 'He doesn't speak English.' I gesture to the police officer.

'Well it's a good thing I speak Italian, then.' Niall gives me a withering look, but I cut him some slack as he's probably feeling as anxious as I am. I return to the cab where Liam's still asleep, but Connor is now awake and groggily gazing out at the scene on the driveway.

'Is that a police car?' my son asks through the open door.

'Yes, but don't worry. Can you hop out of the cab for me, Con? And close the door behind you.'

I walk around to the other side of the vehicle, open the door, reach in and gently shake Liam awake. 'Up you get, baby. Come on, let's go.'

He mumbles and groans, but does as I ask, his eyes still half closed. I take his hand and go round to where Connor stands wearing a dazed expression.

Niall is listening to the female officer who's speaking English. I catch snippets of the conversation as I approach with the boys. I'd rather keep them shielded from whatever's going on here, but now that the taxi's pulling out of the drive, there's nowhere for them to sit out of the way. I'm torn between wanting to know what's happening and wanting to take the boys out of earshot. We're supposed to be on holiday relaxing, not talking to police officers.

'We'll need you to check,' the female officer says to my husband.

'Check what? What's happening?' I ask, my curiosity getting the better of me.

'They want to confirm our identities. You've got all our passports, right?'

I nod and pull them out of my bag.

'The alarm was triggered,' Niall says. 'It alerted the security company who called the police because the Masons didn't answer their phone straight away.'

'Was anything taken?' I hand our passports to the male officer who checks our photos. My stomach lurches at a horrifying vision of the villa being trashed. Of all our stuff stolen.

Niall shakes his head. 'They said it doesn't look like anything was touched.'

I exhale in relief.

'But we'll have to go in to make sure,' Niall continues. 'Apparently the window in the downstairs toilet was open. They think they must have climbed in that way. You must have forgotten to close it.'

'I didn't open it,' I retort, and stop myself from adding that he could also have checked the windows before we left the house, if he was so worried. Instead I pause and say, 'I'm certain everything was locked before we left. I checked and double-checked. Anyway, we wouldn't have been able to set the alarm if any of the windows had been left open.'

'Not necessarily,' Niall says. 'There might not be a sensor in the downstairs bathroom.'

I try to think back to when we left the house earlier this morning. It was all so hectic, getting ready, trying to round up the boys and making sure we locked up the house properly. Could Niall be right? Was it my fault that someone broke in? I'm certain I didn't leave any windows open, but I've been feeling quite groggy in the mornings since we got here, absent-minded. Perhaps he's right. Perhaps it *was* my fault. I wipe a prickling sheen of sweat from my forehead and top lip.

'So, you go in to see if anything is taken,' the female officer says, ushering us towards the front door.

'Can we take the boys inside?' I ask. 'Is it... safe?'

'There's nobody inside,' she confirms. 'Just the security company doing some checks.'

'Did the intruder make a mess?' Niall asks.

'No, not at all.' The woman removes her hat for a moment and wipes her forehead. 'I think the alarm must have scare them before they do any damage. There was no one here when we arrive.'

'That's a relief,' I reply, thankful we don't have to face a mess.

'I recommend you to change the locks as soon as you can,' she adds.

Niall and I spend the next hour going through the house and checking our belongings, along with the Masons' possessions. Nothing appears to have been touched, but of course we can't be absolutely certain.

Once the police and security firm have gone, I go upstairs to our bedroom and sit heavily on the end of the bed. With a certain amount of dread, I take out my phone and call Amber for a video chat. At least nothing was taken and there's no mess to clear up, but I'm still worried she might blame us for not locking the villa properly.

The phone rings and rings, but she's not picking up. I'm reluctant to leave her a voicemail or text, not about something so serious. I end the call and decide to try again in ten minutes. I won't be able to relax until I've spoken to her.

I stand, deciding to have a quick shower to wash away the travel grime, when the phone rings in my hand. It's Amber returning my call. My heart thumps with nervousness as I tap to answer.

Her face appears on the screen, her skin radiant, dark hair glossy and lustrous, her lips a deep shade of plum and her eyes gazing into mine. I pat my hair ineffectively, realising that I look a fright – crumpled and tired from our day trip and the shock of the break-in. Amber's eyes darken with concern.

'Beth...'

I attempt a half-hearted smile.

'Beth, is everything okay? You look worried.' She's standing outside the cottage in our garden.

I'm hit by a wave of homesickness as I catch sight of the back door and the warmth and lights of our kitchen through the window behind Amber.

'Beth? You called me... I'm returning your call...'

'Sorry, yes. I did, um, I needed to let you know something. Well, I still do, need to let you know, I mean...' I'm rambling like an idiot.

Amber quirks a perfectly shaped eyebrow.

I inhale, attempting to order my thoughts and speak more clearly. 'I'm so sorry, but there's been a break-in at your house. Nothing's been taken or damaged that we can see, but—'

'It's fine, Beth. I've already spoken to the police and the security firm. They filled me in.'

'You have?' My shoulders drop.

'They needed to confirm that you were who you said you were, and that you weren't intruders yourselves.' She laughs and gives me a smile.

Thank goodness she isn't angry. I wonder why she didn't call me after she found out. 'I think the alarm must have scared them off. It doesn't look like anything was touched. I'm pretty sure we locked up properly, so I'm not sure how they even got inside—'

'The police said a bathroom window was left open.'

I feel my cheeks blaze with guilt. 'I'm so sorry, I don't know how we missed—'

'Honestly, don't worry, Beth. Of course it was a bit of shock to hear about what happened, but as long as no one's hurt, well, that's the main thing, isn't it?'

'Yes, yes, of course.' Relief courses through me. 'I hope Renzo's not worrying. We're trying to take good care of your home! It's so beautiful. I hope this hasn't spoiled your holiday too much.'

'Not at all. And it's me who should be worrying about you,' she says, putting a hand to her chest. 'We've never had anything like this happen before. You must all be quite shaken up.'

'We're okay,' I lie. No sense in telling her how unsettled the whole thing has made me. 'The police asked us to check if anything had been stolen. Niall and I didn't notice anything missing, but maybe I should walk you round the house so you can check.'

'Good idea.' She nods, casting a glance over her shoulder into the house. When she turns back, I notice the tip of her nose is red.

'You look cold, Amber. Why are you in the garden at night, if you don't mind me asking?'

'I didn't want the children to hear about the break-in,' she replies.

'Oh, yes, I know what you mean. Okay, I'll be quick so you can get back into the warm.' I scan each room with my phone so she can verify if anything's missing. She confirms that it all looks good.

'I think you guys should relax and drink lots of wine tonight,' she says with a laugh. 'You deserve it after such a shock.'

'We will. You too. Oh, and the police officer said that you should get the locks changed as soon as possible,' I add. 'We can try to arrange it from here, if that's easier.'

Amber looks thoughtful. 'I doubt we'll get anyone to do it

over the weekend. Don't worry. I'll try to get something booked for Monday, if that's okay with you guys?'

'Sure. But what if whoever it was comes back in the meantime?'

'Just make sure all the windows are shut and the alarm's on when you're out.' She says the words lightly, but I can't help thinking that it's a dig. That she blames us for leaving the bathroom window open. I'm ninety-nine per cent sure I didn't. But, of course, there's always that one per cent of doubt.

I end the chat with Amber, feeling worse than I did before I called her.

This whole thing feels so surreal. Today we visited one of the most beautiful places in the world, and then we arrived back to this nightmare. I guess it could have been a lot worse. At least the Masons' home is still in one piece and no one was hurt, but I'm starting to wonder if this holiday swap is doing more damage than good. If the whole thing isn't straining our marriage instead of healing it.

We'd been planning to go out for dinner again tonight. We were going to head down to the promenade and try out one of the beachfront restaurants. It's Saturday night so there will probably be a nice buzzy atmosphere down there. But it's almost nine p.m. by the time the police and security firm finally leave. We haven't showered or rested since returning from Ravello, and neither of us feels in the mood for getting glammed up. Plus the boys are shattered. Amber's suggestion to chill out and drink wine is probably the best one.

After showering and changing, Niall pours us each a glass of Soave from the Masons' temperature-controlled wine store. Amber told us to help ourselves to their cellar, but we haven't touched any of it until now. I whip up some penne al salmone and a green salad for the four of us, which we eat outside on the terrace. We're ravenous, so it disappears pretty quickly. But the relaxed holiday ambience has evaporated. Everyone's quiet, even the boys. The villa feels different. Violated. It's weird to think that a stranger was in here, possibly going through our stuff. The police said that we shouldn't worry too much. That the alarm going off would most likely deter them from returning. But I think the shock of the situation is only starting to hit me.

I clear the plates on autopilot and send the children upstairs to start getting ready for bed. Early nights for all are probably what's needed. While Niall loads the dishwasher, I close the sliding doors and lock them, gazing out at the gently rippling blue of the swimming pool and the darkness of the garden beyond. I give a shiver. There's far too much glass in this house. Anyone could be out there right now, standing in the darkness looking in. At this moment in time, I'd give anything to click my fingers and be back home in our cosy Dorset cottage, curled up on the sofa with the curtains drawn and the wood burner roaring.

Once the boys are settled in bed, Niall and I don't seem to know what to do with ourselves. It's only ten thirty, but it feels like the early hours of the morning.

'May as well go to bed,' I offer.

'We should double-check all the doors and windows first,' Niall says.

After a good ten minutes of making sure the ground floor is secure, we trudge wearily back up the stairs.

'Ravello was so beautiful.' I give a wistful sigh. 'I can't believe it was only this afternoon that we were there. So much has happened since then.'

'So much for a relaxing day out,' Niall grumbles. 'If we'd taken the car, we'd probably have been home earlier and the house would never have been broken into.'

'Or maybe we'd have interrupted the break-in and been even more traumatised, or hurt even.'

'Maybe.' He goes ahead of me into the bedroom and

through to the bathroom. I think he's more shaken up than he's letting on.

I check the balcony door for the tenth time. It's locked. I wish the Masons had curtains or blinds. It's disconcerting to look out at the black night knowing that if someone's out there, they can see straight in. I get changed in the dressing room where there are no windows.

Finally, we're both in bed with the lights turned out. Niall rolls onto his side, his back to me. The room feels too large. The Masons' covered portrait still hangs opposite the bed, the white-silk covering a ghostly shape in the gloom. My heart is beating too fast and sweat trickles down my back despite the air con. I'm not sure how I'm going to manage to fall asleep tonight. My ears are cocked for any sound. Common sense tells me that a burglar isn't going to return after being scared off by an alarm. They would probably know that the police would have been called. That security measures would now be upped. I'm sure we're safer than we were before. But my body is betraying what my head is telling me.

I freeze at a sound outside our room. It sounds like a door opening. I suddenly have the worrying thought that the intruder might have found somewhere to hide inside the house, and was simply waiting for us to go to bed. Did the police actually check everywhere? What about under the beds and in the cupboards? How could we have been so slack? My whole body is taut as a wire.

'Niall,' I whisper, tapping his shoulder with my forefinger.

'What?' he replies too loudly.

'Shh. I think there's someone outside our door.' My heart is hammering now. I'm scared for the boys in their room down the corridor. Please, God, don't let them get hurt.

The pad of footsteps makes me catch my breath. 'Did you hear that?'

Niall sits up and switches on his bedside light. He looks as tense as I feel.

'Mum, can we sleep with you and Dad tonight?' My body sags with relief as I see Connor standing at the door holding Liam's hand. Liam has dried tear tracks down his face.

'What are you two doing up?' I cry.

'We can't sleep. What if those burglars come back.'

I beckon the boys over and stroke their warm cheeks.

'Of course they won't come back,' Niall says. 'You're perfectly safe. They can't get in here.'

'We want to go h-home,' Liam wails.

'Can we sleep with you, Mum?' My eldest son looks on the verge of tears.

'Of course you can. Hop in here.'

'No wriggling,' Niall says as the boys clamber over me to snuggle in between us. I know he isn't pleased by their intrusion in our bed. He likes to stretch out.

But I feel strangely comforted by the presence of our children. Less nervous. Less alone. We're a little unit. All together. Safe.

TWENTY-SIX

BETH

I wake to an empty bed, and to harsh sunlight streaming in through the balcony doors. A bleary glance at my phone shows it's almost nine a.m. I run my tongue over my teeth and rub the grit from my eyes. I slept even worse than usual last night. The boys wriggled and shifted as I lay there worrying about the intruder, wondering if they might still somehow be inside the villa. I didn't have the courage to get up and look, but I also didn't want to voice my worries to Niall in case the children heard. I would have taken one of my sleeping tablets, but I couldn't in case the intruder returned and I was too out of it to hear them.

At some point I did eventually manage to drift off, because when I awoke again at around four a.m. Niall wasn't in bed. I assumed he'd gone to the bathroom, but if he had, he was taking his time. I wondered if I should get up to see if he was okay. Instead, I fell back to sleep.

The events of yesterday evening come back to me in an unsettling montage of buses, taxis, police and open windows. This villa doesn't feel like the glamorous holiday home it once was. Instead, it's cold, echoing and a little scary. Hopefully, that feeling will fade. Maybe I'm tired.

It's not only the house. Niall is different here, too. He's uncommunicative and irritable. On edge. I still can't stop thinking about that photo of him in Amber's jacket pocket. It's like an unwelcome song I can't get out of my head. I guess I could mention it to her – see what she says – but then I'd have to admit that I was snooping, and that I tried on her jacket. I take a deep, cleansing breath, sit up and stretch out my arms. I should get out of bed and see where Niall and the boys have got to.

I shower and dress in black linen shorts and a strappy cream top. The boys' bedroom is empty and as I make my way down the stairs I hear them chatting in the kitchen. To my surprise, Niall is cooking with their help.

'Hi, Mum!' Liam calls out enthusiastically. He's standing at the island, slicing mushrooms with a sharp knife, his fingers perilously close to the blade.

'Careful with that.' I can hardly dare look, but I'm loath to criticise Liam, or rain on Niall's parade.

'Morning, lazybones,' Niall says, looking up from a bowl where he appears to be whisking eggs.

'Morning. This all looks very productive.'

'We're making a full English,' Connor says proudly.

'I can see. Very nice! What's brought this on?' I ask.

'Other than a bad night's sleep and being starving?' Niall replies. 'If we'd waited for you to come down, we might have been waiting all day.'

'It's not *that* late. Where were *you* last night?' I plonk myself on one of the bar stools. 'I woke up and you weren't in bed.'

'Couldn't get comfortable with Connor kicking me every two minutes, so I went and slept in the next room.'

My phone starts vibrating in my hand. 'It's Sal. I hope everything's all right at home.'

'What does *she* want?' Niall frowns. He's never been her biggest fan. He thinks she's a busybody. She's not. She's just friendly, and likes to chat. But her overfamiliarity tends to put people off.

I take the call. 'Hey, Sal. Everything okay?'

Niall rolls his eyes and shakes his head.

I start walking out of the kitchen.

'Breakfast will be ready soon,' Niall calls after me. 'I thought you were going to help.'

I pop my head back in and mouth that I won't be long. Then I make my way upstairs. I can't chat with Sal while Niall's listening.

'Hi, Beth, are you still there?' Sal asks.

'Sorry, yes, I'm just going somewhere quieter.'

'How's your holiday? Hope you're having a good time.' Sal's voice is warm and comforting.

I'm hit with a pang of homesickness. Silly, really. 'Yeah, it's good. Well, it's been eventful anyway.'

'Oh?'

I go into the bedroom and perch on Niall's side of the bed, looking out over the balcony. 'Is everything okay at your end?'

'Yes, fine.' Sal doesn't sound too sure. I wonder if she might be having trouble with her ex again. They rarely speak these days, but maybe something's happened.

'Sal?' I prompt.

'It's probably nothing,' she says.

'That doesn't sound good. Come on, what is it?'

'It's... it's nothing to worry about... just that... I don't really trust Amber.'

'Oh.' My stomach gives an anxious flip. I wasn't expecting that. 'In what way?'

'Well, for a start, she keeps asking all sorts of questions about you and Niall.'

I give a shiver. 'Well, I suppose that's natural. We are living in their house after all. And they're living in ours.'

'I know, but these are like really nosy questions about you, and what you're like. I know it might not sound like much, but you'd know what I meant if you'd heard her.'

Her words are setting off alarm bells, but at the same time I'm hoping Sal has got the wrong end of the stick. 'Are you sure you're not being overprotective?' I ask.

There's a short pause from her, and then, 'I don't know. I got a bad feeling from her, Beth. She's odd. I mean, she's beautiful and seems friendly at first glance. It's just that some of the things she says feel nasty. Like she thinks she's a cut above the rest. And Renzo dotes on her like she's his princess.'

'Sounds nice,' I reply jealously, and we both laugh.

'I know it's sounding like sour grapes,' Sal adds, 'but it's not that. Well, I mean, it is a bit – Renzo's gorgeous and a really nice person – but, no, there's something *wrong* about her.'

I'm unsettled by my neighbour's words, but I tell myself not to be paranoid. Sal doesn't have many friends. She's super-loyal to the ones she does have so she's probably being overcautious on my behalf. I stand up and walk over to the balcony doors. 'Things have actually been a bit weird here, too.'

''Oh?' Sal replies. 'In what way?'

I tell her about yesterday's break-in and she's horrified. 'You poor things! Are the boys okay?'

'Everyone's fine. But it all feels a bit weird here now.'

'I'm not surprised. No one would blame you if you wanted to cut your holiday short and come home early,' she suggests.

'I did think about that, but we're here now. The weather's amazing, and the place is beautiful. We'll see how we get on over the next couple of days. If I'm still spooked, then maybe I'll suggest it to Niall.'

'Well, if you're sure. I think I'll invite the Masons over for dinner. See if I can suss them out a bit more.'

'You don't have to do that, Sal!' I love my friend, but I know she can come across as a bit full-on sometimes. I don't want Amber and Renzo to realise she's spying on them.

'Don't worry, I'll be discreet,' she answers with a smile in her voice.

'Honestly, Sal, don't worry.'

'It's no trouble.'

I don't know how to tell her to leave things alone without offending her, so I change the subject, hoping she might forget about it. 'Everything all right with you?' I ask.

Sal sighs. 'Yeah, same old. I'm already missing our chats.'

'I'll bring you back a pressie.'

'If there's room in your luggage, you can smuggle me back a handsome Italian.'

'Ha! You might have to make do with alcohol.'

'Spoilsport, but okay, that's the next best thing, I suppose.' She pauses. 'Sorry if I worried you about Amber. It's probably nothing, especially as Niall already knows her... but I could have sworn you said you organised the holiday through one of those house-swap sites.'

My blood runs cold. 'What did you say?'

'I said I didn't realise Niall already knew Amber,' Sal repeats.

'He doesn't,' I say. Although I'm already thinking of the photo I found in Amber's pocket.

'Oh.' Sal's reply is followed by a long silence.

My heart is thumping too loudly. 'What makes you think they know each other? Did she say something?'

'Not exactly.' Sal sounds sheepish.

'*What?*' I demand. 'What is it? Spit it out, Sal. We've been friends long enough for you to be straight with me.' I'm pacing the bedroom.

'Beth!' Niall calls up the stairs. 'Breakfast's ready!'

I lower the phone for a second. 'Coming!' I yell back.

'I kind of, sort of stalked her on social media last night,' Sal admits.

'Well, *I* did that before we came here. It's kind of necessary when you're planning to swap houses with a stranger. She's not friends with Niall on Instagram, Twitter or Facebook.'

'No, but she was tagged with him in a Facebook photo,' Sal replies. 'It's not on her page if you scroll down, but I found the photo by searching her name. She works in PR, so she's tagged a lot. I'll send you the link so you can see it.'

'Wow,' I reply, a little shocked by her thoroughness. 'You're good at snooping, Sal.'

'I know,' she says wryly. 'Divorce will do that to you. Hours of gin-soaked nights Facebook-stalking my ex-husband's new wife.'

'Oh. Yes. Sorry.' I remember how cut up Sal was when I first met her. I was suffering from borderline post-natal depression after Liam was born, and she'd just got a divorce. We were a real barrel of laughs back then, but I really do think we saved one another's sanity.

I give a start as the bedroom door flies open and Liam bursts into the room. 'Dad says to come down now because breakfast's ready.'

I nod and hold out a finger. 'I'll be two minutes.'

'He said you had to come *now*.'

'Okay, I'll be there. Can you close the door?'

Liam gives me a stern look that at any other time would have me laughing, but right this minute I'm too concerned by Sal's discovery. I shoo my son out of the room and close the door, walking back over to the bed. In the back of my mind, I register the fact that Niall's going to be annoyed with me for not helping him with breakfast and for not coming down when he called, but it can't be helped. I glance at the bedroom door and lower my voice. 'I found a photo of Niall in one of Amber's jacket pockets,' I admit to Sal.

'Oh... that's not good,' she replies.

Her tone makes me want to defend my husband. 'Niall said it was a promotional photo, so she's probably a fan. Or maybe they met on one of his book tours. Like you said, she works in PR.'

'O-kay, well, that might explain it. There were a couple of other people in the photo too,' Sal admits, but she still doesn't sound completely convinced by my explanation.

Nonetheless, my panic subsides a bit. 'I'd better go. The boys are waiting.'

'Yes, of course.' Sal sounds oddly formal and a little awkward. 'I hope you don't mind that I called about this. It's probably nothing. I just wanted to—'

'Oh, no, of course, sure, it's fine,' I reply. But actually, I'd really rather she hadn't called me with her doubts. I was already feeling wobbly about everything and this has only made me more unsettled. This holiday isn't turning out to be anything like I imagined. Far from it.

TWENTY-SEVEN

BETH

Niall is sullen throughout breakfast. He doesn't even ask me about Sal's phone call, for which I'm grateful. Instead, he pointedly talks to the boys and leaves me out of the conversation. My stomach is in knots and my head is spinning with everything Sal told me. I realise there's probably an explanation for the Facebook photo of Niall and Amber, but added to all the other little things, I can't help thinking that there could be something behind it. Something that I don't want to know.

'Can we go swimming now?' Connor asks, putting the last piece of toast and scrambled egg in his mouth.

'Let your food go down first,' I reply. 'That was a lovely breakfast, boys. Well done.'

'Go up to your room for half an hour,' Niall says. 'You can swim later.'

Liam's about to protest, but I see Connor shake his head at his brother. He already knows when not to upset his father.

'Clear your plates first,' Niall adds.

Connor and Liam do as they're told, and then take themselves out of the room. I manage to give them a wink before they go.

The silence in the room is heavy. I sip my coffee. 'That was absolutely delicious. Thanks.'

'It was delicious, was it?' Niall asks.

'I think the boys really enjoyed making it with you.'

'Oh, really? How would you know that? You weren't here. You were upstairs talking to your friend. It seems these days you prefer talking to your friends than spending time with your family.'

I swallow, trying to think how best to defuse the situation. Niall's angry that I took the call from Sal. That I didn't praise him enough for making breakfast. That I didn't come down as soon as he called. I know he's being unreasonable, but at the same time, I also know there's no point arguing with him about it. My husband has the capacity to sulk for days.

I think about all the meals I've cooked where he's never said so much as a thank you. Or where he's told me that he's not hungry right now, or he's too busy to eat. I've never called him out on it. Maybe I should have. I always thought I'd rather have an easy life, than an argumentative one. Or was I making a rod for my own back?

'Sorry about that,' I say, giving him a soft smile. 'It was Sal. She wouldn't stop talking. I kept trying to cut her off, but you know what she's like.' I send out a silent apology to my friend. Bad-mouthing Sal is the only way I can see to turn Niall's anger away from me.

'I honestly don't know what you see in that woman,' Niall grunts. 'She's a leech. You should distance yourself from her, or she'll only get more clingy.'

'It's better to keep the neighbours onside.' I shrug. 'It's fine. She's harmless.'

'What did she want anyway?' Niall asks, his eyes boring into mine.

I open my mouth, but have no idea what to say. My mind has gone blank. I don't want to tell him that Sal is suspicious of

Amber, and I'm certainly not going to mention the Facebook post; not until I've seen it myself.

The doorbell chimes, saving me from answering the question. Please don't let it be Luciana. Much as I like her, the last thing I need is another friend dropping round to prove Niall's point.

'Who's that?' he asks. 'It's Sunday morning, for Christ's sake.'

'I'll get it.' I turn and head for the front door, grateful for the distraction. As I pull open the door, a glare of sunlight makes me squint and shade my eyes. Two large, dark-haired men stand at the door. They're wearing suits and sunglasses. For a moment I think they must be police officers with news of yesterday's break-in, but there's something about them that doesn't quite look 'official'. Their suits are too well tailored, their tans too even, teeth too white.

'Hello,' I say uncertainly.

They glance at one another. 'You are English,' the younger of the two says. I notice several tattoos on his neck.

'Yes.'

Niall comes up behind me. 'Can I help you?' he asks, his voice deeper than usual.

'You are not the Masons,' tattoo man says.

The older man says something to his companion in Italian and points to us. I don't think he speaks any English, but he looks like the one calling the shots. Perhaps they're father and son, but the age gap doesn't look big enough. Brothers maybe.

'We wish to speak to the Masons,' tattoo man says.

'They're on holiday,' Niall replies. 'Can we take a message?'

'Who are you?' Tattoo man removes his sunglasses and stares from Niall to me, and back again. 'You are family?'

I open my mouth to reply, but Niall cuts me off. 'We're staying here on holiday.'

'When they are coming back?'

'Not for another ten days. What did you say your names were?'

'On holiday, where?' Tattoo man narrows his eyes and I realise these men might be dangerous. I wonder if they're the ones who broke into the house yesterday. Suddenly, I'm scared. I'd like to close the door on them, but at the same time, I'm nervous of doing something that might make them angry.

'We don't know,' Niall replies.

Tattoo man confers with his companion for a moment. The older man seems very agitated. He keeps gesturing to the house.

'You are the Masons' family, yes? You tell us where they have gone.'

'We're not family,' I reply. 'We booked the house through an agency. We don't know the owners. This is a holiday home.' I hope I sound convincing. There's no way I'm giving these guys our address.

'We come in,' tattoo man says. 'We see if the Masons are in the house, okay?'

'We have young children,' Niall says. 'I'd rather you didn't disturb them.'

'It's fine,' tattoo man says. 'I have children too.'

'The thing is,' I say, 'we had a break-in last night. A robbery.'

'You have a robbery, here? Last night?' The man looks surprised and they both talk quickly in Italian for a moment.

'Yes,' I confirm. Their surprise seems genuine, so perhaps they weren't responsible for the break-in. I clear my throat. 'We're expecting the police to arrive in a minute. They're coming to take a statement about the robbery.' I'm hoping my lie will make them leave. There's something shady about them. I get the impression that they won't want to hang around if they think the police are about to show up.

'Okay,' tattoo man says, putting his sunglasses back on. 'We come back another time.'

'After ten days,' Niall says firmly.

They don't reply. Instead they turn and walk back down the drive towards a gleaming black Range Rover that's parked in the street.

Niall ushers me inside and closes the door. 'Who were they?' he whispers.

'I don't know, and I don't want to know. Is it safe to stay here, do you think? Maybe we should check into a hotel.'

'It's fine. We'll be fine,' Niall says unconvincingly. 'Good thinking, saying the police are on their way. That should put them off coming back.'

'I wonder what they want with the Masons.'

'Who knows.' Niall heads back through the hall.

'I should call Amber.' I follow him into the kitchen.

'No,' Niall replies. 'Let's leave it. There's no point getting ourselves into a drama that doesn't involve us.'

'But we should at least find out who those people are.'

'Look, Beth, let's just enjoy the holiday. Those guys have gone now and I doubt they'll be back now we've mentioned the police. I'm going for a swim. You coming?'

'In a minute.'

'Fine.' He goes out onto the terrace and takes off his polo shirt, dropping it onto one of the sun loungers before diving into the pool.

I don't think those shorts he's wearing are even swimming shorts. Niall is obviously as rattled by the encounter as I am. So why won't he discuss it with me? Is he really content to stay here in this house after we've had a break-in and a visit by two very suspect men? Is he actually prepared to risk our safety? Why on earth didn't we just stay home?

My phone pings. It's a text message from Sal. The link to the Facebook post she was telling me about. I wonder if I really want to get into this now.

The boys clatter down the stairs. 'Dad's in the pool!' Liam cries.

'Does that mean we're allowed in too?' Connor asks hopefully.

I stare at their eager upturned faces, their little bodies already tanned from hours of swimming. 'Give Dad another fifteen minutes. He's having a quiet swim.' I glance over to the pool where my husband is powering through the water, swimming fast, agitated laps.

'But Dad said—' Connor starts.

'Just fifteen more minutes upstairs, okay? That's not long to wait. And make sure you both put on sunscreen.'

'Fine.' Their shoulders slump and they trudge back the way they came.

Sod it. I click on Sal's link. Facebook opens. I glance outside. Niall is still swimming laps, his bronzed shoulders rising and falling. The post pops up on my screen. The photo was taken outside a restaurant or bar at night. There are four people in the photo – three men in suits, one of whom is my husband, and a woman in a fitted cream sleeveless dress, her sleek, dark waves tumbling over one shoulder – Amber. She and Niall are standing very close together, closer than the other two men. So close that their arms are touching. They're smiling, relaxed. Almost cosy.

I leave the kitchen and stand in the hall, my pulse racing, a queasy feeling swirling around my stomach. It doesn't mean anything. It's just a photo. Niall must have met hundreds of people over the years. Readers, bloggers and bookshops love to tag him in photos. So why then do I have such a bad feeling?

My eye is drawn to a delicate gold eternity bracelet on Amber's wrist. I tap the photo and zoom in with my fingers. The bracelet is inset with diamonds. My breath hitches and my fingers start to tremble. I know that bracelet. It's exactly the same as the one I always wear. The one Niall gave me when Connor was born.

TWENTY-EIGHT

AMBER

'Hellooo!'

Renzo, the kids and I are dawdling up to the front door of the cottage when we hear someone calling out behind us. My heart sinks, realising that it's none other than busybody Sal from across the road. If it were just me here, I would pretend not to have heard her, but my family betrays me by turning around and giving her a warm greeting in return.

'Hello, Sal,' Renzo says. 'How are you?'

She puffs up the pathway, her cheeks reddened by the biting wind. 'I'm well, thanks, Renzo. Hope you've—'

'Can we go in, Mama?' Franco asks. 'My hands are cold.'

'Of course,' I reply. 'Renzo, you've got the key, can you open the door so the kids can go inside?'

Renzo tuts. 'In a minute. Franco, don't be rude. Say hello to Sal first.'

'Hello,' he says morosely.

I stifle a smile. He sounds how I feel.

'Hello, Sal,' Flora says before she can be told off too.

Sal's gaze skips over me as she smiles at my family. 'Sorry, I won't take up too much of your time. It's too chilly to stand out here for long. Although at least the sun's been shining. I hope you've all had a good day.'

'We have, thanks,' Renzo replies. 'A lazy morning, then a wander around Sherborne town centre.'

'How lovely,' she says. 'We have some great little boutiques and cafés.'

'You certainly do. Would you like to come inside?' Renzo offers.

'No, no, it's fine, I won't keep you. I saw you passing and just wondered if you'd all like to come over for dinner one evening this week?'

There's an awkward beat of silence, during which I guess that she's probably been watching out her window, waiting for us to come back so she could extend her unwanted invitation.

'Obviously, don't worry if you've got too much planned, or if you'd rather not...' She gives a nervous laugh.

'No, that would be lovely,' Renzo replies, giving me a look that says I need to agree with him.

'Really lovely,' I add without much enthusiasm. I really don't see why we should have to give up a peaceful evening for the sake of politeness to a woman we'll never see again after this holiday.

'Wonderful.' Sal beams. Funnily enough, she still hasn't given me a single glance yet. All her words have been directed at my husband and children. Maybe her thick skin isn't quite as thick as I'd first thought. Perhaps she's finally realised I'm not a fan. But that begs the question as to why she'd then want to invite us over. Interesting. I wonder what she'd say if I told her not to worry, that I'd stay home while she pretended my family were hers. The thought makes me smirk. Sal must have seen my change of expression, for she returns my grin with a smile of her own – although I can't work out if it's actually genuine or not. 'I also wanted to see if you're all okay after yesterday's news,' she adds.

'News?' Renzo asks.

My blood ices over at her words.

Renzo's brow creases and he glances from Sal to me, and then back to Sal again.

'Yes,' Sal charges on. 'The break-in at your house back in Italy. It's good they didn't take anything, but still, it must have been a shock for you all.'

How the hell does she know about that? She must have spoken to Beth.

Renzo freezes, his face blanching. Franco's expression turns anxious, and Flora simply looks bemused. I glare at Sal, pointing surreptitiously to the children and shaking my head. She instantly understands her faux pas, realising that the children know nothing about any break-in. But what she also doesn't realise, is that I haven't told my husband about it either.

'Sorry,' she stammers. 'I think I've got my wires crossed. Obviously, I didn't mean...' She trails off and her cheeks grow even more crimson, if that's possible. 'Anyway, drop me a text, let me know if you're free one night this week... for dinner.' She steps back and trips over a loose paving slab, almost going flying. But Renzo catches her arm and sets her back on her feet.

'You okay?' he asks.

'Yes, fine, sorry. Thanks for catching me.' She barks out a nervous laugh before heading off.

My husband turns to me, his face dark, and mouths, 'Break-in?'

I shake my head and mouth back, 'Later.'

I watch Sal walk awkwardly away as Renzo heads to the front door.

'What did she mean?' Franco asks me.

'Nothing,' I cut him off.

'But she said there was a—'

'I said *nothing*.' My tone brooks no argument.

Franco snaps his mouth shut and follows his father into the

house. Flora takes my hand and we walk through the front door together into the warmth of the cottage. The atmosphere, however, is several degrees cooler than the temperature.

'Okay, kids.' Renzo claps his hands. 'You can go up to your room and chill out for a while.'

Franco doesn't need telling twice. Any excuse to go on his phone. Flora's a little more reluctant, but she does as she's told and follows her brother up the stairs, giving us a baleful look over her shoulder.

Renzo strides through to the kitchen and opens a bottle of red wine. He pours himself a generous glass and takes a few large gulps.

'Renz? You okay?'

'What? Yes, fine. She's an odd one, isn't she? Sal.'

'Tell me about it,' I reply. It's strange that Renzo hasn't mentioned the break-in yet. I wonder if I should bring it up myself.

He tops up his glass. 'Sorry, do you want some?' He reaches up to the cupboard to get another glass.

'Go on then.' I remove my coat and scarf, dumping them on the table.

'Do you know what Sal was talking about?' Renzo asks, his back to me while he pours my drink.

'Okay. Yes. I do.' I wince, waiting for him to be shocked and upset with me for keeping him in the dark about such a big thing.

He turns and hands me a glass. His face is blank.

'Renzo, are you okay?'

'Uh...' He swallows and huffs out a breath. 'Yeah... so what happened?'

'It's fine, everything's fine. There was a break-in at the house yesterday—'

'I can't believe you knew about it,' he says accusingly.

'But nothing was taken and no one was hurt,' I add quickly.

'How did you hear? Did the Kildares call you?'

'I got a call from the alarm company, and then Beth rang.'

'Yesterday?'

I nod sheepishly.

'Why the hell didn't you tell me!' Renzo's voice booms through the kitchen, making me jump.

I inhale, give him a pointed look and gesture upstairs.

He shakes his head and repeats the question more quietly. 'Tell me what happened, Amber.'

I take my wine and sit at the breakfast bar. 'Not much. The alarm went off while the Kildares were out, but the intruder left without taking anything, so no harm done.'

Renzo is still shaking his head, his expression unreadable.

I don't get fazed by much, but I don't like my husband's reaction. Either he's really hurt that I didn't tell him, or really angry. Probably both. Bloody Sal and her big mouth. I take a glug of my drink.

'Sorry I didn't tell you, Renz, but I didn't want to spoil our holiday with bad news. Nothing was taken or damaged so I didn't think it would matter.' I realise my explanation is weak.

'I'm not a child, Amber,' Renzo says through gritted teeth. 'I don't need protecting from bad news. You should have told me straight away.'

'I know. You're right. I'm sorry.' I lower my head and put my hands in my lap to hide my trembling fingers. Renzo's mad. He'll get over it. He never stays angry for long. But if that's the case, then why is my heart pounding so hard? Why do I feel as though everything is sliding away? Was yesterday's break-in a coincidence? A practise run? Whatever it was, I don't think my nerves can stand much more.

'So nothing was taken?' he asks for confirmation.

I lift my gaze. 'That's right. The police said the alarm must have spooked them.'

'How did they get in?' Renzo drains his glass and pours a refill.

'Through the downstairs bathroom window apparently.'

'They broke it?'

'It was left open.'

Renzo clenches a fist. 'I still can't believe you didn't tell me, Amber.' His eyes are misted with hurt.

'I'm sorry.'

'I'm going upstairs for a while.'

'Don't be mad, Renz.' I get to my feet. I want to put my arms around him, but he's holding himself so stiffly, I don't think he would welcome my embrace. I force myself to stay where I am, watching my husband leave the kitchen. I badly want to go after him to smooth things out between us, but it's probably better if I let him calm down for a few minutes. There are so many conflicting emotions running through me. So many what-ifs circling my brain. It's too late to change things now.

I try to let my mind go blank. The evening sun streams in through the windows striping the room. Renzo's footsteps creak overhead. I stand in the middle of the kitchen, unsure what to do with myself.

This is ridiculous. What am I doing wallowing in regret? I've made this plan and I'm going to stick to it. I go to the counter, top up my glass with the last of the wine, and head upstairs to make amends with my husband.

I walk past the children's room. It's quiet in there. Good.

I open our bedroom door and give a shiver. It's freezing! It's also empty. I cast my gaze around the room and see that the balcony doors are open, letting in a stream of icy air, the curtains shuddering and billowing in the breeze.

'Renzo?' I take a step towards the balcony. There's no reply. The light out there is blinding as the sun sinks lower. I blow on my hands and take another step. 'Renz, are you out here?' I pull aside the curtains and open the door wider to see my husband standing stiff-backed and unresponsive, looking out over the garden. 'Renzo?'

'Look at this sunset,' he says softly.

I brave the cold and stand next to him. 'Are you sure it's safe out here? It feels a bit rickety.' I glance around at the mossy flagstones and rusted railings.

'It's fine,' he replies, drawing me near. 'Can you believe those colours? It's like a painting.'

I exhale and stare out at the display of reds and oranges bleeding across the sky. 'Looks like the sky's on fire,' I murmur. 'Pity it's so bloody cold out here.'

'Sorry I got cross earlier,' Renzo says, rubbing my arm to warm me up. 'It was a shock, that's all.'

'I'm sorry too.' I lean in closer. 'You're right. I should've told you.' I look up at him. 'Are we okay?'

'We're never *not* okay, Amber.'

At his words, I feel my fears start to drift away. As long as I have Renzo, then nothing else matters.

TWENTY-NINE

BETH

The evening air whispers warmly over my skin, but my hands remain icy. I clench and unclench them at my sides, trying to get the circulation going. Maiori's tree-lined promenade teems with people out for their *passeggiata*, an evening walk where the locals hang out, catch up with friends and soak in the beautiful surroundings.

I didn't want to come down to the beachfront. I'd rather have gone to a low-key bar closer to the villa, but Niall insisted that as it's only the two of us we should take advantage of the situation. He's booked a table at some posh restaurant in a thirteenth-century Norman tower that juts out over the sea. He doesn't realise that this isn't a romantic evening out. This is something different. Something necessary.

Ever since I saw that photo of Niall and Amber on Facebook, I haven't been able to think about anything else. I've spent the day stewing about it until I could stand it no longer and realised that I have to do something. I have to get the truth from my husband. Even if it turns out that I discover something I don't want to know.

My darkest fear is that he had an affair with Amber. That

he's still seeing her. That maybe this whole house swap is some kind of twisted game. I'm doused with terror at the thought of my family splitting apart. What will happen to us? To the boys? Our home?

I thought about calling Amber first to hear her side, but I dismissed that idea. If I'm wrong, then she'll think I'm a paranoid lunatic, and Niall will be furious at me for spreading our personal issues around. No. I have to speak to my husband first. Get him to tell the truth. I'm sure I'll be able to tell whether he's lying or not.

Niall slings his arm around me and breathes in deeply. 'Now, this is what I'm talking about. A nice night out, just the two of us, finally able to relax for the evening.' He pulls me in for a quick squeeze. 'Great idea to drop the kids off at Luciana's, Beth. *Now* I know why you befriended her – free babysitting.' He grins.

I know he's expecting me to laugh along with him, but all I can muster is a weak smile. While Niall was having his siesta earlier this afternoon, I called Luciana and asked if the boys could hang out with her two this evening as Niall and I had some things to discuss. She was a little taken aback at first, but then she seemed to embrace the idea, saying that Marco and Gianni would love it. They could all have pizza and a videogame tournament.

I knew that I'd never be able to have a proper talk with Niall if I was worrying about the boys overhearing our conversation. This way, I'll be able to say what's on my mind without being interrupted. Only, Niall seems to think this is my attempt at a romantic evening. I did tell him that I didn't want a fancy night out, just a drink, but he didn't listen.

As we saunter along the promenade, the grey stone tower looms up ahead, set among rocks above the indigo sea. Warm orange light glows from the arched windows studded along its walls. The sight should be dramatic and inspiring, but instead it fills me with dread. I've never liked confrontations.

Back at the villa, I knew exactly what I was going to say to my husband. I was determined and confident. As we draw closer to our destination, part of me wonders if I might have been overreacting. If that Facebook post isn't simply what it looks like – a photograph of people at a book event. *But what about the bracelet?* A little voice asks. *How do you explain that?*

I realise my sudden reluctance to question my husband is only my nerves coming out to play. I try to summon my earlier confidence, but it seems to have evaporated into the balmy night air. I tell myself not to think about any of it yet. Wait until we're seated in the restaurant, let the conversation come about naturally. My mouth is dry. I lick my lips, desperate for a drink. An aperitivo would go down really well about now.

We reach the top of the promontory and I stare down at the steps that lead out to the tower. I pause for a moment.

'You should probably have worn some slightly more sensible shoes.' Niall looks disapprovingly at my open-toe stilettos, assuming my reluctance is down to my footwear.

'I'll be fine,' I say. 'These shoes are actually quite comfortable.' That's a blatant lie. After walking all this way they now feel like instruments of torture. But denying it somehow makes me feel better. More powerful and in control.

'Good job,' Niall says. 'That's a hell of a lot of stairs.'

Finally, we reach the restaurant where we're seated at a table next to a Gothic arched window that looks out over the Mediterranean and down onto the rocks. The place is busy, echoing with soft chatter and laughter, and the clink of cutlery and silverware. A cool breeze flows through the window making me shiver even as I welcome it. Niall orders us each an Aperol spritz and asks to see the wine list.

'Hope you're hungry,' he says, leaning forward to look out the window. 'The food is supposed to be amazing.'

I'm the opposite of hungry. My feet are throbbing and my brain feels woolly. Should I ask him about the photo now? Get it over with? But then we'll be interrupted by the waitstaff as they ask about wine and take our orders. I rearrange my maxi dress so it won't get creased. I decide that I should probably wait until the food arrives before saying anything. With that decision made, I'm able to relax a little.

Niall chats to me about the history of the tower, but I'm not really listening. Just making all the appropriate responses, and arranging my face into various expressions of interest, fiddling with my bracelet and shifting in my seat. My drink slides down too easily.

Niall orders us a bottle of the house red. We decided to skip starters and go straight for a main course. Usually I would take my time and quiz the waiter about each dish, enjoying the discussion of where it's from and how it's cooked. But this evening my heart isn't in it. I select something off the menu, instantly forgetting what I decided upon.

Niall is doing all the talking while I try to maintain interest. The whole time, my mind is flipping between whether to ask him about the photo or whether to forget about it and simply focus on enjoying the night. My phone is on the table, the Facebook post bookmarked so I don't have to waste time locating it.

'You're quiet,' Niall says, observing me.

'Am I?' Heat floods my face.

Niall's eyes narrow.

I pick up my wine glass again and start sipping.

'Yes. What's wrong?' His tone is terse rather than concerned.

This is when I should ask him about the photo. This is the perfect opener.

'Fillet of beef for you, sir.' The waiter sets the plate in front of Niall who smiles appreciatively. 'And the tuna for signora.'

The food is good, probably incredible. But I can barely

taste any of it. I've been reaching for my wine glass instead. We're already on our second bottle of house red and, unusually, it's me who's drunk most of it. At least the arrival of our main course has distracted Niall from his concern over my quietness. After a few mouthfuls of tuna, I give up and lay down my knife and fork, settling for another glass of wine instead.

'Maybe we should buy a case to take back with us,' Niall suggests with an eye-roll.

I nod, purposely misconstruing his sarcasm for a genuine suggestion. I'm suddenly overcome with a rush of anger. Why shouldn't I have a few glasses of wine? We're on holiday, aren't we? I pick up my phone and tap the Facebook app, deciding that there's nothing wrong with asking my husband about the photo. I'm curious, that's all.

'Remember that photo I found of you in Amber's jacket pocket?' I ask.

Niall looks up, his laden fork hovering in front of his mouth. 'Huh?'

'The photo. Of you. In Amber's pocket.' My words are slurred. I think I'm a bit drunk, which is unfortunate. But maybe it's a good thing. I don't think I'd have had the courage to ask Niall otherwise.

'What about it?' He jams the food into his mouth and chews, his eyes clouded with irritability for a moment before they clear and he adopts a more nonchalant expression.

'You said you didn't know her.' I watch his face carefully.

'I don't.'

'So why's there a photo of the two of you together?'

'*What?*' He puts down his knife and fork and glares at me, his face reddening.

'Look.' I thrust my phone across the table, under his nose.

He takes it from me and stares at the screen before shaking his head and handing it back. 'There are probably hundreds of photos of me with random people. How am I supposed to remember them all?'

'She's wearing my eternity bracelet.'

'She's wearing your...?' He reaches out a hand to take back the phone. 'Let me see.'

'The one you gave me after Connor was born.' I point to my bracelet. 'She's wearing the exact same one.'

He squints at the photo. 'It looks like this photo was taken at a book signing in Rome. I bought you the bracelet when I was on the same book tour. It's probably a popular design over here.' He tosses the phone down on the table between our plates. It lands with a clatter. 'What *is* this? Are you trying to accuse me of something, Beth? Because if you are, I don't appreciate it.'

'I'm not accusing you of anything,' I reply, realising this conversation is escalating quite rapidly. We're skirting around the edge of a really serious argument. 'I'm curious, that's all. It seems like quite a coincidence that we're staying at this woman's home and she has a photograph of you in her pocket, and another one with her on social media.' My heart is hammering in my chest. All my suspicions are pouring out now. This wasn't how I'd planned to speak to my husband, but I can't seem to stop myself.

'Maybe she's just a fan of my books. Did you think about that possibility?'

'Yes. But Sal said Amber was asking her questions about us. Personal questions.'

Niall chokes out a disbelieving laugh. 'Oh, well, if *Sal* is suspicious then I *must* be guilty!' He reaches for his wine glass but it's almost empty. He drains the dregs and snatches up the bottle, but that's also empty. He thumps it back down on the table in disgust. 'I think you're drunk, Beth, and it's giving you an overactive imagination. And I've warned you that Sal is an interfering busybody with nothing better to do than stir up trouble so I don't know why you're even listening to her.'

'She's not a busybody. She's my friend. And I'm not that drunk. Anyway, I was having these thoughts before I even touched a drop of alcohol.'

'Is this what tonight has all been about?' Niall's face darkens, his billowing anger palpable across the table. 'Here's me thinking you wanted a romantic evening for the two of us. But, *no*. You engineered it so you could throw these pathetic accusations at me. Well, thanks a lot, Beth. Great holiday this is turning out to be.'

'That's not fair,' I reply, stung. 'You'd be the same if you found a photo of me in a strange man's jacket pocket.'

'Yes, I would. But that's because you don't give out promotional photos to the general public.' His voice softens a little. 'Beth, this is my job. My *work*. There are probably hundreds of photos of me out there.'

I bite my lip, knowing that what he's saying makes sense, but still somehow unable to fully believe him. 'So if I were to call Amber and ask her outright if you knew her, she would tell me the same thing.'

'For goodness' sake, Beth! You sound like a jealous crazy person! I've had enough of this.' He scrapes his chair back and rises to his feet, takes his wallet from his pocket and extracts a wad of euros that he slams onto the table. 'If you call Amber, spouting all this ridiculous stuff, she'll think you're a nutcase. But by all means, go ahead if you don't believe me.'

'What are you doing?' I ask.

'What does it look like I'm doing?' he sneers. 'I'm leaving you to your drunken ramblings. You can come home once you've sobered up and can start thinking straight again. You've never been able to handle your drink, Beth.'

'You're leaving?' I can't believe Niall's actually walking out on our conversation. I wonder if it's because he's genuinely outraged or if it's because I've touched a nerve.

He rests his hands on the chair-back and leans across the

table. 'Well, I'm not staying here to be accused of all this nonsense,' he hisses at me.

I freeze in my seat, too confused and shocked to say any more as my husband turns and stalks out of the restaurant.

That went as badly as it could possibly have gone.

And I'm still no nearer to discovering the truth.

THIRTY

AMBER

'Look at that!' Renzo sits back on his heels to admire the wood burner where a fire now crackles and spits against the smoky glass.

'Well done, Renz. It's good to know mankind can still make fire,' I drawl from my spot on the sofa with Flora curled up next to me.

He grins up at me. 'That was more fun than the one at home. More primitive somehow.'

'Can I light the fire tomorrow?' Franco asks.

'And me!' Flora cries.

'Okay,' Renzo replies. 'Not on your own. Mama or I have to be with you.'

The four of us are in the living room about to watch *Paddington* with supper on our laps. We're trying out Beth's homemade meatballs with fresh spaghetti. I'm not exactly dying to eat her food, but we're all too weary to go out, the takeaway places all take too long to deliver, and neither of us could be bothered to cook from scratch tonight.

Flora and I remain seated while Renzo and our son head off to the kitchen to bring in the food. We've watched *Paddington* many times before, but it's a favourite we always return to when we're stuck for a family movie. God knows I need something to take my mind off the situation I'm in.

Some people might say it's my own fault, but I think I just got unlucky, that's all. At least instead of whining about it, I'm doing something. I close my eyes, place a hand on my sternum and inhale deeply.

'Are you meditating, Mama?'

I can sense Flora studying me.

'Yes. You have to be quiet when someone's meditating.' I open one eye to see her shift position, copy my pose and close her eyes. She's imitating me. We breathe together for a while and I'm overcome by a rush of something – not exactly emotion. More like sentimentality. It's nice.

'Okay, here we go!' Renzo and Franco come into the living room and hand Flora and I a tray each with a bowl of hot food. Wine for me and lemonade for her. They make the return trip to the kitchen to fetch their trays and we settle in to watch the film.

'This is really tasty,' Renzo says with his mouth full. 'Seriously good.'

I scowl. He's right, but it would gall me to admit it out loud. I'm three mouthfuls in, when my mobile starts to ring. I glance down at the screen to see Beth's name flash up.

'Who's that?' Renzo asks.

'Work,' I reply, setting my phone to *silent*.

Renzo pauses the TV to cries of annoyance from the children. 'It's Sunday!'' he says. 'Don't they know you're on holiday? Do you need to take it?'

'No, it's fine.'

'Okay.' He presses play again and we settle back into our film and food.

Thirty seconds later, my phone starts to vibrate. It's Beth again. My heart starts to pound as I wonder why she's calling. I should definitely answer it, but I'm delaying because I want to be in the here and now with my family. I don't want to step back into what's happening over there. Not yet.

The phone falls silent.

I exhale and place a forkful of spaghetti in my mouth.

A moment later, my mobile buzzes to let me know I've received a voicemail. I should just switch off the damned thing. I realise I've been zoned out of the movie for a while. I force my attention back to the television. The kids and Renzo are laughing. It's the part where Paddington is cleaning his ears with a toothbrush. I try to get back into the spirit of things, but my heart isn't in it.

'Actually, Renz...'

'Huh?' He frowns and drags his gaze over to me from the TV screen.

'I think I will have to call this client back, after all.' I put my tray on the coffee table, reach for my phone and stand up.

'Really? That's a shame.' He pauses the TV again.

'Dad!' Franco cries. 'This is the best bit!'

'We'll pause it until you come back,' Renzo says to me.

'No.' I shake my head. 'Keep watching. I'll be back in a few minutes.'

'You sure?' he asks. 'You should at least finish your food first.'

'I won't be able to enjoy it while I'm thinking about work.'

He nods knowingly. 'Okay, but don't be too long.'

I leave the room and close the door behind me. I'm nervous and excited and terrified and giddy. Beth's call could be nothing. But the fact that she rang twice means it's probably something important. I press play on the voicemail, and start walking up the stairs. I wish I'd thought to bring my wine glass with me. Beth's message begins.

Amber... sorry to bother you on a Sunday evening, but I need to ask you a question. I'd rather have spoken to you directly than left a message but you're not picking up so I guess you're busy or maybe you're having an early night, I don't know. I wish I'd had an early night myself...

She's gabbling. Actually, she sounds like she might be drunk. How funny. She doesn't seem happy at all. I go into the bedroom, turn on the bedside lamp and sit on the edge of the bed, listening to the rest.

Anyway, she continues, *my question is this: Do you know my husband, Niall? I mean, I know you know him through the house swap, but were you friends beforehand? Because I'm embarrassed to say that I found a photo of him in your jacket pocket. I wouldn't normally look in someone else's pocket, but I was playing hide-and-seek with my kids, and, uh, well... I found the photo. So, if you could just tell me, that would be great. It's been bugging me and I thought I'd ask.*

She pauses. *Hope you don't mind!* She says this last part really breezily, as though that will negate her previous drunken, paranoid rant.

I swing my legs up onto the bed, lean back against the pillow, and shake my head in gleeful wonder. *Wow,* I really messed with Beth's head, didn't I? Putting that photo in my jacket pocket was genius, even if I say so myself. I wasn't sure if she'd be the snooping kind, but, let's face it, all human beings are the snooping kind. If there's an opportunity to be nosy, we'll take it. So little miss perfect Beth Kildare isn't quite so perfect after all.

The message is still running, but it's only background noise now. She's obviously forgotten to end the call.

Amber...

Oh, my mistake, she's still going.

There's something else... I don't suppose... do you own a gold eternity bracelet? Because I think it's similar to one I own. She pauses. *Actually, don't worry about the bracelet. But if you could let me know about Niall, I'd be grateful. Thanks. Bye.*

The message ends.

Beth's voice message has given me clarity and a timely reminder of why I decided to do all this in the first place. I don't think I'll call her back yet, even though it's tempting. If only to see what other pathetic questions she might want to ask about her husband.

The sound of the TV filters up through the floorboards. I should really go back downstairs to join my family on the sofa. There's just something I want to try first.

I get up off the bed and take a few steps to the door where my black handbag hangs from the hook. I unzip it and rummage through to find the small packet of tools I bought from the local hardware shop in town yesterday. I managed to slip away from my family for a short while under the guise of stocking up on a few toiletries from the chemist. Then I nipped into the hardware shop to pick up my order.

I step out onto the landing and pause, listening out. The TV is still playing downstairs, Flora's laughter mingling with the soundtrack. I cast my gaze over the packet in my hand, and slip one of the tiny rake tools into my palm, along with the tension bar. Since I arrived here, I've been secretly watching YouTube videos on how to pick locks, so I'm quite confident I can do it. Of course, my plan was to try this while everyone was out of the house, but I have no idea when that will be, and I have no time to lose.

As I stand outside Niall's locked study, adrenalin races through me. I'm stupidly excited about doing this. I slide the little metal rake into the lock and jiggle it about, before inserting the tension bar and pulling it down. Nothing happens, so I try again. Still nothing. My fingers have become sweaty, making the tools slippery. I wipe my fingers on my jeans and try again. Still no luck.

Trying not to let frustration take over, I substitute the rake for a different one. Taking a deep breath, I slot it into the lock and wiggle it up and down a few times like a lever, trying to imagine it pushing up the lock pins. I slot in the tension tool at the base of the opening, pull it down, and feel a lift of joy as the lock gives way with a click. I turn the door handle and the study door swings open.

I shove the packet of tools into the back pocket of my jeans and step into Niall Kildare's sacred office.

It's disappointingly predictable.

A traditional mahogany desk at the window with a tan leather insert, stuffed bookshelves, framed prints of his book covers, a shabby rug. It smells musty with a hint of aftershave. It screams *I'm an important author*, and the fact that he keeps it locked is so offensive to me. Either he doesn't trust his family. Or he has something to hide.

I use the light from the landing and scan the bookshelves. There are multiple copies of his own books, along with plenty of other fantasy and historical series, a lot of classics, and a couple of shelves of writing-craft books.

The desk is tidy. There's no PC or laptop – I guess he must have taken that with him. I start pulling open the desk drawers. They're stuffed with notes and old bits of stationery. The three drawers along the top all have locks. The right drawer slides open. It's filled with phone-charging leads, earbuds and other cables. The central drawer also slides open, but it turns out to be a flat tray that extends the desk. The left-hand drawer, however, is locked.

I don't waste time looking for a key. Instead, I use my lock-picking tool kit and open the drawer easily. To my disappoint-ment, it lies empty. I purse my lips and blow out a breath of disappointment. I don't even know what I was expecting to find in the room. Perhaps he simply locked the door because he didn't want our young children disturbing his workplace – a reasonable action to take. I'm imagining more secrets where there are none.

I sit at his desk chair for a moment, gazing at my reflection in the dark window, wondering what Niall would think if he saw me here in his private office, going through his things. I can't help smirking. I stare at the open drawer and put my hand inside, reaching into the far corners. There's nothing there. I turn my hand over and run my fingertips across the ceiling of the drawer. The lining is papery and hanging down slightly.

I frown and slide the whole drawer out of the desk, placing it on the floor. I kneel and shine my torchlight into the empty hole. Taped to the top of the drawer space is a slim sheaf of papers... or are they photos? My heart begins to pound. I carefully detach them from their hiding spot and turn them over. I can't believe he still has these. Next, I take out the cheap little phone I brought with me to England.

It's time to do this.

Everything is in place.

It's now or never.

THIRTY-ONE

BETH

I collapse onto a low wall and remove my stilettos before massaging the balls of my poor blistered feet. I'm heading home on Corso Reginna, the main street that leads off the coast road. After walking back from the restaurant, up all those stairs and back along the promenade, my feet are swollen and throbbing. I literally couldn't walk another step right now. Not until I've had a decent rest.

I can't believe how badly I've handled things this evening. First, I drank too much, too quickly, blurting out my accusations at Niall without any subtlety whatsoever. Second, I called Amber and did exactly the same thing. I'm actually pretty mortified about that. I cringe at how incoherent and rambling I must have sounded to her. She must think I'm an idiot. My carefully planned evening is in tatters. My husband is furious with me, and I've no idea how Amber feels as she still hasn't called me back. As for myself, I'm tired, humiliated and anxious, while still not entirely believing Niall's story. In short, I've achieved precisely nothing.

I sigh, realising I'm still pretty tipsy. I'd kill for a glass of water right now, but I didn't bring my wallet out with me tonight. I stare around glassily at the beautiful stone buildings with their tall, shuttered windows and Juliet balconies. At the dim shape of the hills beyond the town, a spray of glittering lights studding the darkness. Such a beautiful place. Too beautiful for me to feel such sadness and despair.

I let my gaze fall back down to the street. There are still quite a few shops open, clusters of people in restaurants and bars, the sound of happy chatter spilling into the square. A busy pizza takeaway has a queue outside, snaking along the grey cobbles. I'm suddenly quite hungry – I barely ate anything at the restaurant so a slice of that pizza would be welcome right now. It would also help to soak up some of the alcohol. I curse my current lack of funds.

The last time I was here, it was market day. Only two days ago. I really enjoyed that morning shopping with the boys. It's a pity Niall didn't join in with the spirit of things, but that seems to be a theme lately. I don't understand how our relationship has gone from being so passionate and all-consuming to a place where I feel as if he's almost a stranger. I realise that it shouldn't be like this. I shouldn't be nervous of him. I shouldn't mistrust him so deeply. He's my husband, for goodness' sake. The father of my children.

I suddenly recall how I saw him speaking to that Italian guy here that day, the one he insisted was an overenthusiastic time-share salesman. I didn't believe *that* either. The two of them looked too pally. Like they knew one another well. Like old friends catching up. If that's the case, then why would Niall lie to me about it? It makes no sense. Unless the guy was part of the whole Niall-knowing-Amber situation.

I feel like I'm going crazy. I don't have any proper proof of anything. Just a couple of photos and a gut feeling. Is that enough to put my marriage in jeopardy? Should I have kept my mouth shut?

My phone starts ringing, and Niall's face flashes up on the screen. My stomach flips with dread. I should answer it, but I can't face another argument right now. I need to sober up a bit. Work out what I want to do. Whether I should keep pushing for answers. Or if I should forget the whole thing. Maybe I should even apologise so that we can get back to normal. I can't decide. I slip the phone back into my bag and let it go to voicemail.

A movement and a cry from further down the street catches my eye. I turn to see an elderly man outside a ceramics shop remonstrating with two men. He's shouting and gesticulating at them. There's something familiar about the scene. I blink to clear my vision, and get to my feet, taking a couple of steps closer. But not too close.

I freeze as I realise that they're the same two men who came to the villa this morning looking for the Masons. I quickly turn my face away, scared in case they see me and come over. I'm worried for the man they're harassing, but I'm not brave or stupid enough to confront them. What could I do anyway? I can't even speak the language. Should I call the police? Or might that make it worse?

There are a few people glancing in their direction, but no one intervenes. I can't get involved in this. It's none of my business and, anyway, I think I have enough to deal with right now.

I'm unsure what to do. In order to return to the villa, I would need to walk past them, unless I could find another route. I suppose I could chance trying to slip by them, but what if they recognise me? What would be the point in taking such a risk? No, I'll have to turn around and find somewhere to wait it out until they move on.

With fumbling fingers, I slip my shoes back on, stand and start to walk away. Not too quickly as I don't want to draw attention to myself. My heels tap, the sound ringing out, but there's nothing I can do about that. I resist the temptation to glance back, instead, I keep my eyes focused straight ahead. My palms are sweaty and my breaths come in short gasps. Seeing those men is the last thing I expected tonight. I'm surprised at how shaken up I am.

Again, I wonder what they wanted with the Masons earlier. I'm certain it couldn't have been anything good. I still have a really bad feeling about all this. Much as it pains me, I think we should leave the villa and find somewhere else to stay. Somewhere where those men can't find us. The chances are that they won't return, but I don't want to risk it. They're obviously some kind of thugs. My mood plummets further at the thought of leaving our beautiful holiday home less than halfway into our holiday.

For a moment, I allow myself to think about the possibility of staying at the Villa Cimbrone in Ravello. But it's probably not as child-friendly as being in Maiori by the beach. The hard thing about moving our accommodation will be convincing Niall. Especially as he's so angry right now. This evening's argument comes racing back at me. No. Niall and I probably aren't going to get back into the holiday mood anytime soon. If we weren't involved in this bloody house swap, I'd suggest flying home. But we can't exactly kick out the Masons. Or can we? After all, we didn't bargain for a break-in or a visit from two scary men. We'd be within our rights to insist on cancelling the holiday swap.

I think wistfully of our cosy cottage. Of flopping on the sofa with the boys watching a movie or playing board games. Instead, my husband hates me, and I'm hobbling down an Italian street alone at night in the hope that two terrifying thugs don't spot me. Not exactly the perfect holiday I'd envisioned.

I should probably call Luciana to check that Connor and Liam are okay. She said to stay out as late as I liked. That she rarely goes to bed before one a.m. But I don't like to take advantage.

A ping from my phone startles me back into my current

surroundings. It's probably from Niall. I pray he's calmed down. I'll check it in a minute. I'm almost back at the promenade now and my phone pings again. I dart recklessly across the main road, forcing a small Fiat to slow down. The driver – a young guy – shouts something at me out of the window. I'm not sure if he was being rude or complimentary. Either way, I'm too preoccupied and too drunk to worry about it. I keep going as my phone pings a third time. *All right, Niall, keep your hair on.*

Back at the promenade, I spy an empty bench further up. Hopefully, if I just stay here for half an hour or so, those two men will have gone, and I can go back to the villa and try to sort things out with my husband. But the thought of walking back there on my own is not a particularly pleasant thought. Maybe I should have stayed where I was and waited for the men to leave. At least then, I'd have a better idea of where they are now.

I stop to slip off my shoes again, then pick my way carefully along the promenade. I weave past strolling couples and families, past dog walkers and boisterous children, heading towards the bench, hoping no one else nabs it before I get there.

I finally reach my target and sink gratefully onto the seat, swallowing and licking my lips. I'm so thirsty. I'll have to go home soon, if only to get a long, cool drink of water. I pull my phone from my bag and psyche myself up for a stream of angry messages from my husband.

But none of the texts I've received are from Niall. They're from an unknown Italian number. Probably local network messages.

I click on the number and the message opens. They're not texts, they're photos. I frown and blink, trying to make sense of them. As realisation dawns, I become still with horror and disbelief. The blood pumps through my veins, pounding my pulse points and ringing in my ears. My vision blurs for a moment and I blink to clear it, staring again at the photographs.

This has to be some kind of sick joke.

Surely this isn't true.

It can't be.

THIRTY-TWO

I wasn't certain if we were in this together. But now I know for sure, I'll be able to do this with more purpose. With clarity.

Maybe now, the bitter jealousy that runs through my veins will start to ease.

Maybe now I can get some peace.

THIRTY-THREE

BETH

The blood whooshes in my ears as I stare at the images.

There are three photographs.

The first is of Niall and Amber with their arms around one another. They're laughing into the camera. It was taken a while ago as Niall's hair is longer and there's no grey in it. It's obvious that they're more than just friends here. My husband and Amber must have been romantically involved in the past. Even though this is what I suspected... to see them together like that... my heart is cracking, splintering. I can't believe Niall lied to me about it. Even worse, that he suggested we come here on holiday. *To her house.*

The second photograph is of Niall and Amber kissing. My hand flies to my mouth. It's so shocking to see them together like this. Their eyes are closed. Her hand cups his face.

But the third photo... the third photo is the one I can't take my eyes off.

It shows Amber with both hands on her stomach. Scrawled across the photo in black marker pen are the words:

Niall, this is your other baby, are you going to acknowledge it?

Is this a joke? My fingers clutch at my throat, my nails scraping the skin on my neck.

It's dated twelve and a half years ago. If it's true, then this child would have been conceived while I was pregnant with Connor. If it's really to be believed, then Amber's eldest child is Niall's son.

As I try to absorb the enormity of this, I feel the bit and pieces of my marriage fracturing around me. Like a shattered mirror reflecting all the lies and betrayals. The love I gave. The dreams I gave up. The hopes I still carried... up until a moment ago. All broken.

Who even sent these? *Amber?* The phone number isn't familiar but that doesn't mean anything. She could have sent them from another phone to mess with me.

I jump as my mobile starts ringing. It's Luciana. I should answer it, but I can't. *I just can't.* I don't think I can speak to anyone. Everything feels too close and too far away at the same time. The darkness, the beach, the villa, home. It's all a jumble in my mind. My phone's ringtone is quiet and loud, familiar and strange. I don't know what to do with myself. What to think. What to feel. I think I'm in shock. That blurred drunken state I was in a moment ago has been replaced by a sharp ache that starts in my gut and finishes behind my eyes.

Niall had an affair with Amber during our marriage... She had his child. The thought of it chokes me. My throat is tight, my eyes burning. Are they still seeing one another? Is that what this holiday is about? Some unfinished business? I feel ill at the thought. It makes no sense. She's in England and we're here. She has a family of her own.

'There you are!' I startle at the sound of my husband's voice behind me. Familiar and yet not familiar any more. 'Why didn't you answer your phone?' he cries. 'I've been calling you. I've been worried sick!'

I stay where I am on the bench, clutching my phone. I don't even turn to acknowledge him as he comes to sit next to me.

'I thought you'd follow me home, catch me up,' he says, like he didn't tell me not to bother coming back until I'd sobered up. 'I went back to the villa, but you never came. Have you been sitting here all this time?' I feel him trying to catch my eye, but I don't move. It's as though I'm frozen solid. As if I've become part of the bench. If I stay seated and unmoving, perhaps he'll give up and go away. I don't want to talk about any of this. It's all too big. I know that once I open my mouth, it will all spill out, and everything will start to crumble and slide away. This moment, right now, is the moment before my life officially changes.

'Beth! Look at me!'

I swallow. My throat is dry. Swollen. I see the three photographs in my mind, flashing up like an old-fashioned slideshow: Amber and Niall embracing. Amber and Niall kissing. Amber and Niall's unborn baby.

How do I even start this conversation?

I loosen my grip on my mobile and tap the screen until the photos reappear.

'What are you doing, Beth? Why won't you look at me? I know I said some stuff earlier, but so did you! Your accusations really hurt me.'

I hand him the phone without looking up.

'What's this?'

My heart pounds as I wait for the images to do their work.

'*Shit*,' he says under his breath. I can almost hear his brain spinning and whirring next to me. Eventually he sighs. 'Okay.' He pauses, rubbing a hand across his mouth.

As I wait for him to continue, I can barely breathe. It feels as if all the oxygen has been sucked from the vicinity. I finally catch his eye as he looks up.

His eyes narrow. 'Who sent you these?'

I don't reply.

Niall shakes his head and stares back down at the images. 'So, I'll admit Amber and I did have a brief fling years ago. But that was before you and I even met. I'm allowed to have a past, aren't I?'

His words are pathetic. The only reason he's admitting anything is because I've presented him with the evidence. He doesn't bring up the fact that he's lied to me about it. I asked him multiple times if he knew Amber, and he said he didn't. So how can I trust anything he says?

'Is this the reason you're out here sulking? Because of something that happened years ago?' He shifts in his seat, bending down to try to catch my eye again. 'You know, it's hard to have this conversation while you're sitting there like a statue. At least say something.'

'Say something?' I reply softly. 'What should I say after finding out my husband was sleeping with a woman while I was pregnant with our child?' I throw him a look of contempt. 'While you were impregnating someone else?'

Despite his tan, Niall's face is grey. 'Surely you don't believe that?' He glances down at my phone again. 'Who sent these anyway? Was it Amber? Look, I didn't tell you about her because she's... well, she's unhinged. She was obsessed with me and lied about me being the father. For Christ's sake, the dates don't even match. She and I were finished before you and I even met. She was using it as a way to get me back. But it didn't work.'

I let his words sink in, and try to weigh up whether or not they could be true. Amber said that Franco is eleven. Niall and I met around three years before her son was born, so if Niall's telling the truth, then Amber's dates are so far out there would be no point in her pretending the child was Niall's. It doesn't seem likely that she'd tell him he was the father of her newborn if they hadn't slept together for three years.

'I don't believe you,' I say, looking him straight in the eye.

He blanches and swallows, and in that instant I know I'm right. It's like being hit in the stomach with a bowling ball. That realisation.

'Why are we here, Niall? Why did you drag us all this way to stay in the house of your... *lover*? Your *ex*? *The mother of your child*? I don't even know what she is to you!'

He lays my phone on the bench and gets to his feet, pacing back and forth for a minute. 'That stupid bitch,' he mutters.

'Just. Tell me. The truth. That's all I want, Niall.' I sit on my hands to stop them shaking. I'm too numb and shocked to even cry. My body is heavy with the weight of it all.

He shakes his head and takes a breath, but still doesn't answer me.

'Niall! Just tell me!'

He runs his hands through his hair and then shoves them in his pocket. He looks so vulnerable right now. Nothing like my self-assured husband. He looks like a little boy. He nods. 'Okay, you're right,' he replies almost irritably. And then more softly. 'You're right.'

'Right about what?' I reply. 'Right that you need to tell me, or right about Amber?'

He looks up at the sky and then drops his gaze to the ground. 'Both.'

My heart judders. I blink, waiting for him to continue, the blood ringing in my ears.

'Amber got in touch with me after years of silence. Said she needed a last-minute holiday and suggested the house swap. I told her it was out of the question. She said if I didn't agree, she'd tell you we'd had an affair.'

'So you *did* have an affair?' I ask.

He hesitates, and then his shoulders sag. 'Yes.'

The air whooshes out of my body. '*Why?*' I whisper.

My husband is silent.

I try to find my voice. 'Why would you do that, Niall? I thought we were happy. I thought we had the perfect marriage. A wonderful life planned out. I was pregnant with our first child! Why would you risk all that? Why would you *want* to?'

'I...' He trails off and looks down. 'I don't know. I wish I could go back and undo it, but I can't.'

'Did you love her?'

'I don't know. *No*. She was...' He throws his hands up. 'I can't explain.'

'You can try! You owe me that much.'

'Okay, then, I was stupid. Flattered by her interest. I ended it. It was over before it began. But then she told me about the baby...'

I shake my head at his words. 'And there was me thinking I was paranoid. That I was the one with the problem. You made me feel terrible the whole time we've been here. Like I'm imagining things! When all along, I was right.'

'I'm sorry, Beth. I really am. I was worried about our marriage. This was all so far in the past. I didn't want it to get in the way of us. I didn't want to jeopardise what we have!'

I give an incredulous laugh. 'You didn't want to jeopardise what we have? So then, why did you sleep with her in the first place? Is she the only one? Have there been other women?'

'No, of course not!'

'Well, I don't know, do I?' I stand shakily and walk down to the edge of the promenade to stare out over the black ocean, my hopes plummeting into the inky darkness. Niall follows, but I don't want him next to me. I turn and walk back to the bench. I pick up my phone and slip it into my bag. I want to storm away from my husband, I can hardly bear to look at him. But I don't know where to go. Back to Amber's villa? The thought makes me sick.

Niall has followed me again. He stands awkwardly, pulling at his fingers.

'What about her son, Franco?' I spit. 'Is he yours? Tell me the truth.'

He's silent for a moment. 'I'm not sure. But I think so. Yes.'

'You don't know! How can you not know? Didn't you ask for a paternity test?' I'm almost yelling the words and people are starting to stare, but I don't care. My whole life is imploding.

'I suppose I took her at her word. I'm pretty sure she was in love with me back then. She wasn't sleeping around.'

I exhale. 'And? So... what? You pay her maintenance? You visit him in secret?' I realise that everything I thought I knew about my life is a lie. It's all been a colossal sham. Maybe Niall paying Amber maintenance is why he's always been so guarded over our finances. Why he's kept me in the dark.

'No.' He stares at the ground again. 'I've never met him. I don't think he even knows about me.'

'So you just left her to raise your child alone? You didn't offer any support?'

'What should I have done?' he cries. 'Left you to be with her? Had us all be one big happy family together? It was a bloody nightmare, Beth.'

'Oh, my heart bleeds, Niall.' I think about Connor and Liam. About the fact they have a brother they know nothing about. What does this even mean? 'You should have told me at the time. You shouldn't have done it in the first place!'

'I know. I'm sorry. I couldn't tell you.' His eyes are filling with tears. 'You would have left me.'

'Maybe I would, maybe I wouldn't. But at least our marriage wouldn't have been this enormous lie. At least we'd have been going into parenthood with some degree of truth. Instead of this... *farce*.' I think back to my pregnancy, trying to recall if there were any signs that should have alerted me to my husband's betrayal, but all I can remember from that period is how happy we were. How Niall doted on me, nipping out to the all-night garage at one in the morning when I had a craving for oranges and white chocolate, rubbing my feet and ankles when they ached. He was the perfect husband. It hits me with a jolt of realisation that his attentiveness was probably down to a combination of fear that he could lose us, and a guilty conscience.

'Beth...' He looks at me. 'I really am sorry. I—'

'"Sorry" doesn't quite cover it, Niall. "Sorry" is absolutely useless, if you must know.'

'I know. I'm...' He trails off. 'What can I do?'

'Right now, you can leave me alone.'

'I don't want to leave you.' A tear drips onto his cheek.

'I don't care what you want.'

'Why don't you come back to the villa? We can talk about this properly. I'll do anything to make this up to you. I know I've been a terrible husband these past few weeks. I've been moody and irritable, and I've taken out my worries on you, when you're the person I should have been good to. I'm a horrible person. I want to make it right.'

'Please just go, Niall.' I collapse back down on the bench and stare past him.

He crouches and tries to take my hands in his. 'Please, Beth, can't you—'

'Get off me!' I shake his hands away as if they're burning hot coals.

He stutters out an apology and stands up again. 'Beth, please...'

'I said GO!'

He nods. 'Okay. I'll go back and wait for you. But don't stay out here by yourself for too long. I don't want to leave you here by yourself.'

'I told you, I don't care what you want. I need you to leave.'

He blinks and turns, starts to walk away.

Despite everything he's done, the space he leaves behind feels vast, cold and empty. I wish I could call him back and have him wrap his arms around me. Tell me it was all a stupid misunderstanding, that he didn't do it and everything's fine now. But I know I'm going to have to get used to that cold, empty space. It's part of my life now. I can barely process what's happening. My mind is spinning, my heart still racing. I'm terrified of everything that's to come. But mixed in with the fear is a growing fury that my husband didn't appreciate everything he had. He kept the truth from me. He wrecked it all. Right now, I wish I'd never even met Niall bloody Kildare. I could kill him for what he's done to me. To our family.

THIRTY-FOUR

AMBER

As I walk back down the stairs to my family, the one thing I can't stop thinking about is the gold bracelet Beth was asking about. *Yes, Beth, I did own a gold bracelet.* I vividly remember the day I threw it at Niall when he ended things with me. I'm amused to think that he recycled that bracelet to give to his wife. Amused and angry at the same time.

After I told Niall I was pregnant, he ended things with me and told me he wouldn't acknowledge our child. That he was happily married to his wife and thought I had understood that. *Uh, no, Niall, I had not understood that, at all.* I was hysterical. I'd been so certain that he was going to be happy at my news. That my pregnancy was going to be the push he needed to leave his wife and be with me instead. I was heartbroken at his rejection of me. Of *us*. Pathetic really to have been so naïve. To have wasted so much energy on a man who didn't deserve it.

I had actually believed that Niall was in love with me. That he was my soulmate. I'd envisioned our lives together – the brooding, creative author and his vibrant, beautiful publicist. We would have made a formidable team. Instead, he chose to remain with his boring wife – a pale imitation of me. No career, no passion, no personality. Just a shadow of a woman. *His loss*.

Thankfully, the pain I felt all those years ago has gone. I met Renzo the very same month that Niall and I broke up, and we fell in love. It was a quieter sort of love than I'd felt with Niall, but it was exactly what I needed at the time. It was easier to let Renzo think that Franco was his son. Less drama, less pain. For everyone.

Renzo may not be an artistic genius, but he's the better man. As far as I'm concerned, Renzo is Franco's father. He was with me through most of the pregnancy, he was the one who sang him lullabies and soothed his tears. Taught him how to kick a ball and cook a meal. I won out in the end. But I never forgot the pain that Niall caused.

I walk back into the warmth of the living room where my family are still seated. I glance at the TV. It looks like they're already halfway through the movie.

'There you are!' Renzo smiles up at me and pauses the movie. 'Sit down. Want me to heat up your food?'

'No, I'll have something later.' I shake my head and settle myself next to Flora who snuggles into my side. I stroke her hair absent-mindedly.

'Are you sure? You hardly touched it.'

'Honestly, I'm not hungry.'

'Everything all right with your work?' he asks.

'Oh yeah. Just a needy client who wanted me to talk through everything with her.'

'That's a bit much on a Sunday.' Renzo rolls his eyes.

'Tell me about it.'

My phone pings with another message. I glance at the screen and adrenalin flows hot in my veins.

'Not again,' Renzo says.

'No, it's nothing,' I say, my voice sounding strange to my ears.

'Sure?'

'Yeah. Let's watch the film.'

He nods and presses play. I lean back into the sofa. I realise my hands are shaking so I shove them between my thighs. The TV is loud, competing with the intensity of my thoughts. I should concentrate on the movie. Block out the doubts.

It's too late for that.

THIRTY-FIVE

BETH

The evening cools and the promenade empties. I remain seated on the bench. Numb. I should move. Do something. Go somewhere. My worst fear right now is that Niall will return and start talking to me. Break into my shock and stir me into feeling something, when all I want to do is stop time. Stop everything. Because I know that once I move, I'll have to face it all.

The only things I'm allowing myself to feel are physical. My thirst. The blister on the sole of my right foot. The skin on my face, dry and taut. My eyes, scratchy and tired.

A thought creeps in. My children are with Luciana. I need to collect them. But how can I face them and act normally? Maybe I could ask her to keep them overnight. Would she mind? If I had my wallet, I'd check into a hotel rather than return to the villa. But I don't. So I guess I'll have to go back there. I'd stay on this bench all night if I wasn't worried about being out here alone, or moved on by the police. No. I'll go back and sleep in one of the spare rooms. I don't have to talk to Niall. Not until I'm ready. I don't think I could even bear to look at him right now.

Every time I think about what he did, a new wave of hurt

and fury crashes over me. All those wasted years on a man who didn't deserve my love. He was faithless right from the start. Is that why our marriage has felt so precarious all these years? Because of his deceit? If he kept this from me, then what else has he been hiding? Knowing Niall, he'll think he can talk his way out of it. But there's no way I can ever forgive him for this. He needs to understand that he's crossed a line. That he has to pay for what he's done.

In the middle of all this turmoil, the thought pops into my head that I really should message Luciana about the boys. I pick up my phone and tap the screen, but it's blank. I try again. *Nothing.* Pressing the power button has no effect. I realise the battery's dead. I wonder what the time is. Not too late, I hope. I slip on my shoes and stand. My body is stiff and cold, my dress crumpled. I need to go back. I think briefly of the two men I saw earlier on the Corso Reginna. The fear I had of running into them is gone. I find I don't care about them at all. I don't think anything could scare or intimidate me right now. I'm just so far past that.

I start to walk. There's hardly any traffic now. Just the odd car and moped cruising by. The shops are all shut and the restaurants are closing, lights gradually winking off and doors being locked. My footsteps ring out on the grey paving stones. I'll go back to the villa, have a long drink of water, plug in my phone and message Luciana. Ask if she wouldn't mind keeping the boys overnight. After that... *what?* Sleep? I doubt it. A fleeting thought tells me to leave the confrontation until tomorrow. Until I've calmed down a little. But I'm not sure I can do that.

As I approach our road, my stomach clenches and my throat tightens. The air is still. A dog barks in the distance and a car zips past blasting out a dance tune. I walk towards the villa trying to fend off a hailstorm of conflicting thoughts and worries. Is this really the end for me and Niall? Should I confront him now or let it be? Should I call Amber and get her side of the story? No. My earlier decision to leave it all until tomorrow is the better one, even though my blood is buzzing with the desire to scream at him. To really let him have it.

When I reach the house, I'm surprised to see it shrouded in darkness. I cross the drive and approach the front door, but the security lights don't come on. I pause, feeling a momentary flash of fear before shaking it off. There's not enough room in my body for fear right now. Not after my whole life has been upended.

The front door is already unlocked, the hall beyond is dark. Not even the fancy staircase has been illuminated. I turn on the lights, kick off my shoes and head straight to the kitchen where I take a bottle of water from the fridge and pour myself a glass. I gulp it down in one long draught, and then pour myself another. I feel its cold descent down my gullet towards my belly. When I'm done, I grip the counter and close my eyes for a moment, steadying myself. I can't believe I'm still dry-eyed. I'm sure I must be in shock.

The house is silent. I open my eyes and cock an ear, listening out for Niall. I was certain he would have waited up for me and tried to talk me round. Maybe he's asleep already. Another dark plume of rage opens up inside me. He couldn't even be bothered to wait up! I would have cut him dead anyway, but I'm beyond furious to realise that he thinks so little of me. That he could go to bed without even trying to win me round after such a horrific revelation. That he can sleep at all.

A muffled thud from upstairs lets me know he's still up. All thoughts of leaving a confrontation until tomorrow are gone. I'll never be able to sleep with these fierce emotions coursing through me. I grit my teeth and exit the kitchen. As I march barefoot up the staircase, I don't feel like I'm even connected to my body. My thoughts are racing, blazing, too big to be contained inside. I need to lash out. To tell my husband exactly what I think of his betrayal and lies. I storm along the landing and take a deep breath before shoving open our bedroom door.

It's dark. The sliding doors to the balcony are open. I don't switch on the lights because I don't want to attract the bugs. I shake my head. Why the hell am I worrying about that? Habit, I suppose. *Strange*. The room is empty, our bed unslept in. I walk through the dressing room to the en suite, bracing myself to face my husband, to let rip. But both rooms are dark and empty. *The balcony*. He's probably out there, brooding in the dark. That's so like him.

I return to the bedroom and stride across the room, more than ready to tell him exactly what I think. My fists are clenched, adrenalin floods my veins. I step out onto the balcony.

It's empty.

I realise we still haven't made use of these two sun loungers. When we first arrived, I remember thinking how nice it would be to have our morning coffee up here, overlooking the pool. Together. Well, that's never going to happen now. I give a silent, bitter laugh. Why am I even torturing myself with these thoughts?

I grip the balcony and stare impotently out at the dark garden for a moment, listening to the hiss of the water sprinklers on the lawn. A noise from inside the bedroom makes me jump. It must be my husband. I'm about to whirl around and tell him exactly what I think of him. But at the exact same time as I have that thought, my attention is snagged by something beneath the balcony. A dark shape on the patio below.

Not a shape.

A man lying face up.

I let out a small shriek. I can't believe what I'm seeing. He's lying so still and there's a horrible dark stain around his head. It looks like he's dead...

It's my husband. It's Niall.

THIRTY-SIX

BETH

As I stare down from the balcony at my husband on the terrace below. I feel sick with shock. His face is unmoving. His body twisted at an unnatural angle.

'*Niall*,' I cry out in a whisper.

My breath starts to come in gasps. I have to get down there. I have to call an ambulance. I fumble in my bag for my phone while at the same time remembering that the battery's dead. I leave the balcony and rush out of the bedroom and hitch up my dress as I fly back down the stairs, through the kitchen and over to the sliding doors. They're locked and my fingers shake as I turn the key. I pull the door back and pause a moment as I see my husband's broken body on the terrace, a dark pool of blood around his head.

'Niall!' I cry once more.

Is there any chance that he might still be alive? I take a step towards him, horrified by his stillness, his slack jaw, the blood on the patio, the way his legs are bent. I crouch and tentatively touch his cheek. It's still warm, but it feels different. His skin is pale and waxy looking. I can't accept that this still figure is my husband. *How can this be?* I can't help thinking of the warmth of Niall's skin, the sound of his voice, his large presence. Even after tonight's terrible revelation about his infidelity and my murderous thoughts towards him, I would never want this! My body starts to shake.

Can this be real? I need to call an ambulance... the police. I need to go inside to plug in my phone, but I can't seem to move. It seems wrong to leave him out here.

Did he fall? I glance up at the glass balcony that's almost chest height. Impossible to accidentally fall over that, even if you were drunk.

Surely he wouldn't have done this himself. I know we had a bad argument, but I can't believe he would do something so final. No. That's not something I could imagine Niall would ever do.

So then, the only other alternative...

I freeze in absolute terror, as a man calls out softly behind me. Someone with an Italian accent. My legs soften and my heartbeat thrashes.

'*Amber*,' he says. 'You are here.'

Who *is* that? I'm too terrified to even open my mouth. I slowly turn around and move back, away from my husband, and away from this intruder.

Did that man called me Amber? Or did I imagine it? Is this one of the men who was looking for the Masons? Does he mean me harm? If I could, I'd move further away from him, but my back is now right at the pool's edge. There's nowhere left to go. I'm terrified that he'll lunge for me. Did this man push Niall off the balcony? Cold sweat prickles my skin.

Is this my fault? If I'd come home with Niall, maybe this would never have happened.

Or maybe we'd both be lying dead on the terrace.

The man stands in the shadows. He's nothing more than a dark outline thrown into relief, like a sculpture carved from black ice. Until he takes a step forward into the light shining out from the kitchen. I give a sharp scream. I can make out his features now – dark-haired and incredibly handsome in dark suit trousers and a white shirt, open at the neck. His eyes glitter strangely. I've never seen this man before. He's not either of the thugs who paid us a visit this morning. Perhaps he works with them. My whole body is trembling. Does he plan to kill me too? My brain races. Did he call me Amber just now, or did I imagine it?

'Who *are* you?' I demand weakly. 'Did you kill my husband?'

He looks at me, confused. Angry. He ignores my questions and asks his own. 'Who are you? What are you doing here?'

'My name's Beth. We're here on holiday.' My voice is high and shaky. I sound pathetic. Like another victim.

His cologne wafts towards me, a warm musky scent. Unfamiliar. It catches in my throat and for a moment I think I'm going to throw up. I swallow and try to breathe normally, but my mind and body are in turmoil.

'*Hello!*' A woman's voice calls out from beyond the kitchen and I hear footsteps on the tiles. 'Beth? Are you here?' It's Luciana. Thank God! I pray she hasn't brought the boys with her.

The man's eyes widen and he shoots a quick glance behind him.

'Get help!' I try to yell to Luciana, but it only comes out as a half gasp. My throat has constricted. I take a few steps sideways along the length of the pool, wondering if I could possibly make a dash for it around the man without him catching me.

As I move, he takes a step towards me. I squeal and edge sideways. I heave up one of the potted plants at the corner of the pool and hurl it at him. It shatters on the tiles, short of my target, but does the job of stopping him and he turns and flees into the house. I exhale, my heart banging in my chest, my knees weak.

Suddenly, I find my courage and my voice and follow the man. 'Look out, Luciana!' I yell. 'There's an intruder! He's coming towards you!'

'Mum!'

Oh no! Connor! My stomach lurches at the sound of his voice. Please don't let this man hurt the boys, and don't let them see their father lying out here on the terrace.

'Connor! Liam! Get out! Run and hide!' I scream, almost sprawling across the tiles in my haste to get to them. I race across the kitchen to see the man shoulder his way past Luciana and the boys who she's trying to shield behind her.

The front door is wide open and I spot another figure standing there. A man. Could it be an accomplice? 'Look out behind you!' I call to her, pointing at the second man.

'Matteo!' Luciana cries. She screams something in Italian and I realise with a jolt of relief that the other person is Luciana's brother.

As I reach the bottom of the stairs and gather my children to my chest, I see Matteo tackle the intruder to the ground with a thud and a crack.

Luciana is still screaming at them. Now that I have care of the boys, she runs over to the front door where Matteo and the intruder are still tussling on the ground. It looks like Matteo is trying to keep him pinned, but they're rolling, kicking and punching. Luciana looks as though she wants to help her brother, but they're a tangle of arms and legs on the ground.

'Be careful, Luciana!' I cry. 'Call the police!'

'I do it!' she replies.

If only I'd charged my phone as soon as I got home. 'Are you boys okay?' I pant.

Connor nods. I'm trying to keep their faces turned away from what's going on. Liam has his face buried in my chest, but Connor keeps trying to glance towards the door, wide-eyed with disbelief. 'Is that the burglar from yesterday?' he asks.

Liam has started crying. 'I want to go home, Mummy.'

A yelp of pain from either Matteo or the intruder makes the three of us jump. Luciana is talking into her mobile phone, gesticulating wildly. Tears are streaking her face now.

The intruder is slipping out from beneath Matteo. He's up on his feet. I push the boys behind me in case he comes back in the house. I daren't send them off to hide in case they somehow catch sight of their father outside. At the thought of Niall lying out there, my knees buckle and I have to stop myself collapsing to the floor.

I hope Luciana has managed to get through to the police. Please let them get here quickly. Matteo is crying out in pain and calling to Luciana. She goes over to him and drops to her knees. He speaks quietly and rapidly. She cries out and is immediately back on her phone again.

I'm torn between keeping my children as close as possible, and checking that the intruder has truly gone. I turn to Connor. 'Sit here at the bottom of the stairs. Don't move. I'm just going over to Luciana, okay.'

Thankfully, he doesn't protest. He takes Liam's hand and sits down. Once I see they're seated, I rush towards the front door where Matteo is sitting up, white-faced and panting. I have to tell Luciana about Niall, and ask her to call an ambulance, but I don't want the boys to hear.

'The man, he had a knife!' Luciana cries, grabbing hold of my arm. 'He stab my brother!'

I switch my gaze back to Matteo and I'm appalled to see a small knife sticking out of his shoulder. Bright crimson blood stains his white chef's tunic. Not too much of it, but enough for me to realise he needs urgent medical help.

Luciana's talking into her phone and gesticulating to her brother.

'Is he all right?' I cry.

'I'm okay,' he pants. But he certainly doesn't look it.

Luciana looks at me with panicked eyes. 'You are hurt too?' she asks.

I shake my head. 'No, not me.' I think of Niall, and a wave of dizziness overcomes me. This all feels like something out of a horror movie.

'Your husband?' Luciana cries. 'Where is he? Upstairs?'

'Shh.' I put a finger to my lips and peer back around the doorframe to check the kids can't hear her, but they're both huddled together, heads down, talking.

'Niall is hurt?' she asks, lowering her voice.

I shake my head and press my lips together. I can't say the words out loud.

'What?' She frowns.

'Niall... he's...' I shake my head again.

'*What?*' Her eyes widen as she realises what I'm trying to say.

I nod. 'He's... he's outside on the terrace.'

She takes my hand and squeezes it. 'The police and ambulance are coming now.'

My throat tightens. 'It's too late for an ambulance. I should check on him, but I need to look after my boys and I don't want them to see...' My voice cracks. I know Niall is gone, but my mind doesn't want to accept it.

'Of course you must be with your boys,' Luciana replies. 'You stay here. Please keep an eye on Matteo. I will check on your husband.'

'Are you sure?'

She nods and speaks in Italian to her brother before disappearing through the kitchen and out onto the terrace. I wait with my arms around the boys. Matteo is sitting on the hallway floor leaning back against the wall.

'How are you feeling?' I ask uselessly.

'I'll be fine,' he replies, but his face is pale and he's obviously in pain. 'I tried to stop the man, but he had a knife so I couldn't...' He shakes his head and winces.

'I can't believe you tackled him,' I reply. 'Thank you for trying. I'm so sorry you got hurt. I really am.'

Matteo closes his eyes. I hope the ambulance doesn't take too long to arrive.

Luciana returns with a glass of water that she holds to her brother's lips. She glances over at me and shakes her head briefly with sorrow in her eyes.

I swallow and let her confirmation settle over me. Niall is really gone. It doesn't seem real.

'Where's Dad?' Connor asks.

My heart lurches.

'Your father is not here right now,' Luciana replies.

I bite back a sob, but I can't cry. Not yet. I have to be strong for my kids. For the news I'm going to have to give them. How will I tell them that their father is dead?

THIRTY-SEVEN

BETH

The police and ambulances finally arrive and everything becomes a blur of people, lights and police radio chatter. They speak first to Matteo and Luciana, none of which I can understand. They're waiting for a fluent English-speaking officer to come and interview me. After a short while, Luciana comes over to where I'm sitting on the driveway wall with the boys.

'How are you feeling?' she asks, placing a hand on my shoulder.

I shrug and shake my head, unable to speak.

'The officers say that if it's okay with you, Connor and Liam can come back with me to stay tonight, while you speak to the police here.'

I get shakily to my feet. My first thought is that I want the boys to stay with me. But I know that it would be better for them to be gone when I speak to the police. I nod at my friend, trying to sound suitably grateful, when it's all I can do to even form a sentence. 'That's great, Luciana. Thank you.' I beckon her to follow me out of earshot of the boys. 'Um...' I swallow. My mouth is dry and my mind is numb, but I have to ensure my children are okay. 'Connor and Liam don't know about Niall yet, so please don't say anything to them.'

'Of course, of course. I won't say anything. I told the police about your husband. They are waiting for the special team to come. The ones who look at the place of the crime.'

'Crime scene investigators.'

'I think.' She nods.

I take a deep breath. 'I'm sorry about Matteo. Are Marco and Gianni okay? Did you have to leave them home alone?'

'My neighbour is there with them. They'll be okay. And Matteo will be fine. The paramedico say is nothing too serious, but they will take him to the hospital to be treated.'

'I'm so relieved it's not serious,' I reply, wrapping my arms around myself. 'I'm so grateful you both showed up when you did.'

'Well, I called you earlier to see if you want the boys to stay overnight with Marco and Gianni, but I kept getting your voice message. I sent texts but you no reply.'

'I'm sorry. My phone died.' I don't tell her Niall's revelation about Amber, or our subsequent fight. It's all too much for me to process right now, let alone talk about out loud.

'Okay.' Luciana pats my hand. 'Well, I worry and I think maybe something has happened. So I decide to bring the children to see if everything okay. Matteo say he will come with me because he didn't like for us to go alone at night. And then we get here... and then...' She throws her hands up in the air and makes a sound like a bomb going off.

'I thought that man was going to kill me.' I hug myself tighter and bite my lip to stop from crying. 'I think... I think if you hadn't shown up when you did, I might be dead.'

Luciana shakes her head and says a few words to herself in Italian. She takes my hand and squeezes it but I can barely feel her touch due to the numb tingling in my fingers.

'I'm so sorry about...' She hesitates for a moment. 'About

Niall. You must be in shock. You don't stay here tonight. After you speak to the police, you come and you stay with me, okay? You get one of the officer to drop you at the restaurant.'

'Thank you.' My voice sounds distant over the buzzing in my ears. 'I don't think I ever want to set foot in this place again.'

'No, of course not. It's a horrible thing. I so sorry for you and what happened. It was an attempted robbery, yes?'

I shrug. 'I don't know. The man...' I gulp. 'The man who stabbed Matteo, he thought I was Amber. I think he knew her.'

Luciana's eyes widen at that piece of news. She doesn't know the half of it, but I don't have the strength to talk about it all yet. I'm still not sure how much I should tell the police. Does my argument with Niall have any bearing on what happened? Not really. Other than the fact that Niall came back to the house alone. *Niall.* I can't believe I'll never see him again.

'Okay, so I take the boys back with me now?' Luciana asks.

'Thank you,' I reply, terrified at the thought of them leaving me here, but knowing that Connor and Liam should go as soon as possible in case they get a whiff of what's happened.

As another car draws up on the road, Luciana gives a decisive nod. 'I take them now.'

'Thank you. I'll come to yours as soon as I can.'

'You should charge your phone,' she suggests. 'In case you need it.'

'I will.' But the thought of going back inside the house starts me shaking again.

Luciana heads over to my sons. I want to keep them close, but I know this is the best thing for them right now. They need to stay calm and try to get some sleep. Time enough to break their hearts tomorrow.

I hug and kiss them both. They're glassy-eyed with exhaustion and shock. Every fibre of my being wants to go with them, but I have to stay to talk to the police. I have to find out what's happened here.

'You're going to go back with Luciana now, okay?' I tell them.

'When's Dad coming?' Connor asks.

'I want to stay with you.' Liam flings himself at me and buries his head in my stomach.

'Why are there so many police?' Connor asks.

Their questions are making me panic. Should I tell them the truth? One look at Liam's tear-stained face tells me it would be too much for them right now. I'll tell them both tomorrow.

'Okay, boys.' I try to inject some brightness into my voice. 'We've all had a bit of an exhausting night, so right now I need you to go back with Luciana and keep her company, okay? Can you do that?'

Both boys look at me with anxious expressions. Connor opens his mouth to speak to me again, but Luciana cuts in by clapping her hands together and telling them that they have to go because Gianni and Marco will be wondering where they've got to. I throw her a grateful look as she shepherds them away.

As Luciana leaves with the boys, three men, dressed casually in jeans, exit the car on the road and come into the driveway. One of them speaks to my friend for a moment. She points in my direction and he lets her leave.

One of the men, youngish with fair hair, nods at me, but continues walking over to the other officers. The other two approach me, both of them dark-haired and dark-eyed.

'Mrs Kildare?' one of them says in almost perfect English. He's wearing dark-blue jeans and a pale-blue shirt with the sleeves rolled up. At a guess, I'd say he's in his early forties. His colleague looks around a decade or so younger.

'Yes, I'm Beth Kildare,' I reply, my voice trembling.

'My name is Stefano Motta, and this is Aldo Di Napoli. We're investigating officers. I understand you had an intruder here tonight. I'm so sorry to hear about your husband.'

'Thank you.' I can barely get out the words. This all feels so surreal.

'We can talk here, or you can come to the station if you prefer?'

'Here please. Not in the house though.'

'That's fine. Can you wait here for two minutes? We need to speak to our colleagues inside, and then we'll come straight back to you.'

'Okay.' I realise I'm glad of the reprieve.

The two of them head inside the villa. I feel awkward and strange standing in the middle of the drive on my own, so I head over to the wall and sit back down. The image of my husband lying on the terrace keeps jumping into my head. I don't think I'll ever be able to stop thinking about it. How do you unsee something like that? I'm shivering again. My whole body judders as if I'm possessed.

A uniformed female officer approaches me. She's carrying a grey woollen blanket, which she drapes around my shoulders with a kind smile. I nod my thanks, but I can't move my mouth to smile back. She walks back to the house. I wait for the two investigators to return, wondering how long they'll be and how long they'll take to interview me. I wish I could just curl up into a ball and not have to think about or talk about any of this. I pull the blanket tighter around me.

A short while passes and the female officer returns with a white mug of black coffee, which she puts in my hand. The warmth of the mug helps to stem my shivering. I sip the liquid, not caring that it scalds my tongue and the roof of my mouth. It's bitter yet sweet. I don't normally take sugar. The officer has disappeared and I realise I never thanked her. Never even acknowledged her kindness.

I must have zoned out, because when I look up, the two investigators are back. They're standing in front of me and it feels odd to be sitting while they loom over me, but I don't think I could stand right now.

'How are you feeling, Mrs Kildare?' the older one asks, Stefano, I think he said his name was.

I shake my head. 'Call me Beth.'

'Okay, Beth. So we're going to record this interview. My colleague Aldo will use his phone, okay?'

I nod.

Aldo states our names and the time and location. He also speaks English, but with a thicker accent.

Stefano crosses his arms. 'We already know you had a break-in here yesterday. Can you confirm that this is not your residence, and that you're a UK citizen here on holiday?'

'Yes,' I reply. 'We swapped houses with the Masons who live here.'

'So they're holidaying in your house in the UK, correct?'

'Yes.'

'Are you able to tell us what happened here tonight?' he asks.

I take a last sip of my coffee before setting the mug on the wall next to me. I start hesitantly, beginning my story from the moment I returned to the house. The two investigators prompt me along the way, asking for more detailed descriptions. I do my best to remember everything as it happened. I end my account with the officers showing up at the house. 'Do you think you'll catch him?' I ask. 'The man who... the intruder?'

'We have officers out looking for him now.' Stefano replies grimly. 'We got a good description from your friends. My colleagues have sniffer dogs out tracking him, and we're going house-to-house in the neighbourhood to see if anyone saw anything suspicious.'

I swallow, looking down at my bare feet, but I feel Stefano's eyes trained on me.

'Are you absolutely sure you heard the man say "Amber"?' he asks. 'Could you have been mistaken at all?'

I blink rapidly and try to recall. 'It all happened so quickly.'

'Out of ten, how certain are you that he said her name?'

'Um, maybe a six? He seemed angry to see me, like he was expecting to see someone else.'

'Or could he have been angry because you and your husband interrupted him while he was robbing the place?'

'I don't know.' I look up at both men. 'Do you really think it was a robbery gone wrong?'

'That's what it looks like, but we're not ruling anything out at the moment.' Stefano's eyes soften. 'Do you have anywhere to stay tonight? Maybe with friends? I think the crime scene officers are going to be a while here.'

'Thanks, I'm staying with my friend Luciana.'

He nods.

'I haven't told the Masons yet. I don't think I can call them tonight. It's too much.' My voice cracks.

'Of course.' Stefano bows his head. 'We'll call them. Let them know what's going on.'

They ask for the contact details, and then Aldo offers to drop me at Luciana's place. It's only round the corner, but I take him up on his offer, and follow him to the car.

As he pulls away from the kerb and leaves the villa behind, I think about my poor husband still out on the terrace surrounded by police officers. *Strangers*. He would have hated that.

Niall and I may have been fighting, and on the verge of a break-up, but I feel his absence as keenly as I would miss a limb. He's been in my life for fifteen years. He's the father of my children. He was the man I loved. I can't believe this is happening to me. We were just a normal couple, a normal family, weren't we? Things like this don't happen. Not to us.

I push aside the thought that there's possibly another of his children out there, currently staying in our home. A stray thought hits me. The reason Niall was so adamant he didn't want to sleep with the Masons' family portrait at the foot of our bed was probably because he would have been facing the image of the son he denied.

I try to set all that aside. The tangle of secrets that my husband has left me can be unravelled another time. I lean back in the passenger seat and close my eyes. It smells of cigarette smoke and air freshener in here.

'Are you okay?' Aldo asks as we get to the end of the road. The car idles and he turns to look at me.

I shake my head and give a strangled laugh. 'No.'

'You try to get some sleep tonight,' he says, and turns into the empty road. 'You eat, you sleep.'

It sounds so easy.

But I can't imagine anything will be that easy again. Not after tonight.

THIRTY-EIGHT

AMBER

'Are they in bed?' I ask, looking up from my corner of the sofa. After the movie, both kids were yawning, so we decided they should have an early night. Franco protested, but I was firm.

'Flora fell asleep the minute her head touched the pillow,' Renzo says with a fond laugh. 'And Franco won't take long to follow. They're both tired today.' He sits next to me and draws me in close for a kiss.

I kiss him back briefly. Reluctantly, I pull away.

He jerks his head back and looks at me. 'What is it?'

I'm usually good at hiding my worries from him, but he's picked up on my jittery mood. I don't answer straight away.

'Amber?' He cocks his head.

'Something's happened,' I say. 'Back home.'

Renzo's face pales. He sits up and adjusts his position slightly so he can look at me properly. 'What is it?'

'I've just had a call from a police investigator, Stefano Motta.'

'About yesterday's break-in?'

'Kind of.' I twist my fingers in my lap and take a breath. I don't know what's wrong with me. I'm not normally so tied to my emotions. I need to get a hold of myself.

'Amber, talk to me.' His eyes narrow. 'Is it something to do with the break-in?'

I give myself a shake. 'Sorry, yes. There's been another one.'

'*What?* Another break-in?' He swears under his breath and gets to his feet, rubbing a hand over the top of his head.

'It's worse than that,' I say.

Renzo holds his hands out. '*Worse?* How?'

'It seems that Niall Kildare must have interrupted the guy, and...' I tail off.

'And?'

'The investigator, Motta, said it looked like the intruder might have pushed Niall off the bedroom balcony.'

'*No!*' Renzo's mouth drops open.

'He landed on the terrace and...' I shrug and wince.

'And *what*? He's hurt?'

I shake my head.

'What, he's *dead*?'

'Apparently. Yes.'

Renzo starts pacing the living room. 'I don't believe this. I don't believe it.'

I peel myself off the sofa and put a hand on his arm.

'This is bad,' he mutters. 'This is so bad.'

'I know, but there's nothing we could have done about it,' I say, trying to calm him.

'Did they at least catch who did it?' he asks, frozen as he waits for my reply.

'No.' I shake my head. 'He ran off.'

Renzo's shoulders slump at the news.

'Apparently, Luciana and her brother were at the house.'

'Who?' He frowns.

'You know, from the restaurant Terrazza Luciana,' I clarify.

'What were *they* doing there?'

'It's a long story, but the intruder stabbed Luciana's brother in the shoulder before he ran off.'

'*No!*'

'He's fine though. Well, he will be fine.'

'Okay, that's good, I guess. But this whole thing is a nightmare.' Renzo runs his hands through his hair.

'I know. It's terrible, but it's not our fault. If you think about it, we've had a really lucky escape. Imagine if we'd been home at the time? That could have been any one of us. I'm just glad it's not *you* that it happened to.' I try to hug my husband, but he's stiff in my arms.

He shakes me off with an anguished stare. 'You don't understand!' he cries. A tear slips down his face and he starts shaking.

I stare at my husband. The news I've given him is shocking and terrible, but it doesn't warrant this kind of reaction. My husband is emotional when it comes to family issues, but these people are strangers. 'Renzo, what's the matter? I know this is shocking, and it's terrible, what happened, but we're safe. We're okay. It could have been so much worse if we were home. It doesn't even bear thinking about.'

He blows out air through his mouth. 'Oh, Amber, I'm sorry. I've been keeping something from you.' He swallows. 'Something bad.'

My heart starts to pump faster. Renzo's been keeping secrets? That's not like him. I'm the one who keeps things hidden, not him. My husband is an open book. He always has been. That's why I love him so much. I need his straightforwardness, his honesty. Without it, our family is lost.

He walks over to the front window and pulls open the curtains. Stares out into the dark, quiet street, at the hazy pools of light from the streetlamps.

'Renzo, what are you talking about?' I take a step towards him, but not too close. He's giving off an aura of needing his space.

He puts both hands behind his head. 'The break-ins, Niall Kildare's murder... it's not random.' He's still facing away from me, gazing out the window so I can't see his expression.

'What makes you say it's not random?' I swallow and give a shiver of dread.

'We're in trouble, Amber.'

My stomach dips. What's he talking about?

'Financial trouble,' he clarifies, dropping his arms to his sides once more.

What? This makes no sense. We've always been extremely well off. With his luxury jewellery stores and my PR clients, we've been lucky enough to never have to struggle financially.

As I try to wrap my head around what he's saying, he turns slowly to face me, catches my eye for a brief second and then stares at a spot on the floor. 'You remember a couple of years back when the business wasn't doing too well?'

'Vaguely,' I reply. 'But I thought you turned it around.'

He gives a short bitter laugh. 'I did. But I ended up making things worse.' He glances around. 'I need a drink.'

'I'll open another bottle,' I say, leaving the lounge and heading out to the kitchen where a bottle of red sits on the counter. I open it, grab two clean glasses and take them back through to where my husband is now perched on the edge of the sofa, his head in his hands. I pour us each a glass and hand him one. I can't believe he's kept this from me. I've been so wrapped up in my own situation that I haven't been paying enough attention to Renzo. I should have seen that something was going on with him. How could I have missed that?

He looks up, gives me a nod of thanks and takes a large swig. 'Amber, I didn't want to have to tell you any of this.'

'I thought you could tell me anything,' I reply, pulling one of the armchairs closer. I sit, facing him, waiting for him to continue.

'I borrowed money to tide the business over. It was fine. I

was paying it back on time. Business picked up and I finally had enough to get rid of the debt.' He clears his throat. 'But the people I borrowed the money from—'

'Wait a minute,' I interrupt. 'You didn't borrow from the bank?'

'No. I borrowed from a friend of a friend. It was a better rate of interest, and seemed simpler.'

'What friend?' I'm already getting a really bad feeling about this.

'Not a friend exactly. You know Tony. His dad owns the ceramic shop round the corner from the store.'

I shake my head. 'I think I know the shop, but I don't know Tony.' I grit my teeth. I already hate Tony.

'Well, we got chatting one night and he mentioned that he knew some good people.' Renzo takes another large glug of wine. 'Only they weren't good people.' He presses his fingers to his forehead and lowers his voice as though someone might be listening. 'They wouldn't take my final payment. Told me the deal had changed and now they wanted me to clean cash for them through my business.'

My skin goes cold at his words. 'You're joking, right?'

'I wish I was, Amber.'

I'm lost for words, my mouth hanging open.

He continues. 'When you told me about the holiday-swap idea, I thought it was a good opportunity to get away. To think about what I'm going to do. I already told them I'm not going to do it, but they weren't too happy about that. I think they originally assumed I was going to default on the loan, and they'd be able to force me into laundering their cash. So me coming up with the final payment put the kibosh on their plans. Now they want me to do it anyway. They wouldn't accept my final payment. I still don't know what I'm going to do.'

'So you think the break-ins at our house are something to do with it?'

'Has to be, doesn't it? I knew they might try to intimidate me, but *murder*? What if they killed this Niall guy, thinking he was me?'

'No.' I shake my head emphatically. 'I don't think so. You didn't do anything wrong. You've paid them back – well, most of it, and you've offered them the rest. They're not going to kill someone for paying them back. The police investigator said he thought it was a simple robbery gone wrong. Don't worry, Renz. It'll be fine.' I'm shocked at his confession, but at least he's told me now. We can sort it out together.

Renzo's eyes fill with tears and he covers his face. 'I screwed up, Amber. I'm so sorry. Can you ever forgive me?'

'There's nothing to forgive.'

'I should have told you; I know I should.'

I go over to the sofa and wrap my arms around my husband, kissing away his tears.

'It was *them*,' he sobs. 'I know it was them who killed Niall. It's too much of a coincidence for it not to be. Honestly, I feel sick...'

I try to calm my husband with soothing words and gentle hands, kissing his salty cheeks and holding him close while he lets out all his fears. 'It will be all right, Renzo. You're safe. I promise you.'

'No, Amber.' He pulls away from me sharply. 'This isn't going to go away, and now someone innocent is dead. Because of me. Because of a stupid decision I made.'

'Listen to me.' I take his head in my hands and make him look into my eyes. 'This is not your fault, okay?'

Renzo takes my hands away and bows his head. 'It *is* my fault.' He swipes at his tears with the back of his hand. 'But I'm going to put it right.'

I don't like the sound of this. 'What do you mean?'

He takes a breath and pulls his phone from his pocket. 'I'll call the police and tell them what's happened.' He looks up at me with determination in his eyes.

I think quickly. 'No. Renzo, that's a really bad idea. If you tell the police about those people, it could put us all in serious danger. You, me, the kids...'

'We're already in danger!' he cries. 'They murdered someone, thinking it was *me*! At least if I tell the police, they might be able to help us somehow. Better than trying to deal with it on our own.'

'Renzo, you can't call the police.' I try to take his phone from his hand, but he moves it from my grasp.

'Sorry, Amber, but—'

I cut him off. 'You can't call the police because there's something *I* haven't told *you*.'

A look of confusion clouds his face. He takes a step back and looks at me questioningly.

I bite my lip and pull at my fingers as I debate how exactly I'm going to tell my husband the truth.

He can't call the police.

Because it wasn't those people who killed Niall.

I know exactly who killed Niall Kildare.

THIRTY-NINE

BETH

It's dark. The beige sofa is soft, sagging in the middle. The room is warm with the faint smell of stale food and other people's deodorants and perfumes. I'm lying in the living room of Luciana's flat that she shares with her children above the restaurant. The floor has been divided into two apartments – one where her brother lives, and one where she lives with her sons. It's small, but homely, still decorated with her parents' furnishings and ornaments.

When I arrived earlier, I looked in on Connor and Liam, who are sharing a bed in Gianni and Marco's bedroom. All four of them were sound asleep. I wanted to go in and hug my boys tight, but I left them sleeping. Time enough for hugs tomorrow.

It's been a few hours since Luciana went to bed. We talked for a while after Aldo dropped me off, but I could see she was exhausted too, so I told her to get some sleep and we'd talk more in the morning. Matteo is being kept overnight at the hospital. He's going to be fine, but they wanted to keep an eye on him, just in case.

I don't think I'll be able to get any sleep tonight. I can't get the image of Niall's body out of my mind. His face. The blood.

I'm living a nightmare. And I don't even want to think about the photos that were sent to me. I think the worst thing is that I'll never know if Niall and I could have overcome his lies. He was taken before we had a chance to really talk about what happened. Before we could reach any kind of closure.

Right now, more than anything, I want to return to Dorset. I want Amber and her family out of our cottage. The Italian police have said that I have to stay in the country until they finish their investigation. Goodness knows how long that's going to take. They seem certain it was a robbery gone wrong, but I'm really not so sure. I try to remember the sequence of events, and especially the words of the intruder. Did he say Amber's name? An icy chill snakes down my back. Could she have had anything to do with what happened tonight?

I sit up. I'm wearing a pair of Luciana's cotton pyjamas. They smell of unfamiliar detergent. I need to get back into my clothes. I quickly shuck off the pyjamas and slip my dress back on. It's a crumpled rag, but I don't care. I left my shoes back at the villa so I creep into the hall and glance around. A door stands ajar. I pull it open and am rewarded with a coat cupboard and a rack of shoes beneath, most of which are kids' trainers. I pull out a pair that look around my size. I pull them on. They're a little tight, but they're better than going barefoot.

There's a yellow Post-it pad on the hall table. I scribble a quick note and stick it to the front door. Then I open the door and slip out, pulling it quietly shut behind me before creeping down the stairs and out into the street.

It's still dark outside, not quite dawn. It's cool and dry. I shiver and wonder if I'm stupid to go back to the villa now. The police might still be there. They may not let me in. Common sense tells me to stay, but a wild voice in my head pushes me to go. I have to try. I need to see if I can make some sense of what happened. If nothing else, maybe being back there will jog my memory. Help me to remember more clearly.

I ghost through the empty streets, my feet in Marco's borrowed trainers hardly making a sound on the pavement. A few minutes later I'm back on the Masons' road, heading towards their home. I should be nervous, anxious, traumatised... something, but my emotions are dampened, numbed. It's as if my brain has overloaded and shut down. It helps that everything is so quiet and dim, just the air around me, fresher and cleaner than during the day.

I stop outside the villa. It's dark. The police and all their vehicles seem to have gone for now. Security tape criss-crosses over the driveway entrance. It's a crime scene. I shouldn't go in. But my prints will be all over the house anyway. I'll try not to touch anything, and if anyone asks I'll tell them I've come to grab some spare clothes to take back to Luciana's. That's actually not a bad idea anyway.

As I slip beneath the caution tape, I wonder about the possibility of staying with Luciana for a few more days. I don't like to ask as I don't want to be an inconvenience. Her apartment is small, and it's probably not fair on her boys to make them share a bed. Maybe I should look into renting somewhere for a week. I'd rather do that than stay here at the villa.

I wish the police didn't need me to remain in Italy. The thought makes me feel trapped. I wish I could take the boys back home. After I tell them about Niall, they'll need some normality in order to grieve. So will I. I don't even know what to tell them about what happened. Maybe it will help to say that he was brave. That he tackled an intruder to protect his family. No matter how much Niall wronged me, he was still their father, and I want them to have a good memory of him.

I unlock the front door, slip under another raft of security tape and straighten up in the hall, listening, in case there may be a lone officer left in the house. But it's dark, so I doubt it. Now that I'm inside, my heart is beating louder, my memories of Matteo's struggle with the intruder rushing to the fore. I put a hand out to the wall to steady myself. *What am I doing here?* I must be crazy to have come back on my own. I don't think I'm in my right mind yet. I'm still in shock.

I quickly decide that there's nothing to be gained from being here other than further traumatising myself. I think I'll grab a couple of changes of clothes for me and the boys and then I'll get the hell out of here.

I daren't put the light on, so I use the torch on my phone to illuminate my way up the staircase. I charged up the battery back at Luciana's earlier. The place feels like a mausoleum with its high ceilings and shiny surfaces. First, I go into the boys' bedroom and shove a few items into their case. I grab their toothbrushes from their bathroom. I close up the case and wheel it along the landing towards the master bedroom, trying not to think about the last time I was up here.

I push open the door and walk in. The bedroom is still and cool, the air con still doing its thing. The balcony doors are shut. I think about going out there and looking down at the terrace, but I daren't. I'm sure they've taken Niall away, but I couldn't face seeing the aftermath of what happened. The blood, the smashed pot... Bile rises in the back of my throat. I leave the suitcase and rush through the walk-in wardrobe to the en-suite bathroom where I drop my phone on the floor and throw up in the toilet. There's hardly anything in my stomach. I'm more or less just retching. It doesn't last long. I flush the loo and sit back on the bathroom floor, trembling and sweating.

After a moment, I grab my phone, climb shakily to my feet and rinse out my mouth in the sink. Again, I wonder what on earth I was thinking, coming back here. There's nothing new to learn. Nothing to be gained from re-living the trauma. I'll pick out some practical clothes and head back to Luciana's.

Returning to the bedroom to retrieve the suitcase, I see that the shawl covering the Mason-family portrait has slithered to the floor, revealing their four happy faces. I can't help staring at

Franco, trying to see if there's any resemblance between him and Niall, or Liam and Connor for that matter. But all I see is a smiling boy.

I give myself a shake and take hold of the suitcase, wheeling it into the closet. A soft sound behind me makes me freeze and catch my breath. Did I close the front door behind me when I came in? The fine hairs on the back of my neck stand up and my arms prickle. I'm gathering the courage to whirl around when a large warm hand covers my mouth and a man speaks softly into my ear.

'Don't make a sound or I'll kill you.'

FORTY

AMBER

'What are you talking about?' Renzo shakes his head in confusion. 'This has got nothing to do with you. Don't try to shoulder the blame for me, Amber. I appreciate it, but this is my mess, and I'm going to get us out of it, okay?'

I love my husband for being so noble. For taking it all on himself, but I can't let him do it. And I especially can't let him call the police. 'I'm not shouldering any blame for you, because it's not what you think. I need to tell you something.' My mouth dries and my insides turn to water as I consider coming clean. I walk across the living room, away from my husband, and sit on the edge of one of the armchairs, clasping my hands in front of me as though I can ward off the future.

Is this the time for truth? Or should I stay silent? Once I open my mouth, there's no going back. But I don't think I really have a choice. Now I've sent her those photos, Beth knows about Niall being Franco's birth father, so I doubt that's going to stay a secret for long. I had my reasons for sending the photos tonight – Beth finding out about me and Niall gives her a clear motive to kill her husband. If it comes down to it, this will shift the blame from my shoulders and onto hers. The only downside is that Renzo is going to discover what I did. *And that's a big downside.*

If I'm honest with myself, I also wanted to twist the knife. Niall chose Beth over *me*. That decision has always stung. I sent her those photos because I wanted to hurt her and I wanted Beth to confront Niall with the decision he made. To cause stress in their marriage. I've been wanting to do that to them for twelve and a half years, but now that it's done, all I feel is fear. *Terror* that I'm about to lose everything.

'Amber, you're scaring me.' Renzo takes a couple of steps towards me and then stops.

'I have to tell you a few things, Renzo. You're not the only one who's been worrying. I've had a lot on my mind recently and...' I swallow. 'Maybe I haven't handled it as well as I should have.'

'It can't be worse than what I've told you. Surely?'

I give a bitter laugh in response. 'Sit down, Renzo. Please.'

He stares at me for a moment before doing as I ask. He sinks onto the sofa opposite.

I dig my nails into the palms of my hands. They're sweaty and my heart is racing with dread. 'These things I'm going to tell you, they sound worse than they are, because I have to tell you everything all at once. Please realise that this all stems from one thing that happened years ago, before we met. And it's the only thing that wasn't my fault. The only blame that lies with me, is that I didn't tell you the truth at the time. This is going to hurt you, Renzo.'

Shadows flit across his face. He holds himself still. Waiting.

I don't know which secret to start with. Is there a right order in which to do this? Why did I think it was a good idea to tell my husband how terrible I am? Maybe because I know that it's all about to come out. Maybe because I'm a destructive person and I like to break things before they have the chance to break *me*.

I can't even look at him. Instead, I stare down at my hands in my lap as I start to speak slowly and clearly. 'The man who killed Niall Kildare is called Luca Silvestre. I'm not proud of myself, but last year, in Naples, I had a brief fling with him. I'd never been unfaithful to you before, and I never will be again. It was a terrible mistake. I'm so sorry.'

I glance up at Renzo. An expression of devastation crosses his face before he clenches his jaw tight.

I massage my throat, look off to the side, and force myself to continue. 'I told Luca I'd made a mistake and that I didn't want to see him again. I thought he would accept it, and that would be that. But... it was awful, he became obsessed with me. He wouldn't stop calling and texting. He started showing up in Maiori. His texts became really scary and I thought about going to the police. But I knew that if I did that, then the truth would come out, and I was too scared to tell you.'

Renzo still hasn't said anything. His face has gone blank. I've never seen him like this before. I wish he would respond. Say something. *Anything*. If only I could rewind what I did, but it's too late for that. I'm in the centre of this and I have to keep going forward.

'Luca said that if I wouldn't leave you, he'd get rid of you himself. I was terrified for your life so I made a plan to get us out of the country.'

I shift in my seat and pull at the top of my jumper. 'It's so hot in here.' Sweat beads my upper lip and prickles under my armpits. 'Are you hot?' I look at my husband, but my words empty into a well of silence.

'Luca told me he was going to kill you. I thought that if the Kildares were there when he tried to carry out his plan, then maybe he would do it and never know that the person he killed wasn't you. I thought the police would catch him.'

'Amber! No!' Renzo gets to his feet. He's staring at me in horror as he realises what I planned.

'You know I'm not a sentimental person, Renzo. I'm not soft-hearted and emotional. You always knew this, and you always accepted it about me.'

His jaw has gone slack and he's shaking his head, his eyes hooded. 'That's because I thought you were guarded. Vulnerable! I thought you were too scared to show your heart. *That's* why I treasured you. Because you showed your heart to *me*!' He coughs out a breath. 'But to do what you did... I don't know which part is worse!'

'You *do* know me, Renzo. I'm the same person I've always been. I made a mistake with Luca, that's all. Just one mistake.... Like you, with the business.'

'That's not the same at all, Amber, and you know it!' Renzo's expression has hardened again. He's looking at me as if he hates me. 'You... you slept with someone else. You set up Niall to die in place of me. You let your lover kill an innocent man!'

'It's not like that,' I reply. And then before I can stop myself, I say, 'Niall isn't innocent.'

Renzo frowns and shakes his head. 'How do you know that? Who are you, Amber? Are you my wife? Because I don't think I know you at all!'

I'm only halfway through my story and I've already lost him. I don't know how I ever thought he would accept this. I don't think I did, really. I should just give up, pack my bags and leave.

'Well?' Renzo says, holding his hands out. 'Aren't you going to finish telling me about these things that happened, that aren't your fault?' That last line of sarcasm pierces my heart in several places.

'Renzo...' I stand and try to take his hands, but he shakes off my touch as if I have the plague. I let my hands drop down to my sides and try to steel myself against his reaction. I tell myself that this is simply the shock talking. That he'll come round, given some time. But I've yet to tell him the worst part of all.

I don't think I can do it. I can't tell him that Franco isn't his son. It will kill him and it will finish us for good. I'll just have to pray that Beth doesn't say anything. That this secret will stay between us. I'll tell her I lied to hurt her and Niall. I'll deny it. She'll be glad that it's not true. Or maybe she won't care. Not now that she knows her husband was unfaithful. Not now that he's dead.

'There isn't anything else, Renzo. That's it.'

His eyes narrow. 'I don't believe you. But for now it's enough. Tomorrow I'm going back to Maiori with the children.'

'We'll go home and face it together,' I say desperately. 'We can sort out those men with the loan—'

'No!' His voice booms around the room and I flinch. He takes a breath and continues in a quieter tone. 'I am going back to Italy with the children. *You* are not coming with us.' He gives me a look of disgust that cuts me in two before leaving the room, closing the door behind him.

My body is hot and cold, my pulse pounds in my ears and I feel as though I might collapse onto the floor and never get up again. This can't be happening. Renzo is my *person*. My *only* person. If I don't have him then I don't have anything.

FORTY-ONE

BETH

My knees go soft and I feel like I'm about to pass out. It's the intruder... the *murderer*. He's back. *What's he doing back here? What does he want?* My heart clatters and I can't get my breathing under control.

'I have a knife,' he says softly.

I feel the tip of the blade press into my back as he lets me know he's not bluffing.

'I'm going to take my hand away from your mouth. If you scream or make a noise I will stab you. If you try to run away, I will catch you and kill you, okay?'

Black spots appear at the edge of my vision. This is it. I'm going to die. I make a pathetic noise that he takes for my assent.

He takes his hand from my mouth and I gasp, trying not to scream, trying not to sink onto the floor. I wish I had the courage to make a grab for the knife and flee, but I can barely stay upright. I have to stay safe for my kids. They've already lost one parent.

'What do you want?' I ask in a shaking voice, turning around slowly, my hands raised at chest height.

He reaches forward with his free hand to take my phone

from me and I let him have it. There's no denying that this man is incredibly handsome, with almost movie-star good looks. But there's something off about him. His skin is waxy and his eyes are too bright and staring. I wonder if he might be high.

'We will talk,' he says, jabbing a black-handled kitchen knife in my direction, and motioning me to go ahead of him. 'Move. Into the bathroom.' He illuminates my way with the phone light. I do as he asks, stumbling through the dressing room to the en suite. 'Get in the shower,' he says.

I don't move, terrified by what he might do to me. I know he's capable of it. He's already killed my husband.

'Get in,' he repeats.

I balk, my feet rooted to the spot. 'Why do you want me to go in there?' I glance at the huge cubicle, at the photo wall of Amber's naked body. Is this man going to kill me in the shower? He's blocking the room's only exit, so there's nowhere for me to run. He's over six feet tall and broad-shouldered. I would never be able to make it past him safely.

He mutters a few words of Italian angrily under his breath. He glares at me and holds up the knife as a threat.

I take a reluctant step towards the shower.

He nods encouragingly, and, although every cell in my body is telling me not to do this, I step inside the glass box, cringing back against the wall. To my relief, he doesn't follow me in. Instead, he slides the door shut after me, but remains outside. Now that I'm in, I see his posture relax slightly. Okay, so maybe he simply wants to keep me contained. He hasn't hurt me yet. If he wanted to kill me, surely he would have done it by now. I allow myself to cling onto this sliver of hope.

'Who are you?' he asks, his voice muffled by the closed shower door. 'And where is Amber?'

'My name's Beth,' I reply in a weak voice. I clear my throat and try not to sound so terrified. 'My family and I came here on holiday.' My words reverberate around the cubicle.

'You are friends with Amber?' He frowns. 'Where is she?'

'No. We swapped houses with the Masons. We came to Italy for a holiday. They went to our house in England.'

The man's face pales. His arms slacken and drop to his sides. He still has hold of the knife and my phone, but it seems that all the tension has gone out of his body.

'Why did you kill my husband?' I ask, emboldened by his change in attitude. 'Who *are* you?'

'I killed your husband?' he asks slowly, incredulously.

I wonder if maybe he's unwell. Surely he can't have forgotten. 'Yes. Did you push him off the balcony? *Why did you do it?*'

He puts a hand to his forehead and rubs at the skin as though he's trying to remove a stain there.

'Hey!' I try to get his attention. 'Answer me!'

He frowns and snaps his head up. 'No! You're lying. It was Amber's husband. I pushed Amber's husband, Renzo.'

'Why would I lie?' I cry out, suddenly uncaring that I might anger him. 'I don't even know who you are. All I know is that you killed Niall. You murdered him.'

'No, no, no,' he moans. Both my phone and his knife drop from his grasp and clatter onto the tiles. And to my utter surprise he follows them, sinking to the floor where he covers his face and begins to sob.

Slowly, carefully, I ease open the shower door and reach down to retrieve my phone. I wince as I make a lunge for it, terrified the man will grab my hand and stop me. But he doesn't move. He's still a mess on the bathroom floor. I tiptoe past him out of the room, moving away as quickly as I can while dialling the emergency number that Aldo gave me earlier.

I wait as it rings.

Praying they answer.

Praying they get here quickly.

Praying that I get out of this alive.

FORTY-TWO

BETH

ONE YEAR LATER

Everything is on track so far, having prepared as much as I could in advance. I sit down at the counter for a second to catch my breath. I need to stop worrying. I slide the tray of rosemary roast potatoes back into the oven – they're crisping up nicely. Next I check on the spiced butternut squash soup – it smells delicious. I used to be a great chef; I just have to have faith that I've still got what it takes.

I'm catering my first paid event tonight. It's a fortieth birthday for a rich, divorced hairdressing client of Sal's. The woman is having a dinner party for her and her seven pals. They're already four bottles deep into the Sauvignon Blanc, so I'm not too worried. But it would be great if they're sober enough to appreciate the food so they can recommend me to their friends and family.

This last year has been the hardest of my life. I never could have imagined that our perfect family holiday would have turned into such a nightmare. The boys have suffered worse than me. Especially Connor. Bless him. He was convinced that if he hadn't been over at Luciana's that evening, he could have saved his father's life. I've had to get him some therapy to help with his feelings of grief, guilt and shock. I think his counsellor's helping, but it's a slow process. Liam has recovered more quickly, but had nightmares for several months afterwards and most mornings I'd wake up to find his small body pressed up against mine. Comfort for both of us.

'Everything going all right in here?' my client asks brightly as she heads over to the wine cooler and pulls out another two bottles, waving them at me with a grin.

'Yes, the first course will be with you in five. Can I bring out any more bread or nibbles in the meantime?' I ask.

'No, we're all good, thanks. Smells delicious!' As she sashays away, I put the soup bowls in the oven to warm.

Connor wasn't the only one who needed therapy. I've also been talking to a counsellor about what happened. I was reluctant to go at first, but after a couple of months of nightmares and sweats, the anxiety and the sudden feelings of dread that would hit me out of nowhere, I realised that I needed some help.

I'm slowly beginning to untangle the mess of emotions that were tied up with Niall's death. The fact that I was never able to properly tell him how much his infidelity hurt me. The counsellor suggested that I write him a series of letters. Get it all down on paper as a way to unburden myself. I thought it was a daft idea as he's not around to read them. But surprisingly, it's helped to lighten some of the dark feelings. I would never want either of the boys to come across such a display of raw emotion – I poured all my hurt and anger into each letter – so I burned each one after writing it.

I toyed with selling the cottage. After all, it's brimming with memories of Niall – of our marriage – and it's also where Amber stayed with her family. But, in the end, I decided we should stay put. The last thing the boys needed back then was more upheaval. Instead, we redecorated and, just before Christmas, we cleared out Niall's study. It was a painful thing to do, but it's the largest of the three bedrooms and I thought Connor should have it. I thought it might help him to feel closer to his father. I said he could make it his own, decorate it however he wanted. He's kept it simple, not wanting to change too much. He loves it in there with his father's desk and a couple of the bookcases.

Liam is gradually getting used to having a room to himself, but he's still not crazy about it and uses any excuse to try to sneak into his big brother's room. The two of them have grown even closer since everything happened. It's been the only silver lining this year. Sharing tears at first but chatting and laughing together more and more.

I thought long and hard about the photos Amber sent me – at least I'm pretty sure it was her who sent them – and I decided to keep the revelation about her son to myself.

Soon after Niall's death, I had a visit from Renzo Mason. He called me and said he was in Sherborne and could we meet. I was nervous to see him, and a lot of those nerves were down to the fact that I didn't know how much of the truth he knew.

We met in a local restaurant for lunch. As soon as I got there, he put me at my ease, and I felt an instant affinity with him. We'd both been wronged. Although Renzo didn't know about my husband's lies regarding his relationship with Amber, so he was under the impression that Niall was as innocent as me.

He apologised for his wife's actions, and said they were getting a divorce and that she was going to appear in court for her dubious part in my husband's murder. He was genuinely devastated by everything that had transpired. I got the impression that he was reluctant to bad-mouth his wife, despite everything; that, as the mother of their children, he still felt some degree of loyalty towards her.

I realised that keeping Franco's paternity to myself was the best thing I could have done. The way Renzo talked about his children; you could tell he was besotted with them. That they were giving him a reason to go on. I wasn't certain whether Amber had already told him the truth or not, but if she had, Renzo didn't mention it. So, neither did I. If I'd told him that Niall was Franco's father, who exactly would that have benefitted? *No one.* Niall didn't want Franco as a son, and Renzo adores him. It's as simple as that. It's not my place to destroy their happiness.

Amber has never contacted me about it or tried to warn me against telling Renzo. I thought that was the first thing she would have tried to do. But perhaps she thinks it's better to let sleeping dogs lie. I certainly never want to see or speak to the woman again. I wish I'd never heard of Amber Mason.

Despite everything that's happened, I still grieve for Niall. For our marriage. For the family I wished we could have been. But I realise that he wasn't ever the person I thought he was. His infidelity and secrets made a mockery of our relationship, and put my family in danger. I'm angry with myself for not trusting my instincts years ago. For trying to smooth over the cracks instead of digging them out and repairing them properly.

The oven timer beeps and I turn off the burner, slip on the oven gloves and crouch down to take the bowls out of the oven. I place them on one of the large gold lacquered trays I brought with me. One by one, I ladle the soup into the bowls, drizzle crème fraiche on the top and sprinkle over toasted pine nuts and raisins.

The first course is ready.

I take a breath and square my shoulders. Here I go... I'm doing this for my boys. For our little family, and also for myself.

To regain something I've lost. To take charge of my life like I should have done all along. The past has been a disappointing and frightening place, but the future beckons and, even though it's all still uncertain, I realise that finally I'm not scared any more.

FORTY-THREE

AMBER

My mistake was thinking it could all be done cleanly. That I could conceive of an idea and it would happen exactly as I had imagined. I'd always been great at planning. Some might prefer to call it 'plotting' or 'scheming', but it all amounts to the same thing.

Most of my plans turned out to be great successes. Being beautiful and intelligent helps, of course it does. But those things can only get you so far. I'd always subscribed to the idea that if you want to succeed, you have to plan down to the tiniest detail.

I created an interesting and thriving business for myself. I found a handsome, successful and kind husband. *Kind* is just as important as the other things. *Kind* is imperative. That's where I went wrong the first time – with Niall. He was not a kind man, too selfish to give me the love I deserved. I had two gorgeous children – one of each. My home was perfect, set in one of the most beautiful places in the world. Yes, all my plans were a resounding success.

But, in the end, I pushed for just that little bit too much and it all came tumbling down.

I don't know which is worse – my spiralling thoughts, or the depressing scene through the smeary apartment window. I grip the sill and scowl as my gaze drags across telephone poles and electricity pylons, grey tower blocks interspersed with scrubby patches of dirt, a pack of dogs lolling in the shade of a convenience store down below. Even the blue sky and sharp sunshine can't make this view beautiful. I unfocus my eyes and let my memories pull me back.

Luca wasn't who I thought he was. The man pretended to be a potential wealthy client. He seduced me thoroughly, and I'd thought that our weekend of fun wouldn't hurt anyone. But he was a fraud. A handsome, charming, unhinged fraud. And I paid the price for that weekend.

I had told him that there was nothing between us. That whatever had happened in the past, it was now over. That I had a husband. A family. But he didn't listen. His threats became more and more disturbing, until a couple of months ago he messaged me to say that he knew where I lived and he would kill my husband so that we could be together. Now I'm not the sort of person to scare easily. But that text terrified me.

I agreed to go to Naples to meet him. To try to talk him out of it. But that was a mistake. The fact that I showed up, only encouraged him. It gave him the wrong message. I would have been better to ignore him.

That meeting made me wonder what I had ever seen in him in the first place. I must have been mad to jeopardise my marriage. But I'd always thought myself untouchable. That I had the luck and the balls to get away with anything. At that last meeting, it was obvious that there was something wrong with Luca. Whether he'd hidden it from me when we first met, or he'd subsequently started to lose his mind, I have no idea. All I knew after that meeting was that he was dangerous, and capable of doing what he said he would.

He messaged me regularly to let me know his terrifying

plans. At first, I would message him back to tell him not to do anything stupid, but eventually, I stopped responding.

I toyed with going to the police, but then it would have all come out. Renzo would have known that I'd been unfaithful. He would never have forgiven me. Now, I realise that I should have reported it. The man was so delusional that I probably could have got away with calling him a liar and denouncing that I'd ever had an affair. But it's too late for wishing.

I was scared and believed that he was going to try to hurt Renzo. So I arranged for us all to get out of the country for a free 'holiday' by getting back in touch with Niall, after years of no contact, and blackmailing him. I told Niall that if he didn't agree, I would tell his wife about our son. A son who was conceived while she was pregnant. Of course, I had no intention of doing any such thing, but it suited my purposes to have Niall under my thumb and agree to the house swap.

I uploaded the details of our home onto one of the holiday-swap sites, and told him to do the same.

The other part of my plan was to pray that Niall would be mistaken for Renzo. I knew they looked pretty similar, and it was a bonus that Beth is also the same height and colouring as me, with her dark hair and curvy figure. So, with any luck, Luca wouldn't realise. I know this part was a bit of a gamble in my plan, but Luca was so intent on killing that I doubted he would stop to check references. Luca had never met Renzo, and Niall was living in my house – who else would it be? Luca also wasn't thinking straight, which helped.

I did feel a little remorse that Niall would get caught up in Luca's demented plan. But I also felt this was a measure of revenge on Niall for abandoning me with his child all those years ago.

To put it crudely, I was killing two birds with one stone: revenge on Niall, while getting my stalker to kill the wrong guy, get arrested and get out of my life for good.

My fallback plan if Luca wasn't caught, was for suspicion to fall on Beth. After all, she would be the jealous wife who had just discovered her husband had cheated on her and had a child with someone else. She would have had the motivation.

I thought I'd planned everything so well. That I had every angle nicely covered. I didn't take into account that bloody Luca would show remorse for killing the wrong person. That he would confess everything to the police.

The stupid man had a total breakdown, in my bathroom of all places. When he discovered he'd killed Beth's husband by mistake, he gave himself up to the police and told them everything.

His confession included showing the police our texts. Thankfully, I hadn't put anything incriminating in them – I'm not *that* stupid. But the police investigators were suspicious that I may have taken my family out of harm's way while putting an innocent family in the crosshairs. They were suspicious of the fact that I didn't report Luca to the police. Of course, I vehemently denied their accusations and told them that I was too scared to tell the police in case it angered Luca further, which was partly true.

There was a court case, but they couldn't prove I'd done anything wrong. I didn't plan to murder anyone. I simply went on holiday with my family. I shook and sobbed and told the jury that I never truly believed the man would do anything that drastic. And they believed me. Renzo didn't say anything to implicate me. I don't know why – he could have told them about my confession to him. Perhaps he didn't want the mother of his children going to prison. Or maybe he worried about the whole money-laundering business coming out. Either way, it doesn't matter.

Thankfully, I managed to get my security guy into the villa after the police left. He removed all the hidden cameras and replastered where he needed to. They'd been so cleverly situated, that I'm not surprised they remained undetected. I'd been nervous that the police might have discovered them, but I had my story ready. I would have told them that the cameras were part of our home-security system, but we'd disabled them for the house swap. Luckily, my cover story wasn't necessary, and I had them uninstalled without even Renzo finding out.

Luca went to prison and he won't be getting out any time soon, thank goodness. Of course, the whole thing was in all the papers and on the news so it's totally ruined my business and my reputation. I may not have been found guilty of any crime, but the media enjoyed speculating and making my life a misery.

Renzo managed to sort things out with his loan situation – at least that's what he told me when I asked. He barely speaks to me these days. He's taken the children and moved back to his beautiful family home. They're still in Maiori, so there's no disruption to the children's schooling and friendships. Renzo's father has been living there alone since his wife died, and so I've no idea how he's adjusting to having a full house again.

I haven't fared so well. I've lost my home – which was heavily mortgaged. I've lost my livelihood because of the bad publicity. And, of course, I've lost my beautiful family. I now live here, in this cheap, inland, rented apartment. I hate it. It's cramped and stuffy, the neighbours are noisy and the neighbourhood isn't somewhere I feel safe to walk alone.

I miss my beautiful house and my work. I miss my Renzo. He pays me a little maintenance, which is something I suppose. Oh, I see Franco and Flora every other week, but it's not the same. I'm not a motherly person. I'm not great with the children on my own, not without Renzo there to do the heavy lifting. I get exhausted by their childish chatter. I love them, of course I do, but I want us to be all together as a family. It doesn't work without my husband. Nothing works without *him*.

I've lost it all, and I don't know how the hell I'm going to get it back.

I still harbour the hope that Renzo might come around. He's such a good man. I'm hoping he won't meet anyone else, and that he'll want to find the good in me.

Even if I can't find it in myself.

I'll give him time, but I haven't given up on him. *I can't*. I know Renzo so well. I know what makes him happy, what makes him angry, what tugs on his heartstrings. I can use all that to my advantage. I can't believe I had everything, and I let it all slide away. But I'm not the sort of person to accept that. To give up, sit back and mope around. No. I'm driven by a burning need to reclaim my family. To be respected and admired and adored once again. When the time is right, I'll make my move and I'll get it all back.

First, I'll need to ensure that Beth never tells Renzo what she knows. Bloody perfect Beth, who's doing quite nicely now, thank you very much, with her pretty country cottage and her dead husband's fat royalty cheques coming in every quarter.

I have to admit, I'm surprised she's kept quiet about Franco's true paternity for this long. At least I hope she has. I'm sure I'd know if she'd already told Renzo, as he would have come straight to me in a blaze of anguish and fury. It's a drama I can do without. I wish I'd never needed to tell Beth in the first place. Although it was quite a delicious feeling to send her those images.

Perhaps she's waiting for her moment to strike. Keeping me in suspense. Dangling the threat. That's what I would do if I were her. I'd tuck the knowledge in my back pocket, just in case. After all, secrets are power. But I won't allow anyone to hold that type of power over me. *No way*. I can't take the chance of her blabbing.

I turn away from the depressing view and start pacing the tiny living room. I'll have to do something about Beth. And I'll have to do it soon. Perhaps Luca coming into my life was a blessing in disguise, getting rid of the loose ends in my life, the niggles that have dogged me throughout the years. Maybe what Luca started, I can finish on my own. But that would involve another trip to England, which might seem suspicious, especially if I went on my own.

I wonder if I could persuade Renzo to let me have the children for a week. Another bonding trip to reconnect with their British roots seeing as the last trip was cut short so abruptly. Perhaps I could even persuade Renzo to come along. My heart gives a little lift at the thought.

Yes. I think this could be the perfect time to arrange another family holiday...

EPILOGUE

ONE YEAR EARLIER

Luciana stares in horror at the blood staining her brother's shirt. She turns to Beth and grabs hold of her arm. 'The man... he had a knife! He stab my brother!' Luciana's heart beats wildly. Everything happened so fast. They arrived at the villa with Beth's children and then suddenly all hell broke loose.

Luciana tries to think clearly. She pulls her phone from her bag and calls the emergency services. Thankfully, someone answers immediately and she starts giving her details, trying not to gabble, forcing herself to be calm. A wild hysteria is coursing through her veins. The last time she felt like this was when he ex-husband beat her. That final time before she somehow found the courage to leave him. Thankfully he's no longer part of her life, but tonight's violence has brought that fear racing back. Sweat coats her skin and her throat is dry.

'Is he all right?' Beth cries, staring in horror at Luciana's brother.

'I'm okay,' Matteo pants, as the woman on the phone assures

Luciana that medical help will be with them soon, along with the carabinieri.

Luciana realises that she's been so caught up in her concern for Matteo that she hasn't even asked how Beth is. She turns, scanning her friend to see if there's any sign of blood or distress. Beth's face is grey with shock. She seems unharmed, but perhaps she's traumatised in some other way. 'You are hurt too?'

Beth shakes her head. 'No, not me.' Her faces blanches further and she looks as though she might pass out.

'Your husband?' Luciana asks, realising Niall is nowhere to be seen. 'Where is he? Upstairs?'

'Shh.' Beth puts a finger to her lips and peers back around the doorframe to check the kids can't hear, but they're both huddled together, heads down, talking.

'Niall is hurt?' Luciana asks, lowering her voice.

Beth shakes her head and presses her lips together.

'What?' Luciana realises that Beth's husband might also need help. She turns to check on Matteo who gives her a reassuring nod.

'Niall... he's...' Beth shakes her head again and covers her mouth.

'What?' Is Beth trying to tell her that Niall is dead? Her heart starts racing again.

Beth whispers, 'He's... he's outside on the terrace.'

Luciana takes her hand and squeezes it, attempting to soothe her friend. 'The police and ambulance are coming now.'

Beth's eyes are wide and staring. 'It's too late for an ambulance. I should check on him, but I need to look after my boys and I don't want them to see....' Beth's voice cracks and Luciana's heart goes out to her.

'Of course you must be with your boys,' Luciana replies. 'You stay here. Please keep an eye on Matteo. I will check on your husband.'

'Are you sure?'

Luciana nods. She tells her brother she won't be long, before she heads through the vast kitchen towards the terrace. Moving as though in a dream, she shakes her head at the drama of the evening. She wonders what Amber and Renzo will think about all this when they find out. They always seem like an untouchable couple. Like everything is always perfect for them wherever they go. Not like normal people with regular problems and worries. If this truly is a robbery gone wrong, then how lucky for the Masons that they happen to be on holiday. Out of harm's way. Not so lucky for the Kildares.

Reaching the open patio door, Luciana halts as she spots Niall lying at an impossibly awful angle on the terrace, dark blood spreading out in a stain around his head. She gives a shiver. It's pretty obvious from here that the man is dead. Maybe she should just go back and tell Beth that she's sorry, her husband has gone.

Luciana is desperate to get back to her brother. To sit with him while they wait for the paramedics to arrive. She's also not keen on getting any nearer to Niall's broken body. But she promised Beth she would check, so she needs to be brave and take a closer look.

Her stomach tightens in apprehension. She inhales a deep and steadying breath, leaving the bright safety of the kitchen behind. On shaky legs, Luciana walks across the terrace towards the body.

As she approaches, she sees that Niall's face is ashen, his eyes closed, jaw slack, body unmoving. She crouches and places her index and middle fingers next to his windpipe, searching for a pulse, but she can't feel anything. He is most certainly dead.

Perhaps it's just as well. The man was an arrogant bully, and Luciana can't deny that, despite only knowing the couple for a short time, she was worried about Beth's marriage to him. Her obvious fear of him. Her deference. Niall reminded Luciana so much of her ex-husband. That cold condescension and domineering tone. His intolerance of anything other than his way. She recognised the same traits in this man lying here. She can't be sure if Niall was physically abusive, but if not, then it was only a matter of time.

Well, now he's gone and so maybe Beth will find a new chance at a happy life. A life where she gets to have a career and financial freedom. Where she isn't walking on eggshells all the time. Where she doesn't cater to the whims of a bully.

Luciana straightens up and is about to get to her feet when her blood freezes.

Niall's eyes are open.

He's staring right at her.

Luciana's palms begin to sweat, but still she can't move. Can't stop staring at the man she thought was dead.

'Help... me,' Niall croaks.

Luciana is transfixed as she gazes into his eyes. Into his soul. She should run inside and get Beth to come. The paramedics will be here any moment. They'll save him and the surgeons will patch him up somehow. Beth will be so relieved.

But then she'll be trapped in that abusive relationship once more.

Luciana's fists tighten at the memories that assault her. The punches to her ribs, the sneering, jeering taunts, the bone-crippling fear, the terror that her husband would kill her and her boys would be left solely in his care. She's paralysed by a storm of raw emotion that she thought she'd left behind.

And then, suddenly, Luciana's heartbeats slow, her mind clears and her body stops trembling. She continues to stare into Niall's eyes as she cups his head in the palms of her hands. No words are needed now.

She raises his head a couple of inches off the ground and

smashes it back down onto the porcelain tile. She does this once, twice. His eyes lose focus and she sets his head carefully back down and gets to her feet. Makes her way back inside to give Beth the terrible confirmation that, as she suspected, her husband is definitely dead.

A LETTER FROM SHALINI

Dear reader,

Thank you for choosing to read *The Family Holiday*. I do hope you enjoyed it. The Amalfi Coast is one of my favourite places in the world. Pete and I went there on our honeymoon twenty-five years ago and had the best time of our lives – the people, the scenery, the weather, the *food*... it's all incredible. We then returned twenty years later for a family holiday – thankfully with no murders and no Amber.

If you'd like to keep up to date with my latest releases, just sign up here:

www.bookouture.com/shalini-boland

I love getting feedback on my books, so if you have a few moments, I'd be really grateful if you'd be kind enough to post a review online or tell your friends about it. A good review absolutely makes my day!

When I'm not writing, reading, walking or spending time with my family, you can reach me via my Facebook page, through Twitter, Goodreads, my website or mailing list at http://eepurl.com/b4vb45.

Thanks so much,

Shalini Boland x

KEEP IN TOUCH WITH SHALINI

http://someonewotwrites.blogspot.com

facebook.com/shaliniboland

twitter.com/ShaliniBoland

goodreads.com/shaliniboland

ACKNOWLEDGEMENTS

It's always such a pleasure and a joy to work with my sensational and talented publisher Natasha Harding. Thank you for all your hard work on this book during such a difficult time. I truly appreciate it.

Thanks also to the wonderful team at Bookouture. Jenny Geras, Ruth Tross, Peta Nightingale, Richard King, Sarah Hardy, Kim Nash, Noelle Holton, Alexandra Holmes, Emily Boyce, Saidah Graham, Aimée Walsh, Natalie Butlin, Alex Crow, Melanie Price, Hannah Deuce, Occy Carr, Mark Alder, and everyone else who helped get this book off the ground.

Thanks to my excellent copy editor Maddy Newquist. Thanks also to Lauren Finger for your superb proofreading skills. Thank you to designer Lisa Horton for yet another eye-catching and evocative cover.

Thank you to Katie Villa who has narrated all my Bookouture books, under the brilliant production of Arran Dutton at the Audio Factory and Bookouture's incredible audio manager Alba Proko. You guys always do an incredible job of bringing my characters to life.

I feel very lucky to have such loyal and thorough beta readers. Thank you, Terry Harden and Julie Carey. You're amazing!

Thanks to all my lovely readers who take the time to read, review or recommend my novels. It means so, so much. Thanks also to all the fabulous book bloggers and reviewers out there who spread the word. You guys are the absolute best!

Finally, I want to thank my own little family for your endless support, your company, your cheesy jokes, big hugs, the mess, the laughter, all of it.